CHARCOAL SKETCHES
and other tales

The translator, Adam Zamoyski, was born in New York of Polish parents, but has spent most of his life in England. He is the author of *Chopin: a biography, Paderewski, The Polish Way: a thousand-year history of the Poles and their culture,* and a biography of the last Polish king, Stanisław Augustus (forthcoming)

HENRYK SIENKIEWICZ

Charcoal Sketches

and other tales

Translated from the Polish by
Adam Zamoyski

ANGEL BOOKS
London

First published by Angel Books, 3 Kelross Road
London N5 2QS

Copyright © Adam Zamoyski 1990

British Library Cataloguing in Publication data:

Sienkiewicz, Henryk
    Charcoal Sketches : and other tales.
    I. Title II. Sienkiewicz, Henryk. Bartek the Conqueror
    III. Sienkiewicz, Henryk. On the bright shore
    891.8536

ISBN 0-946162-31-X
ISBN 0-946162-32-8 pbk

This book is printed on Permanent Paper conforming
to the British Library recommendations and
to the full American standard

Typeset in Great Britain by Trintype, Wellingborough, Northants.
Printed and bound by Woolnough Bookbinding,
Irthlingborough, Northants.

Contents

Introduction

Henryk Sienkiewicz was once the most widely known of Polish writers. But his fame both at home and abroad rested on those of his works with the greatest thematic impact and, arguably, the least literary merit.

Outside Poland, he was known above all for the novel that won him the Nobel Prize in 1905, *Quo Vadis*, a tale set in Neronian times whose naive and sentimental depiction of the early Christians would fill a modern reader with cloying unease. At home, he entranced several generations with his great historical novels, which are still read by every schoolboy today. These books so far eclipsed his other work that their fall from fashion and lack of literary reputation have to a certain extent blighted the rest of his oeuvre. This is very uneven in quality as well as being inconsistent in style and subject-matter. Sienkiewicz's was not a strong artistic personality, and he was, often adversely, affected by pressures imposed by the political and social conundrums of contemporary Polish life.

He was born in 1846 in that part of Poland which had fallen to Russia in the Partitions of 1792. In 1866 he began medical studies at the Warsaw Main School, which was turned into the Russian University of Warsaw in the following year. He abandoned medicine for philology, in which he graduated in 1870. Sienkiewicz's generation was traumatised by the failure of the 1863-4 Polish Insurrection against Russia, the last of a series of attempts to regain independence through armed struggle. The failure of the Insurrection and its savage consequences brought about a shift in attitude in Polish society and gave rise to a movement known as Positivism. This rejected the struggle for independence and concentrated on cultural survival and the strengthening of the nation through mass self-improvement. The Positivists were influenced by the works of Auguste Comte, John Stuart Mill and Charles Darwin, and they advocated a programme of 'organic work' which was supposed to bring cleanliness, thrift and enlightenment into the peasant's hut and a social conscience, expertise and the entrepreneurial spirit into the gentry's manor.

Like all his contemporaries, Sienkiewicz was seduced by this programme in his student days, and this was reflected in his first literary steps. In 1869 he began contributing articles to the Positivist *Weekly Review*, and although three years later he moved to the editorial board of a less radical paper and then to the conservative *Polish Gazette*, he never lost the typically Positivist didacticism that characterised his early style. But his adhesion to Positivist principles did not last long. His first novel, *In Vain*, published in 1872, revealed a pessimistic streak which was not entirely in keeping with the Positivist confidence in progress. This was followed by a number of short stories and novellas, mainly dealing with oppression, highlighting ignorance and castigating complacency.

In 1876 Sienkiewicz set off for the United States, which he spent two years touring. He returned via France and Italy, and was back in Poland in 1879. This journey had a profound influence on his ideas and his writing, and both grew less parochial. The sight of oppression and injustice everywhere he went, and the clear evidence that material progress was not the universal panacea that the Polish Positivists believed further cut him off from the movement, and his views became more autonomous, if more sceptical. He wrote some of his best short fiction during this trip, including *Charcoal Sketches* (*Szkice węglem*, 1877), in which his strong sense of humour, and particularly of the grotesque, surface for the first time. Another facet of Sienkiewicz that began to emerge at about this time is his fervent patriotism, and this can be discerned in his next major novella, *Bartek the Conqueror* (*Bartek ZwycięΩa*, 1882). The same year saw him turn to history in search of a wider field for expressing his patriotic feelings, and in 1883 he began writing the first novel of a trilogy *(With Fire and Sword, The Deluge, Pan Wołodyjowski)* set in mid-seventeenth-century Poland, which was to absorb him for most of the decade and turn him into a household name. It is a straightforward adventure in the style of Dumas or Scott, and its tremendous pace, its sense of period, its naive view of political events and its unashamed wallowing in the glories of Poland's past, all helped to guarantee it immense popularity with a public that saw only failure and defeat around it.

The 1890s saw Sienkiewicz turn once again to more serious contemporary subjects, in the long novels *Without Dogma* and *The Połaniecki Family*, which reveal his disenchantment with all programmes and a growing scepticism. But he was also drifting back to religion, and this gave rise to his next work, the novel *Quo Vadis?* (1894-6). This was followed by the novella *On the Bright Shore* (*Na jasnym brzegu*, 1897), which contains echoes of Positivist theories, patriotic undercurrents, and a semi-religious rejection of cosmopolitanism. Sienkiewicz went on to write the last of his major works, the historical novel *The Knights of the Cross* (1897-1900), inspired by the wish to challenge the German onslaught in the Prussian partition of Poland. Sienkiewicz's work became more and more overtly patriotic, and when the Great War broke out, he joined with the pianist Ignacy Jan Paderewski in forming a Polish National Committee in Switzerland, where he had settled. This eventually grew into the official representative of Polish interests recognised by the Entente Powers in 1917 as the Polish provisional government. But Sienkiewicz did not live to see this, as he died in 1916 in Vevey, Switzerland.

The present selection cannot of course provide a comprehensive picture of Sienkiewicz's writing, but the three novellas represent a progression that gets away from the accepted idea of him as a historical novelist on the one hand and a writer of sentimental short stories on the other. At the same time, the three tales show all the strengths, as well as limitations, of Sienkiewicz's style, and treat some of his most enduring concerns. They all have more or less contemporary settings.

He is above all a very good storyteller, and his language is flowing, rich and evocative. He sets an engaging pace and has a talent for making scenes come alive. These qualities are to the fore in *Charcoal Sketches*, a headlong satire on village life in Russian-ruled Poland where Tsarist administration encourages corruption and promotes injustice with bureaucratic aplomb. Its by no means simple plot, involving as it does the relationship between the village, the manor and the Tsarist administration, is unravelled in a masterly way, and the life of the locality

is laid before the reader with a familiarity born of understanding. In the role of narrator, Sienkiewicz varies his tone, which
is sometimes almost coldly laconic, sometimes arch, and sometimes lyrical. He also varies his position, standing aside to
observe, and then putting himself inside the mind of one of the
protagonists. A great strength is his sense of humour, of the
grotesque and the fatuous, and his love of hyperbole, which are
used in different ways in each of the three tales. Bathos is a
favourite device, and it too is much in evidence. A propensity
for sentimentality, which mars many of his best stories for the
modern reader, is kept well in check here.

Sienkiewicz is occasionally reproached with producing two-
dimensional characters, and in this respect the present selection is revealing. He is at his best as an observer of character,
and this serves him well in the first two stories, *Charcoal
Sketches* and *Bartek the Conqueror*. But in *On the Bright Shore*,
where he needs to develop the psychology of his characters, he
is perhaps less successful. This last work also suffers from
something that affects all the serious works: his somewhat
problematic sexuality, which is both prim and voyeuristic.
Nevertheless, this story of an affair between an artist and a
beautiful widow of dubious reputation amongst the Polish
community on the Riviera contains some fine vignettes of its
setting and arresting cameos of the variegated types who are
drawn to it.

The style of the three novellas is different in each case: the
youthful archness of *Charcoal Sketches* gives way to the grim-
mer humour and more relentless tragedy of *Bartek*, which is
superseded by the more refined wit and elegant narrative of *On
the Bright Shore*. Yet the themes running through them are
remarkably similar. Sienkiewicz's concern for the Polish peasant, or, in the last story, the Polish orphan, is paramount. All
three constitute a strong indictment of the intelligentsia, which
cares but does nothing, the nobility, which would like to do
something but cannot, and the wealthy, who do not care. In
Charcoal Sketches, even the Church is accused of failing to take
responsibility upon itself.

Charcoal Sketches is set in 1870 in a village in the Russian
partition of Poland, and its action is closely bound up with the
consequences of the political events of the previous decade.

Although it was ruled by Russia, this area had been officially termed the Kingdom of Poland, and it enjoyed at least some form of autonomy. It differed from the rest of the Russian Empire in that the peasants were not enserfed in their persons. Some owned their land, while the majority were tenants of smallholdings on the estates of the gentry. Although there had never been a feudal system in operation in Poland, most tenancies were granted on the basis that part of the rent was paid in cash or kind, and part in labour, thereby guaranteeing the squire reserves of free manpower at harvest-time. Many of the larger estates had with time transferred to cash and done away with the labour-rent, and by the late 1850s the Polish Agricultural Society, an association of landowners, began to discuss reforms, including plans for giving the peasants the smalholdings they worked. The Tsar was already planning the emancipation of the Russian serfs, and invited the Poles to make their own proposals. But the agrarian question coincided with demands voiced throughout society for other reforms, for greater autonomy, and even for separation from Russia. The more radical elements in Polish society, known as the 'Reds', were pressing for sweeping changes and public fervour mounted throughout 1861 and 1862, heightened by brutality on the part of the Russian police and army. In January 1863 the 'Reds' proclaimed an Insurrection, and guerilla war engulfed the whole country. The Insurgent government issued a decree freeing the peasants from all labour-dues and giving them the land they worked, but the Insurrection was crushed after some twenty months, and a period of 'Pacification' ensued, during which everyone who had played any part in the events was subjected to brutal repressions.

Towards the end of the Insurrection, on 2 March 1864, the Tsar published a decree of emancipation for the Polish peasants in an effort to pull the carpet from under the Insurgent government, and in effect sanctioning a situation that it would have been impossible to reverse. The decree varied from its earlier Russian model radically. It appeared to be more generous to the peasants and it penalised the gentry. The aim was to suggest that the Tsar was taking the side of the Polish peasant against the Polish lord, and to ruin the minor gentry, who were the most nationalist element in the country.

The decree abolished labour-rents; turned tenancies into freeholds; distributed land to landless peasants; granted grazing and wood-gathering rights on manorial lands; and set up peasant councils under Tsarist administration which would put an end to landowners' influence over village affairs. The consequences were not long in making themselves felt. The landless peasants were given too little land to survive on. The compensation to the landlords was paid out not in cash as in Russia, but in negotiable bonds which immediately plummeted in value. Most of the resentment in the villages fell on the Tsarist administration with which everyone had to deal, and the intended confrontation between village and manor never materialised. But the old ways of doing things had been swept away, and the paternalism of the manor, which had provided at least some help to peasants in need, was now replaced by a ruthless bureaucracy which the peasants distrusted and feared. The gentry and the clergy also feared this bureaucracy, with the result that they tended to keep out of trouble and look to their own affairs, leaving the peasants largely at the mercy of their ignorance. It is this tendency that Sienkiewicz is most critical of in *Charcoal Sketches*, but his dispassionate understanding for all sides prevents the story from becoming mere propaganda.

It is the same tendencies that are ultimately under attack in *Bartek the Conqueror*, although the circumstances are very different. This story is set in the Duchy of Posen (Poznań), the area taken by Prussia during the partitions. The Duchy had a degree of autonomy under the Prussian Crown, but after 1848 this fell victim to the rise of German nationalism. The area was more prosperous and less backward than the Kingdom, and the peasants here were no less free than their counterparts in western Europe at the time. The threat that they, and the Polish gentry, had to face was Prussian and then German government policy. This branded the Poles as an inferior nation, and strove to turn the whole area into a bastion of the Teutonic world, primarily by the relentless germanisation of the native population. The language of instruction in schools was German, and in 1874 the use of Polish textbooks was forbidden. In 1876 German became the exclusive language of administration and all official business. The second tier of German policy was to fill the area with German settlers and encourage the natives to emigrate to the United States. Germans from other parts of the Reich were given incentives and credit to settle in the Polish areas, while officials and policemen who agreed to retire there were given higher pensions. A Colonisation Commission bought up tracts of land and gave them to German colonists. A series of laws forbade Poles to buy land or build new houses on their land. In the event, the Poles were to win this battle for language and land by dint of clever counter-moves, including the setting up of cooperatives, land purchase banks and so on. But in 1882, when Sienkiewicz was writing *Bartek*, the prospect was gloomy. The failure of the Polish Insurrection against Russia in 1864 had weakened the position of the Poles, while the Prussian victories against Austria in 1866 and France in 1871, the unification of Germany and the promotion of the Prussian kings to the status of German emperors all contributed to a strengthening of the German position. In 1871 the Duchy of Posen was incorporated into the German Reich and lost its autonomy. The only role reserved for the Polish population in this scheme of things was to provide cannon-fodder for the German army. This is the fate reserved for the peasant Bartek, who is not only physically exploited by being forced to fight for Germany, but also demoralised and psychologically destroyed by the experience. Sienkiewicz was concerned that, left to himself, the Polish peasant would be trodden into the ground by the German machine, and he felt that the landed gentry were not facing up to the threat with enough energy.

In 1886 Bismarck made a speech in the Reichstag to support his latest package of measures aimed at squeezing the Poles and forcing them to sell up their land. In it he assured the assembly that, being endemically irresponsible, the Polish gentry would probably welcome his measures, since they would be far happier spending their money at the roulette tables of Monte Carlo than administering their estates. Whether or not he had Bismarck's speech in mind when choosing the setting of the last story in this selection we do not know, but Sienkiewicz was certainly concerned at people wasting their time and their money when they could devote both to the public good. At the same time, he was sensitive enough to appreciate that an élite which is denied a role in all but the lowest levels of the administration, as was the case with the Poles under Russian and Prussian rule, will tend to wander aimlessly abroad. Ironically, most of the characters in *On the Bright Shore* believe that they are doing something for the Polish cause, and Sienkiewicz shows them up as being misguided.

As a writer Sienkiewicz is the victim of his own reputation, for this outstripped his purely literary merit. He started out as a polemicist, almost a literary politician, and he was read as such. In his historical novels he gave his readership what they needed: comfort and a sense of pride. In his later works, he examined contemporary life with the voice of conscience. His concern was to make powerful statements rather than create psychological drama. His contemporaries knew what they wanted from him, and they got it. After his death, his towering reputation made people look for profundities that never existed, and this, combined with a certain degree of natural dating of the subject-matter, convinced many that he was not a very good writer. In Poland he is now read and appreciated more for what he is – a craftsman, a storyteller, a writer who can induce laughter and compassion, a writer who deserves to be read. It is hoped that the present translations will help to reveal him as such outside his native land.

Sienkiewicz has been very poorly served by his translators. Almost all his works were translated into a surprising number of languages during his lifetime, but very few since his death. A new translation of *Bartek* was made fifty years ago, but the other two tales have not been translated for nearly a century. All the original English versions are abysmal. One of his most prolific translators into English seems to have worked from Russian translations: he clearly knew very little Polish and certainly never used his imagination. The early translations of *Charcoal Sketches* entirely fail to put across the element of farce which Sienkiewicz used to such effect. Translators of *On the Bright Shore* do not seem to have even noticed the element of humour in the story. The present translations have been made with this in mind, and it is hoped that they will convey some of the real sense of the originals.

Adam Zamoyski

CHARCOAL SKETCHES

or

An Epic Entitled:

WHAT WENT ON IN WOOLLYHEAD

I

*In which we are acquainted with
the heroes, and which leads us to
expect that something will follow.*

A deathly silence reigned in the Woollyhead village office. The Elder, an ageing peasant named Francis Beet, sat at the desk writing with great concentration. The Clerk, the young and hopeful Mr Skrofulowski, stood by the window picking his nose and swatting the flies.

The office was as rich in flies as a cow-shed; the walls, of which the original colour was a mystery, were crawling with them. The same went for the picture hanging over the desk, the paper, the seals, the Crucifix and the Elder's ledgers.

The flies were crawling all over the Elder himself, as though he were their natural perch, but what attracted them most of all was the pomaded head of Mr Skrofulowski, which gave off a powerful smell of cloves. A whole swarm of them hovered above it, occasionally settling on the parting of the hair in live black patches. From time to time Mr Skrofulowski cautiously lifted his hand and brought it down suddenly with a resounding slap. The flies would noisily shoot up into the air, while Mr Skrofulowski bowed his head, picked out the corpses and flicked them onto the floor.

It was four o'clock in the afternoon. A hush reigned over the whole village, as everyone was in the fields. Outside, a cow scratched itself against the wall, occasionally poking its wheezing nostrils and dribbling mouth through the window. Now and again it would swing its heavy head down to swat the flies off its chest, hitting the wall with its horn as it did so. Mr Skrofulowski would respond by leaning out of the window and shouting: 'Watch it, damn you!' after which he would go back to contemplating himself in the little mirror hanging just by the window, rearranging his hair and picking his nose phlegmatically.

Eventually, the Elder broke the silence:

'Mr Skrofulowski,' he said with a thick Mazovian accent, 'why don't you write this 'ere report . . . I'm a bit clumsy at it. After all, you're the Clerk.'

But Mr Skrofulowski was in a bad mood, and whenever he was in a bad mood, the Elder had to do everything himself.

'So what if I am the Clerk,' he replied grandly. 'The Clerk's job is to write to the Governor or the Head of the District. When it's a question of writing to another Elder, just like you, you can do it yourself.' To which he added with majestic scorn: 'What's an Elder to me, anyway? A peasant, that's all! You can butter a peasant, but he's still a peasant.' He looked in the mirror and smoothed his hair. But the Elder felt insulted, and answered back:

'What d'you mean? . . . Haven't I taken tea with the Head?'

'You don't think I'm impressed by that, do you!' answered Skrofulowski nonchalantly. 'Anyway, I bet he didn't give you any arrack with it.'

'Well, you're wrong, 'cause I got harrack too!'

'Perhaps you did, but I still won't write your report for you.' To which the Elder angrily retorted:

'If your hintelligence is so delicate, then why did you apply for the job of Clerk?'

'Nobody applied to *you;* I just happen to be a friend of the Governor's . . .'

'Bloody good friend! – Whenever he comes here, you start licking his arse so . . .'

'Beet, Beet! Hold your tongue, I warn you. All you peasants and this job are beginning to get on my nerves. An educated man only goes to seed surrounded by people like you. If you annoy me any more, I'll throw this Clerkship to the devil, and you lot with it.'

'What'll you do then, eh?'

'What! I suppose you think I'll starve! An educated man can always manage. You don't have to worry about an educated man. Only yesterday Inspector Stołbicki said to me: "Oh, Skrofulowski, you'd make a terrific sub-inspector; you really understand what makes the world go round!" – Sub-Inspector, see! You only have to drive round the distilleries and play cards with the gentry. You turn a blind eye on a thing or two and your pocket fills out nicely; and where d'you find a distillery without cheating these days? D'you think Mr Skorabiewski here in Woollyhead doesn't fiddle? Tell me another! – I spit on your clerkship. An educated man . . .'

'The world won't end just because you go.'

'No, the world won't end. But it'll get pretty hot for you around here; they'll be dipping a stick into that inkwell and writing on your back with it!' At this the Elder began to scratch his head, saying:

'You don't have to get all worked up about it.'

'Just you keep a hold on your tongue . . .'

'All right then . . . all right.'

Again all was silent except for the Elder's pen, which scraped away at the paper slowly. Finally he straightened up, wiped the pen on his frock-coat and said:

'Well, I've finished . . . with God's help.'

'Read out what you've concocted.'

'I haven't concocted nothing – I've just written everything out as it should be.'

'Come on, let's hear it!'

The Elder took the paper in both hands and began to read out:

'To the Elder of the village of Humbug. In the name of the Father, Son and Holy Spirit. Amen. The Governor said the Army lists must be done just after the Our Lady, but our registers are in your parish with His Reverence, and some of our blokes have been working over with you, see? So you write it all out and send them all back here before the Our Lady if they've got their eighteen years. And if you don't, you'll get clouted . . . Which God grant us all. Amen.'

The worthy Elder heard the vicar round his sermon off in this way every Sunday, and this seemed to him to fulfil all the requirements of decent stylistics as well as being quite essential. But Skrofulowski started laughing.

'So that's it, then?' he asked.

'I'd like to see you do better.'

'I will, because I feel ashamed for the whole of Woollyhead.' Saying this, Skrofulowski sat down, took up the pen, made several circles in the air with it, as though gathering impetus, then started to write quickly.

Soon the note was ready. The author smoothed his hair and began to read:

'From the Elder of Woollyhead to the Elder of the village of Humbug: Whereas the military lists are to be ready by such and such a day of such and such a year, at the request of higher authorities, the Elder of the village of Humbug is hereby notified, re the lists of Woollyhead peasants now at the Parish registry, to remove these from the said registry and to remit them to Woollyhead at the earliest possibility. Peasants from Woollyhead at present employed in the Parish of Humbug are to report on the same day.'

The Elder eagerly drank in the words, while his face expressed rapture and an almost religious concentration. It all seemed so fine, so ceremonious, and so thoroughly official. That beginning, for instance; 'Whereas the military lists etc . . .' the Elder greatly admired this use of 'whereas', but somehow he could never quite fit it in himself, and even if he knew how to begin a letter, he simply could not carry on from there. With Skrofulowski, it just gushed out like water, and they could not have done a better job in the District Office. Now all he had to do was smear the seal, slam it down so the whole table shook, and there it was!

'That's clever, all right,' said the Elder.

'Well,' said Skrofulowski, relenting, 'I mean, Clerks write books and things . . .'

'What? D'you write books too?'

'Didn't you know? And who writes the official ledgers, then?'

'Oh, yes,' said the Elder. After a moment, he added: 'Now the lists'll be ready in no time.'

'You just make sure you get rid of all the loafers in the village.'

'Oh, don't worry, we'll manage to get rid of a lot.'

'Remember that the Governor complained about the people of Woollyhead. He says they don't work and only get drunk.' 'Beet doesn't keep the people in order,' he says, 'and he'll have to answer for it.'

'I know,' replied the Elder, 'I'm always the one who has to answer for it. When Rozalka the blacksmith's daughter gave birth, the court said give her twenty-five, just so she'd remember next time that it's not nice for an unmarried girl. And who ordered it? Me? – Not me; the court. And what's it got to do with me anyway? I don't care if they all have kids. The court ordered it, and then they all jump on me: "Didn't you know corporal punishment's been abolished?" says the Governor, and then a bash in the face, "and you can't beat anyone any more!" and again he bashed me on the head. Well, I suppose that's just my luck . . .'

At this point the cow banged the wall so hard that the whole office shook.

'Here, go to the devil!' the Elder called out with bitterness.

The Clerk sat down on the table and resumed picking his nose.

'It serves you right,' he said, 'why don't you watch yourself a little? It'll be the same with all this drunkenness. One black sheep leads the others astray. Don't we know who the ringleader is, the one who drags everyone in Woollyhead off to the inn?'

'Of course we don't know, and as for the drunkenness, well, everyone needs a drink when they've been out in the fields all day.'

'I'm only going to say one thing; just get rid of Turnip and everything will be all right.'

'What am I supposed to do – pull his head off or something?'

'No, don't pull his head off. They're making out the conscription lists. Just slip him on to the list, make him draw the short straw, and there you are.'

'But he's married, and he's got a year-old son.'

'Who's to know that? He wouldn't go and complain, and even if he did they wouldn't listen. Everybody's much too busy at conscription time.'

'Oh, Mr Skrofulowski, Mr Skrofulowski! You don't care about the drunkenness – you just fancy Turnip's wife . . . and that's a sin against God.'

'And what's it got to do with you? You just remember that your son's nineteen and he'll have to draw a straw too.'

'I know, but I won't let him go. If I can't manage any other way, I'll buy him out.'

'Oh well, if you're that rich . . .'

'The good Lord's put a few coppers in my hands – not much, but it may be enough.'

'You're not going to pay eight hundred roubles with your coppers, are you?'

'When I says I'll pay, I'll pay, even if I have to scrape together all my coppers. And if the Lord God lets me stay on as Elder, then maybe with His gracious help I'll manage to get it all back in a year or two.'

'You may get it back, and on the other hand you may not. I need money too, and I'm not going to let you pocket all the takings. An educated man always has more expenses than a common fellow. But if we wrote Turnip down instead of your son, it would be a saving for you . . . You don't find eight hundred roubles lying around in the street, you know.'

The Elder pondered for a moment. The thought of saving such a large sum began to dance before his eyes and titillate him pleasantly.

'But it's always a risky thing,' he said finally.

'You won't even have to think about it.'

'That's what I'm scared of – you'll think it up with your head, and I'll pay for it with mine.'

'Well, if you really want to pay eight hundred roubles . . .'

'Now I'm not saying I want to pay . . .'

'Why not, if you're so sure you'll get it back? But I wouldn't count too heavily on keeping your post. There are still a few things they don't know about you; if they knew what I know . . .'

'But you dip into the village funds more than I do!'

'I'm not referring to the village funds – I'm alluding to a slightly more distant period . . .'

'I'm not scared; I just did what I was told.'

'I'd like to see you try to explain that to them.' Having said this, the Clerk picked up his green check cord hat and left the office.

The sun was low and the peasants were coming back from the fields. The Clerk met five mowers carrying scythes on their shoulders.

'The Lord be praised!' they said, bowing to him.

The Clerk merely nodded his pomaded head in acknowledgement, instead of replying with the customary 'for ever and ever!', since he felt that this was not fitting for an educated man.

That Mr Skrofulowski was an educated man everybody knew, and this fact could only have been doubted by spiteful or vicious people – the sort who get a flea in their ear and lose sleep over any person whose genius lifts him above the common level.

If we had, as we should, a full biographical dictionary of all our great men, the entry devoted to this exceptional person – whose portrait has for some unknown reason not yet appeared in any of our illustrated papers – would inform us that his first educational steps were taken in Dunceford, capital of the district of Dunceford, in which lies the village of Woollyhead. By the seventeenth year of his life, the youthful Skrofulowski had reached the second form and he would have risen higher just as swiftly had it not been for the fact that stormy times arrived, cutting short the strictly educational aspects of his career once and for all. Carried away by the ardour common to youth, Mr Skrofulowski, who had on previous occasions fallen victim to the injustice of his teachers, stood up at the head of his more passionate colleagues, began to cat-call at his persecutors, tore up his books, broke his ruler and pens, and abandoned Minerva for Mars and Bellona.

There now dawned a period when he wore his trousers tucked into his boots and not over them, and when he sang 'All hail to you great lords!' with an ardour full of bitter and fierce irony. Camp life, singing, clouds of tobacco-smoke, romantic adventures in billets – where young maidens wearing crucifixes on their breasts, their backs and God alone knows where else, refused nothing for the sake of the motherland and her chivalrous defenders – such a life was in complete harmony with the passionate and tempestuous soul of the young Skrofulowski. In it he found the fulfilment of those dreams which had enflamed his imagination when he used to read under his desk in class *The Adventures of Rinaldo Rinaldini* and similar works which form the heart, develop the intellect and awaken the imagination of our youth.

But this life also had its more sombre and risky aspects. His fiery courage often carried Mr Skrofulowski away. Just how effectively it could carry him away would be hard to believe were it not for the fact that even today the people of Humbug point to a fence that the best horse could never jump, and which Mr Skrofulowski – carried away one stormy night by the passionate desire to conserve himself longer for the defence and happiness of the motherland – managed to clear with one leap. Whenever Mr Skrofulowski happens to go to Humbug, now that these times are long past, he contemplates this fence with something approaching disbelief, and thinks: 'The devil! I couldn't make it now!'

After this superhuman exploit, which was even mentioned in despatches, fortune, which had hitherto defended Mr Skrofulowski's back like the apple of its eye, suddenly deserted him – clearly terrified by his courage. Not a week had passed before Mr Skrofulowski's back, which had so heroically and insistently exposed itself, met not a bullet or a bayonet (thanks to Providence, which always knows best), but with a different and equally unfriendly implement of plaited hide adorned with a piece of lead at its extremity. This implement completely riddled the so far inviolate skin on the back and shoulders of our amiable hero.

From that moment, a definite change began to take place in his feelings and his ideas. Lying face down on a straw mattress in the Woollyhead inn, he spent sleepless nights reflecting – just like St Ignatius Loyola – and he finally arrived at the conclusion that every man ought to serve the public good with the weapon best suited to him. Thus the intelligentsia ought to serve with their heads and not their backs, for not everyone has a head, while every peasant has a back, and consequently he had exposed his own unnecessarily. What more could he do for the motherland with the weapons he had used until now? Jump over some other fence? No, once was quite enough – though not everyone could jump like that, he mused.

Was he to go on shedding his blood? No, decidedly not. Quite enough had been spilt already. He would serve the public good in a completely new and pacific manner; with his intelligence, or rather, with his knowledge. As he knew a great deal, and particularly as he knew something about almost every inhabitant of the district of Dunceford, he was able to render quite exceptional service to the common good during the period of Pacification.

And so he started along this new path of public service, which led him straight up to the village Clerkship. Now, as we have overheard, he was even dreaming of a Sub-Inspectorship.

Even in his present post he was far from badly off. Secret knowledge always kindles respect for the bearer amongst other people. Since, as I mentioned earlier, my charming hero knew something about almost every inhabitant of the district of Dunceford, everyone treated him with the greatest respect, mingled with wariness, dreading to displease such an altogether exceptional man. As a result, all the gentry bowed to him, as did all the peasants, taking their caps off from afar and exclaiming: 'The Lord be praised!' Here, however, I see that I must explain more clearly to my reader why Mr Skrofulowski did not reply with the customary 'for ever and ever'.

I have already mentioned that he considered it unsuitable for an educated man to do so, but there were also other reasons. Independent intellects tend to be daring and radical. It is not surprising, therefore, that Mr Skrofulowski had decided, back in those stormy days, that 'the soul's just a lot of nonsense'. On top of this, the Clerk was at this moment absorbed by the publication of a Warsaw bookseller, a Mr Breslauer, entitled *Isabella of Spain, or The Secrets of the Court of Madrid.* This in every respect remarkable novel had enchanted and involved him so deeply that at one stage he even thought of dropping everything and leaving for Spain. 'Marfori succeeded, so why shouldn't I?' he thought, recollecting the passage describing Marfori kissing Isabella's stockings. He might indeed have set off in quest of these, for he was of the opinion that 'one is completely wasted in this stupid country', were he not held back by a different pair of stockings – native ones of which this epic will tell later.

As a result of reading this *Isabella of Spain*, published periodically by Mr Breslauer to the greater glory of our literature, Mr Skrofulowski began to view the clergy and everything directly or indirectly connected with it with deep scepticism. And so he did not answer the mowers with the customary 'for ever and ever', but merely walked on.

He walked and walked, and on his way he met some girls coming back from harvesting, carrying scythes on their shoulders. As they were passing by a vast puddle, they walked in single file, lifting their skirts up from behind and revealing beetroot-like legs.

'How are you, my little darlings!' Mr Skrofulowski exclaimed, stopping on the same path. As each girl passed, he grabbed her round the waist, kissed her and then playfully pushed her into the puddle. The girls squealed and giggled so much you could see their back teeth, and when they had passed, the Clerk listened, not without pleasure, to what they said to each other.

'Oh, he ain't half a nice gentleman, our Clerk!'

'He's all red and shiny like an apple!'

'And his head smells just like a rose – when he grabs you round the waist, you go weak all over!'

The Clerk walked on, his mind full of pleasant thoughts. A little further on, by one of the cottages, he again heard people talking about him, so he stopped behind the fence. On the other side there was a dense cherry-orchard with beehives in it, and two women stood next to these, talking. One had her apron full of potatoes, which she was peeling. The other was saying:

'Oh my dear Stachowa, I'm so scared they'll take my Franek off with the soljers, it makes my skin creep.' To which Stachowa replied:

'You'd best go and see the Clerk – yes, go and see the Clerk. If he can't fix it, then nobody can.'

'But my dear Stachowa, what can I give him? You can't go to him empty-handed. The Elder's easier; you can give him some white crayfish, or butter, or some flax, or a chicken; he's not fussy – he'll take anything. But the Clerk won't even look. Oh, he's terrible ambitious, he is. With him you just got to give money straight away.'

'You bet I won't take no eggs or chickens from you,' muttered the Clerk. 'Do they think I take bribes or something? Go to the devil with your wretched chickens!' He separated the branches of a cherry-tree and was just about to call out to the women when he suddenly heard the rumble of a chaise behind him.

The Clerk turned round to look. In the chaise sat a young student, with his cap cocked over one ear and a cigarette in his teeth. He was being driven by the same Franek the women had been talking about a moment before. Leaning out of the chaise, the student caught sight of Mr Skrofulowski, whereupon he waved and called out:

'How are you, Mr Skrofulowski? What's new? Still smear your head with two inches of pomade, do you?'

'Your servant!' answered Skrofulowski, bowing low. But when the chaise had passed, he quietly called after it: 'I hope you break your neck before you get there!'

The Clerk detested this student. He was a cousin of the Skorabiewskis and always came to spend the summer with them. Skrofulowski not only loathed him: he was also scared of him. The young man was a joker as well as a great dandy, and he regularly made fun of Skrofulowski. He was the only person in the whole neighbourhood who was not in the slightest intimidated by the Clerk. Once he had even barged in on a village meeting, and proceeded to call Mr Skrofulowski a fool in unequivocal terms, telling the peasants to ignore him. Mr Skrofulowski would gladly have taken his revenge – but what could he do? He knew something interesting about everyone else, but he had absolutely nothing on this one.

The student's arrival was rather inconvenient from another point of view as well, so he walked on frowning, not stopping until he had reached a cottage that stood a little way from the road. When he beheld this cottage, his face lit up once more. If anything, it was poorer than the others, but it looked tidy. The front was swept clean and the little yard was carpeted with rushes. By the fence lay a pile of small logs. A log with an axe stuck in it leant against a block. A little further stood a barn with its door open, and beside it a construction which served as pigsty and cowshed. Beyond this stretched an enclosure in which a horse was stepping from foot to foot as it grazed. A great pool of liquid manure with two pigs lying in it glistened in front of the pigsty. Ducks strutted about near the pool, shaking their heads and fishing beetles out of the dung. A cock was scratching about among the woodchips by the block, clucking madly whenever it found a grain or a worm. The hens waited for this call, ready to rush up and peck at the titbit, snatching it away from each other.

In front of the house, a woman was winnowing hemp in a hackle, singing to herself quietly. Beside her lay a dog, its front

paws outstretched, snapping at the flies that kept settling on its
torn ear.

The woman was young – perhaps twenty years old – and
strikingly handsome. She wore the usual peasant bonnet on
her head. A white blouse held in by a red ribbon revealed the
outlines of two full healthy breasts, like a couple of young cab-
bages. Everything about the woman radiated health. She was
wide in the shoulders and the hips and narrow in the waist.
Her figure was supple and doe-like.

Yet her features were fine, her head small and her complexion even a little pale, though at this moment it was gilded by
the rays of the sun. She had large black eyes, fine brows, a
small thin nose and lips like cherries. Rich dark tresses peeped
out from under her bonnet.

As the Clerk walked up, the dog lying by the hackle got to
its feet, put its tail between its legs and began to growl, baring
its teeth in a quivering grin.

'Kruczek!' called the woman in a high harmonious voice,
'lie down, or I'll . . .'

'Good evening, Mrs Turnip,' said the Clerk.

'Good evening, Mr Clerk,' answered the woman, without
stopping her work.

'Your man at home?'

'He's working in the forest.'

'Oh, pity . . . There's some official business for him.'

For poor people, anything to do with officialdom invariably
spells trouble. The woman stopped her winnowing.

'What is it?' she said uneasily, with a look of fear.

The Clerk had come in through the gate and was standing
beside her.

'Give us a kiss and I'll tell you.'

'We can do without that!' retorted the woman. But the
Clerk had already managed to catch her round the waist and
pull her over towards him.

'Let go, sir! I'll scream . . .' cried the woman, desperately
trying to disengage herself.

'Come to me this evening, eh? . . .' whispered the Clerk,
without letting go.

'I won't come tonight nor any other night!'

'My beauty . . . my Marysia . . .'

'Sir! It's an insult to God! Sir!' Saying this, she made even more violent efforts to free herself, but Mr Skrofulowski was strong, and he would not let go. They began to struggle, and finally the woman fell over the hackle and on to the woodchips with the Clerk on top of her.

'Oh my God! Help!' she squealed.

At this point Kruczek came to her rescue. His hair bristled and he leapt at the Clerk, barking furiously. As the latter was lying face down and backside up, and as he was wearing only a short jacket, Kruczek went for that part of the corduroys not covered by it. He got through the cord, bit into the nankeen, got through the nankeen, bit into the skin, got through the skin, and it was only when he felt he had a good mouthful that he began to jerk his head viciously and tug.

'Jesus, Mary!' yelled the Clerk, forgetting that he was an *esprit fort*.

The woman jumped up. The Clerk leapt to his feet frantically, as though he had been scalded, while Kruczek stood up on his hind legs, refusing to let go. The Clerk seized a log and began hitting out blindly behind his back with it, and finally Kruczek, having caught a blow in the small of his back, leapt aside, whining pitifully. After a moment, however, he returned to the attack.

'Get that dog away! Get that Devil away!' screamed the Clerk, waving the log desperately.

The woman called the dog and pushed him out through the gate. Still panting heavily, they looked at each other in silence.

'Oh what a terrible thing! Why did you have to take a fancy to me?' exclaimed the woman, terrified by the bloody turn events had taken.

'Vengeance on you!' shouted the Clerk, 'Vengeance! Just you wait! Turnip'll go to the Army. I wanted to help . . . but now . . . you'll come to me yet . . . Vengeance!'

The poor woman blenched and spread her arms. She opened her mouth as if to say something. But by now the Clerk, having picked up his check green cord hat, was beating a hasty retreat, waving the log with one hand and holding up his miserably torn cords and nankeens with the other.

II

A few other persons and a sorry sight.

About an hour later, Turnip returned from the forest on one of the manor carts with Łukasz the carpenter. Turnip was as tall as a poplar and very tough – built to wield an axe. He went to the forest every day now, as the squire had sold to the Jews all the woods on which there was no easement, and all the pines were being felled. Turnip earned well, for his work was good. When he spat in his hands, grabbed the axe, swung it, grunted and struck, the whole tree would shake, and a chip half-a-yard long would fly off. And he had no equal for loading the wood on to the carts. The Jews, who moved about the wood with their measuring-sticks, gazing at the tree-tops as though they were searching for crows' nests, could not help wondering at his strength. Drysla, a wealthy merchant from Dunceford, would say to him:

'Oh, Turnip, you're a devil of a fellow! Here, six coppers for vodka – no, wait; five coppers for vodka . . .'

Turnip just went on swinging his axe so hard that the sound carried. Sometimes, just to keep his spirits up, he would call out: 'Ho-op, Hop!' The cry would vanish amongst the trees, and then the echo would send it back. Again there would be silence, except for the crash of his axe. At times the pines would break this with the usual soughing of their branches.

Sometimes the lumberjacks would sing, and in this too Turnip had no rival. It was a treat to hear him bellowing out the song he had taught the others:

> 'Something in the wood went crash,
> Down it came with a dreadful smash.
> A poor old gnat fell off a pine,
> He hit the ground and broke his spine.'

And so on.

At the inn too, Turnip was much in evidence. He was

extremely fond of spirits, and became very pugnacious when drunk. One day he made such a big hole in the head of Damazy, one of the manor stable-boys, that Józwowa the housekeeper swore she could see his soul through it. Another time, when he was only seventeen, he had a fight at the inn with some soldiers on leave. Mr Skorabiewski, who was still Elder at the time, called him over to the office, gave him a box or two on the ears, for form's sake, and asked benevolently:

'Turnip, for God's sake! How on earth did you manage? There were seven of them!' to which Turnip replied:

'Well, your honour, their legs go bad from marching and as soon as I touched one of them, he'd just fall over.'

Mr Skorabiewski hushed up the affair. He was always particularly kind to Turnip: the old women even used to whisper in each other's ears that Turnip was his son: 'You can see the son-of-a-bitch has a gentleman's bearing . . .'

This was in fact not the case, although it was true that everyone knew Turnip's mother and no one had ever met his father. Turnip himself had been tenant of a house and four acres of land when the enfranchisement came. From then on he worked the land as his own, and as he was thrifty, things went quite well for him. Then he married, and he could not have found a better woman. So everything would probably have gone very well, had it not been for his exaggerated fondness for vodka. But there was nothing to be done about it. Whenever anyone made an observation, he would immediately retort: 'If I drinks, it's my business, and you keep out of it!'

He feared no one in the village, and only knew manners in front of the Clerk. If he saw the green hat, the turned-up nose and the goatee beard slowly swaggering down the road on long legs, he would go for his cap immediately. The Clerk knew a few things about Turnip. Turnip had been asked to transport some papers during the stormy days, and he had agreed. What was it to him? Anyway, he was only fifteen at the time, just a boy watching the pigs and the geese. Nevertheless, he now felt that he might have to answer for carting those papers about, and consequently he was afraid of the Clerk.

Such was Turnip.

When he got back from the forest that day, the woman ran out of the hut to meet him with tears and wailing.

'Oh, you poor thing! I won't be seeing you for much longer, I won't be washing your shirts or cooking your food. You'll go off to the ends of the earth, you poor wretch!' Turnip was taken aback.

'Have you been eating parsley, woman, or did you get stung by a fly?'

'I ain't been eating nothing, and nothing's bitten me, but the Clerk came here and he says you can't wriggle out of the army in no way now. Oh, you'll be sent to the ends of the earth!'

He started asking her what and how, so she told him everything, only concealing the Clerk's lechery, fearing that Turnip might go and say something stupid to him or, worse still, beat him up, only making matters worse.

'You idiot!' said Turnip at last. 'What are you bleating about? They won't take me into the army 'cause I'm too old, and anyway, I've got a house, I've got land, I've got you, stupid, and I've got that bleeding nuisance too.' Saying this, he pointed to a cradle in which the bleeding nuisance, that is to say a tough one-year-old boy, was kicking away and yelling hard enough to deafen the dead.

The woman began to wipe her eyes on the apron, but went on.

'That doesn't mean anything! Doesn't he know about all them papers you were carting about from forest to forest?'

Here, Turnip began to scratch his head.

'Aye, he knows all right . . .' And after a moment he added: 'I'll go and talk to him – maybe there's nothing to worry about.'

'Yes, go,' said the woman, 'but take a rouble with you. You can't go near him without a rouble.'

Turnip took a rouble from the chest and set off to see the Clerk.

The Clerk was a bachelor, so he did not live in a separate house. He lived in one of the stone farm-hands' quarters by the lake. There he had two rooms to himself with a separate hall-way.

The first room was empty but for some straw and a pair of gaiters, while the second served as both bedroom and sitting-room. There was a bed, which was almost never made up, and on it two pillows without covers, shedding their down. Next to it stood a table; on it were an inkstand, a few pens, some official books, a dozen or so numbers of Mr Breslauer's edition of *Isabella of Spain,* two dirty English collars, a jar of pomade, some cigarette-holders, and finally a candle in a tin candlestick with a few flies drowned in the wax around the reddish wick.

By the window hung a sizable mirror, and opposite stood a chest of drawers containing the Clerk's flamboyant toilette; pants of every shade, waistcoats of magical colours, ties, gloves, patent shoes and even a top hat, which the Clerk would don when he had to go to the district town of Dunceford.

At the moment of which we speak, the Clerk's cords and nankeens were resting on a chair by the bed, while the Clerk himself lay on it, reading the latest number of Mr Breslauer's edition of *Isabella of Spain.*

His condition – the Clerk's not Mr Breslauer's – was terrible. So terrible that one would need the style of a Victor Hugo to depict just how terrible it really was.

To begin with, his wound kept him in agony. His reading of *Isabella,* usually his most pleasant distraction and solace, now increased not only his suffering but also the bitterness he felt after the incident with Kruczek.

He felt a little feverish and found it difficult to concentrate. Terrible dreams visited him from time to time. He was just reading about the young Serrano making his appearance at the Escorial, covered in wounds, after his glorious victory over the Carlists. The young Isabella was pale and moved as she received him. The muslin on her breast heaved with passion.

'General, are you hurt?' she asked Serrano, her voice quivering.

At this point, the unhappy Skrofulowski began to fancy that he was Serrano.

'Oh, yes, I am indeed hurt,' he replied in a dispirited tone. 'Forgive me, most noble lady, but I cannot tell you where . . . etiquette will not permit . . . Oh . . . Oh, damn that . . .'

'You must rest, General. Sit down, sit down. Tell me of your chivalrous deeds.'

'I can tell you everything, but sitting down is out of the question!' exclaimed Serrano in despair. 'Oh, forgive me, my

Queen. That cursed Krucz . . . That cursed Don José . . .
Oooh . . .'

Here pain shattered the dream. Serrano looked round; the
candle on the table crackled as one of the flies soaked in wax
began to burn. Other flies were crawling over the walls. So it
was one of the farm-hands' quarters and not the Escorial, and
there was no Queen Isabella. Now Mr Skrofulowski came back
to his senses completely, lifted himself on the bed, soaked a
kerchief in the jug of water standing under it and changed his
compress.

After this he turned his face to the wall and fell asleep, or
rather, sank into a dreamy torpor and once more found himself
galloping towards the Escorial by special post.

'My dear Serrano! My darling! I'll dress your wounds
myself,' whispered the Queen.

The hair bristled on Serrano's head. He realised the full
horror of his position. How could he disobey the Queen, and
yet how could he submit to such an intimate operation? Cold
sweat was forming on his brow, when suddenly . . .

Suddenly the Queen vanished and the door opened with a
crash, revealing none other than Don José, Serrano's bitter
foe.

'What do you want? Who are you?' called out Serrano.

'It's me – Turnip,' replied Don José bashfully.

Skrofulowski woke up for the second time. The Escorial
had once again turned into the farm-hands' quarters. The candle was still burning, the fly by the wick was crackling and
shooting out blue droplets. In the doorway stood Turnip, and
behind him . . . the pen is trembling in my hand . . . Kruczek
had thrust his head and neck through the open door. The
monster's eyes were fixed on Mr Skrofulowski and something
akin to a leer hovered on his face.

Mr Skrofulowski really did come out in a cold sweat, and
only one thought flashed through his head: 'Turnip's come to
break my bones, and Kruczek's here to help . . .'

'What do you both want here?' he screamed in terror.

Turnip put a rouble on the table and said humbly:

'It's me, your honour. I've come about that draft . . .'

'Out! Out! Out!' bellowed Skrofulowski, whose courage had
suddenly returned. He leapt to his feet and made for Turnip

menacingly, but at that moment pain from the Carlist wound seared through him, and he fell back on to the pillows with stifled moans.

III

Rumination followed by Eureka.

The wound began to fester.

I expect that my fair readers are beginning to shed tears for my hero, so before one of them swoons I will hasten to say that he did not die of this wound. He was destined to live on for a long time yet. Besides, if he had died I should have had to break my pen and end the tale. But since he did not, I shall get on with it.

As we have seen, the wound began to fester, but this unexpectedly turned to the advantage of the Grand Chancellor of Woollyhead. This came about very simply; the wound attracted all the cardinal humours, which promptly left his head, allowing him to think more clearly. And he immediately realised that he had been very foolish until now. Just consider: the Clerk had, as you might say, set his heart on Turnip's wife – and little wonder, for you would not find better in the whole district of Dunceford – so he wanted to get rid of Turnip. Once Turnip had been conscripted into the army, the Clerk could throw all restraint to the winds.

However, it was not all that easy to slip Turnip on to the list in lieu of the Elder's son. A Clerk is a great power, and Mr Skrofulowski was a great power amongst Clerks, but unfortunately he was not the deciding authority in the matter of conscription. He would have to get round the Rural Guard, the Military Commission, the District Governor and the Superintendent of the Guard, and none of these was particularly interested in endowing the army and state with a Turnip in preference to a Beet.

'Slip him on to the recruitment lists – and then what?' my likable hero asked himself. They would check the lists, and since the registers have to be enclosed and since Turnip could not be gagged, they might smell a rat, and he might even lose his Clerk's post, and that would be that.

The greatest men have made mistakes under the influence of passion, and their greatness lies in their readiness to admit this. Skrofulowski admitted to himself that in promising to Beet that he would put Turnip on the draft list he had made the first mistake, that in going to assault Turnip's wife by her hackle he had made the second, and that in scaring her and her husband with the idea of conscription he had blundered for the third time. O exalted moment, when the truly great man says to himself 'I'm an ass!', you came to Woollyhead! You flew in on wings from the place where the sublime rests on the supreme, for at that very moment, Skrofulowski did quite distinctly say to himself:

'I'm an ass!'

But was he to drop the plan now, now that he had already baptised it with the blood of his own (in his excitement, he said: of his own breast), was he to abandon it now that he had consecrated it with a brand new pair of cords (for which he had still not paid Srul the tailor), and a pair of nankeens which he had only worn once or twice? No. Never! On the contrary: now that his appetite for Turnip's wife had been heightened by a desire for vengeance on them both, and Kruczek as well, Skrofulowski swore to himself that it would be lunacy not to make things hot for Turnip.

So he began to ponder over the ways and means for the whole of the first day, regularly changing his compresses, he pondered for the whole of the second, still changing the compresses, and he pondered all through the third, still changing the compresses, and can my reader imagine what he thought up? – Precisely nothing.

On the fourth day the village messenger brought him some diachylum from the Dunceford chemist. Skrofulowski smeared some on to a dressing, applied it, and behold the miraculous effects of this *medicamentum* – almost immediately exclaimed:

'I've found it!'

He had indeed found something.

IV

Which could be entitled: 'The Beast is Netted'.

A few days later, whether five or six I do not rightly know, Elder Beet, Councillor Gomuła and young Turnip were sitting in the side-parlour of the Woollyhead inn. The Elder took up his glass.

'Why don't you quit arguing about it when there's nothing to argue about,' he said.

'I say the Frenchman won't let the Prussian get him,' said Gomuła, banging his fist on the table.

'The Prussian's a clever rascal,' retorted Turnip.

'So what, he's clever? The Turk'll help the French, and the Turk's the strongest of all.'

'You don't know what you're talking about – Garibaldo's the strongest.'

'What are you on about now? Where d'you fish this Garibaldo out of?'

'I didn't fish him up nowhere – didn't they say that six years back he sailed up the Vistula with boats and a lot of men? Only he di'n't like the beer in Warsaw, 'cause he's used to better, so he went back.'

'Don't talk such rot – Every Kraut's a Jew!'

'Garibaldo ain't no Kraut!'

'What is he then?'

'Well, I mean . . . I suppose he's just another emperor!'

'You're bloody clever, you are!'

'You're not much cleverer . . .'

'You'd better have another drink,' said the Elder.

'Your health, friend!'

'Your health!'

'Cheers!'

'Cheers!'

'The Lord grant happiness!'

All three drank, but since the Franco-Prussian war was on, Councillor Gomuła came back to politics.

'The French,' he said, 'are a lecherous people. I don't remember them, but my father used to tell how when they was

billeted on us it was like the Day of Final Judgment in Woollyhead. They was awful interested in the women. Next door to
us lived Staś (Walenty's father), and they had a Frenchman in
the house – maybe even two; I can't remember. One night Staś
wakes up and says to his wife; "Kaśka, Kaśka! Look, the
Frenchman's tinkering about with you." And she says; "Yes, I
know." So Staś says; "Well, tell him to go and get lost!" and
the woman says; "Just you try and talk to him – he don't
understand Polish." So what could he do?'

'Come on, let's have another drink,' said Beet after a while.

'God grant happiness!'

'The Lord be generous!'

'Your health!'

So they had another drink, and as they were drinking
arrack, Turnip slammed his empty glass down on the table and
said:

'Ah, it's good stuff – really good!'

'Have some more,' said Beet.

'Pour it out!'

Turnip was getting redder, and Beet kept filling his glass.

'You can lift a bushel of peas on to your back with one hand
all right, but I bet you'd be scared of going to war . . .' he said
to Turnip after a while.

'Why should I be scared? If it's just a question of fighting,
I can fight!'

'Some people is small and brave, others is big, strong and
yeller,' Gomuła chipped in.

'Rubbish!' retorted Turnip, 'I'm not yeller!'

'Who knows?' rejoined Gomuła.

'I can tell you,' retorted Turnip, showing a fist the size of a
loaf of bread, 'that I'd only have to put this fist in your spine,
and you'd fall apart like an old barrel.'

'I don't think so.'

'Give over,' interrupted the Elder. 'You're not going to
start a fight, are you? Have another drink instead.'

They did have another drink, but this time Beet and
Gomuła only wetted their lips. Turnip knocked back a full
glass of arrack, and it went straight to his head.

'Now embrace each other,' said the Elder.

Turnip almost burst into tears over the slobbering embrace,

which meant that he was pretty drunk. He then began bitterly lamenting a roan calf which had died in his shed one night a couple of weeks earlier.

'Oh, the Lord God took such a beautiful calf from me!' he wailed pitifully.

'Come on, don't get upset,' said Beet. 'The Clerk got a paper from the District Office today, and it says the manor wood's going to be for the peasants.'

To which Turnip answered:

'That's justice! I mean, the squire didn't plant the wood, did he?' But his mind went back to his woes.

'Oh, it wasn't half a good beast. When it nudged the cow during sucking, her arse nearly hit the beams.'

'The Clerk said . . .'

'Damn the Clerk!' interrupted Turnip angrily. 'The Clerk means as much to me as your big toe.'

'Watch out he don't revenge himself. Here, have another drink.'

They had yet another drink. Turnip felt comforted and sat down on the stool quietly. Just then, the door opened to reveal the green hat, turned-up nose and goatee beard of the Clerk. Turnip, whose cap was perched on the back of his head, threw it to the floor, stood up and gurgled:

'Lord be praised!'

'Is the Elder here?' asked the Clerk.

'Yes!' answered three voices.

The Clerk approached, while Szmul the innkeeper rushed up with a glass of arrack. Skrofulowski sniffed at it, made a face and sat down by the table. There was silence for a moment. Then Gomuła started.

'Mister Clerk?'

'What?'

'Is it true about the wood?'

'Yes, quite true, only you must all sign the request together.'

'I ain't signing nothing,' said Turnip, who felt a repugnance common to all peasants towards signing his name.

'Nobody's asking you to. If you don't sign, you won't get anything. It's up to you.'

Turnip started scratching his head, while the Clerk went on

in an official tone, speaking to the Elder and the Councillor.

'Yes, it is true about the wood, but everyone has to fence off his own part, so there are no quarrels afterwards.'

'Yeah! The fence'll cost more than the forest's worth,' butted in Turnip.

The Clerk ignored him.

'The authorities,' he said to the Elder and the Councillor,' are providing money for the cost of the fence. Everyone will make a profit on it, as they're sending fifty roubles per lot.'

Turnip's eyes began to sparkle drunkenly.

'In that case I'll sign. Where's the money?'

'I've got it,' said the Clerk, 'and here's the document.' Saying this, he produced a piece of paper folded in four and read out something that the peasants listened to with delight, though to tell the truth they did not grasp a single word. Had Turnip been a little more sober, however, he would have noticed the Elder winking at the Councillor.

'Well, who's first?' said the Clerk, producing the money.

They took turns to sign, but when Turnip took the pen Skrofulowski pulled away the document and said:

'Maybe you don't want to? Everything's voluntary here.'

'You bet I want to!'

The Clerk shouted:

'Szmul!'

Szmul appeared in the doorway.

'What does Mister Clerk want?'

'Come and witness that this is all voluntary.' Then he said to Turnip once more:

'Maybe you don't want to?' But Turnip had already signed, making a blot about the size of Szmul. He took the money from the Clerk, all fifty roubles of it, put it away in his shirt and called:

'Bring more harrack!'

Szmul brought it. They had a couple more draughts, and then Turnip leant his fists on his knees and started dozing. He lurched once, lurched again, and finally fell off the stool, mumbling as he fell:

'The Lord be merciful to me a sinner!'

His wife did not come to fetch him, knowing she would not go unscathed if he was drunk. It often happened. The following day, Turnip would kiss her hands and beg forgiveness. When sober, he would never say anything unpleasant to her, but when drunk, he would often let her have it. So Turnip spent the night at the inn. The next day he woke up at sunrise. He looked round, his eyes wide with amazement as he perceived that he was not at home but at the inn, and not even in the side-parlour where he had been on the previous evening, but in the public room beyond the counter. He crossed himself, then took a second look round. The sun was already rising and throwing its rays through the multi-coloured windows on to the counter. Szmul, wearing his burial shirt and zizith, stood by the window, swaying as he recited his prayers.

'Szmul, you infidel!' yelled Turnip.

Szmul took no notice. He swayed backwards and forwards, then took something out of his shirt, kissed it, and went on wailing at the Lord God, thanking Him for the dawn and the sun in the sky, for tearing the night off the earth and making day, for being strong and great.

Turnip began to scratch, just like any peasant who has spent a night at the inn, and suddenly he came across the money.

'Jesus, Mary! What's this?'

Meanwhile, Szmul had stopped praying, and, taking off the shirt and zizith, went into the parlour to put them away. He came back slowly, very grave and calm.

'Szmul!'

'What d'you want?'

'What's this money I've got?'

'Don't you know, stupid? Yesterday you agreed with the Elder that you'd go and report to the ranks instead of his son; you took the money and signed the contract.'

The peasant went white as a sheet. He threw his cap to the floor, threw himself on to the floor as well and started sobbing so loud that the window-panes shuddered.

'Now get out, you soljer,' said Szmul phlegmatically in Russian.

Half an hour later, Turnip returned home. His wife, who was cooking, heard the gate open and angrily ran out to meet him.

'You drunkard!' she began, but when she saw him she

shuddered, for he was barely recognisable. 'What's wrong with you?'

Turnip went into the house, but found himself unable to utter a single word. He sat on the bench for a while staring at the floor. The woman started asking and eventually got everything out of him.

'They sold me just like the Jews sold Christ!' he concluded, ignoring the fact that Christ had been sold under somewhat different conditions. Then she began to wail, he joined in, and the child in the cradle started yelling its head off, while Kruczek howled so pitifully in the doorway that women rushed out of their houses, clutching spoons and asking each other:

'What's going on over at the Turnips'?'

'I suppose he must have beaten her up or something.'

She was indeed wailing louder than Turnip, for the poor woman loved him more than anything else in the world.

V

In which we are acquainted with the legislative body of Woollyhead and its leading lights.

On the following day there was a session of the village court. Councillors gathered from all over the neighbourhood, with the exception of the gentlemen, alias the nobility, several of whom were councillors. But these few did not wish to differ from the rest and stuck to the English policy – the principle of non-intervention so greatly extolled by that remarkable statesman John Bright. This did not, however, prevent the intelligentsia from wielding an indirect influence over the fate of the neighbourhood. If some member of the gentry had a problem, he would invite Mr Skrofulowski to his house on the eve of the session. Vodka was brought in, cigars were passed around, and the whole matter would be discussed in a relaxed manner. Dinner followed, and Skrofulowski was politely invited to partake with: 'Please, Mr Skrofulowski, do be seated!' So

Mr Skrofulowski would sit down to dinner, and on the following day he would casually say to the Elder: 'I had dinner with the Mieciszewskis (or Ościeszyńskis or Skorabiewskis) yesterday. Hmmm . . . I know what that means; there's an unmarried daughter.'

At table, Mr Skrofulowski kept up excellent manners and ate all sorts of mysterious dishes just as he saw others eat them, trying to show all the while that this familiarity with the manor did not flatter him unduly.

He was a man of great tact and he knew how to mix in every milieu. As a result, he not only kept his self-assurance, but even joined in the conversation, never failing to mention as he did so 'that kindly Chief' or 'that splendid Governor' with whom only yesterday or the other day he had played a couple of rubbers at a rouble a point. In a word, he would show everyone that he was on excellent terms with all the eminent personalities of the district of Dunceford. He did notice, it is true, that the ladies would stare at their plates in a curious manner during these accounts, but he was quick to perceive that this must be the fashion. Another thing that struck him as strange was the way in which after dinner, before he had even started taking his leave, the squire would slap him on the shoulder and say: 'Well, goodbye to you, Mr Skrofulowski!' Again he understood that this must be the accepted form in high society. It must be added that just as he was saying goodbye and shaking hands with his host, he could always feel something crisp in the latter's hand. He would then bend his fingers and, scraping the squire's palm, scoop that 'crisp something' out of it, never, however, forgetting to add:

'Oh, sir! Between us this isn't necessary. As for your problem, you need not worry.'

And indeed, the host did not need to worry, for Skrofulowski held Beet and Councillor Gomuła in his grip, and between the three of them they held all the other councillors in theirs, so that the latter were only allowed the privilege of approving the decisions of this triumvirate. There is nothing in any way extraordinary about this; in every collegiate body it is always the members of genius who monopolise all the influence and hold the rudder.

With such efficient management, and with Mr Skrofulowski's innate talents, local affairs would have presented no problem, had it not been for one drawback, namely, that Mr Skrofulowski only took the floor on certain occasions, in order to explain to the assembly just how a case should be considered from the legal point of view. Other cases, particularly those not preceded by anything crisp, he would leave to the independent discretion of the assembly, picking his nose with nonchalance, to the great anxiety of the councillors who would feel in these moments that their brains had been amputated.

Of the gentry, or, to be more precise, of the gentlemen, only Mr Floss, owner of Lower Progress, took part in the sessions in his capacity as councillor, claiming that it was the duty of the intelligentsia to do so. For this he was universally condemned. The gentry assumed that Mr Floss must be a Red; the very name 'Floss' seemed somehow to confirm this. The peasants, fired by a democratic sense of their own individuality, maintained that it was not proper for a gentleman to sit on the same bench as a whole lot of peasants – the best proof of which was that 'other gentlemen don't'. Actually, the peasants suspected that Mr Floss was not a real gentleman at all. As Skrofulowski did not like him either (Mr Floss never having tried to make himself worthy of the latter's esteem with the aid of anything crisp, and having once even told him to shut up in public), the ill-will felt towards Mr Floss was universal. One fine morning, the councillor sitting beside him said, in the presence of the entire assembly: 'I suppose you think you're a gentleman, sir? I mean; Squire Ościeszyński – he's a gentleman; Squire Skorabiewski – he's a gentleman too. But you ain't no gentleman, you're just an upstart.' Hearing this, Mr Floss (who had just acquired Crumbledown as well) gave up and left the village to itself.

'He asked for it,' commented the gentry, and to support the principle of non-intervention, they hauled out one of those proverbs that constitute the wisdom of nations: 'You can butter a peasant', etc.

So, without further disturbance on the part of the intelligentsia, the village deliberated on its own affairs unaided, using only the Woollyhead intellect, which, after all, should have been quite sufficient for Woollyhead, on the strength of the theory that the Galician intellect is sufficient to govern

Galicia, and the Parisian adequate for Paris. Besides, it is con-
clusively proven that common sense or 'healthy peasant understanding', as it is called in the Vistula Region, is worth far
more than any sophistry of foreign origin. That the inhabitants
of this country bring this 'healthy understanding' into the
world with them at birth is a well-attested fact.

This became immediately apparent in Woollyhead at the
session of which we speak. A request from the District Office
was read out, demanding that the village repair, at its own
expense, that part of the Dunceford road lying within its
boundaries. This project did not particularly appeal to the
patres conscripti, and one of the senators hastened to express
the enlightened view that there was no point in repairing the
road since one could just as easily drive through Mr Skorabiewski's meadow. Had Mr Skorabiewski been present, he
might have found something to say against this *pro bono
publico*, but he was not present, being a subscriber to the principle of non-intervention. And so the proposal would certainly
have been passed unanimously, had it not been for the fact
that Mr Skrofulowski had been invited to dinner at Mr Skorabiewski's the previous day. During the meal he had enter-
tained Miss Jadwiga with the story of two Spanish generals
being garrotted in Madrid (gleaned from Mr Breslauer's edition of *Isabella of Spain*), and after dinner, while he was saying
goodbye to Mr Skorabiewski, something crisp had changed
hands. So instead of writing down the amendment, the Clerk
stopped picking his nose and put down his pen, which
signified that he wished to take the floor.

'The Clerk wants to say somefink!' repeated voices all over
the room.

'I want to say that you're a bunch of fools!' said the Clerk
casually.

The power of real parliamentary oratory, however concise,
is so great that after this harangue against the proposal and
against the administrative policy of the Woollyhead body in
general, the assembly began to look round anxiously and
scratch its mental organs. This unmistakably denoted a deeper
penetration into the problem. Eventually, after a long silence,
one of the representatives questioned:

'Why's that?'

'Because you're fools!'

'I suppose he's right . . .' said one voice.

'A meadow's a meadow,' added another.

'And in spring you get stuck in it,' concluded a third.

As a result of this, the amendment recommending Mr Skorabiewski's meadow was discarded, the official project was
accepted, and the allocation of the repair costs according to the
estimate could proceed. Another suggestion was then put forward; that the manor take upon itself the entire expense in
return for the undisputed use of its meadow. When this too
was quashed, thanks again to Mr Skrofulowski, the efforts of
all the legislators concentrated exclusively on throwing the
burden off their own and on to another's shoulders – in order
not to deprive the neighbour of that inner warmth and satisfaction resulting from his realisation that he is making the
greatest sacrifices for the common good. But the spirit of justice was so deeply rooted in the minds of the Woollyhead legislators that nobody managed to wriggle out. Except for the
Elder and Councillor Gomuła, who took upon themselves the
burden of making sure that everything proceeded as speedily
as possible.

It must be admitted, however, that such a disinterested
sacrifice on the part of the Elder and the Councillor evoked a
certain amount of jealousy from the other councillors, like any
virtue that surpasses the mundane, and even produced an
angry voice of protest.

'And why's you two not goin' to pay?'

'Why should we pay, since you've already paid?' answered
Gomuła. It was an argument to which neither the healthy
Woollyhead intellect nor, I suspect, any other could have
found a reply. The protesting voice was silent for a moment,
and then spoke in a tone of conviction:

'Ah, yes . . .'

Thus the matter was closed completely, and the sorting out
of others would doubtless have followed immediately but for
the sudden and unexpected invasion of the legislative chamber
by two piglets. They rushed in madly through the badly-
closed door and began tearing around the room without any
conceivable motive, slipping through peoples' legs and squealing loudly. The debates were interrupted while the assembly

engaged in pursuit of the intruders, and for some time the deputies repeated with rare unanimity:

'Shoo! Damn you! Shoo! Here . . .' and so on.

Meanwhile, the piglets had taken refuge between Mr Skrofulowski's legs, staining his second pair of sand-coloured cords with a rather suspect shade of green. Had our newspapers correspondents in the provinces as they ought, we should have heard that this stain was never washed out, in spite of the fact that Mr Skrofulowski tried glycerine soap and scrubbed it with his own toothbrush.

Thanks to the resolution and energy that now as ever characterised the representatives of the community of Woollyhead, the piglets were seized by their hind trotters and ejected, protesting vigorously, and it was at last possible to get back to the agenda.

The next case on the list was that of a peasant by the name of Środa against the aforementioned Mr Floss. Having fed on the latter's clover one night, Środa's oxen had left this vale of tears in the morning and departed to a better bovine world. The desolate Środa placed this sad case before the court, begging for help and justice.

Having penetrated to the heart of the matter with its characteristic sharpness, the assembly came to the decision that although Środa had let his oxen loose on Floss's meadow on purpose, it was nevertheless certain that if there had been wheat or oats growing on it instead of that 'varmint' clover, the beasts would still be in the best and most desirable state of health, and would never have experienced those sorry ailments of bloating to which they had fallen victim. Starting out from this principal premise, the assembly arrived by an equally logical and strictly legal route at the conclusion that the man responsible for the death of the oxen was not Środa, but Mr Floss. Consequently, Mr Floss would have to reimburse Środa for his oxen, and as a future warning, he was ordered to pay the sum of five silver roubles to the court funds. Were he to refuse payment, the money would be seized from his factor, Icek Zweinos.

There followed a series of cases of a civil nature. These were all judged quite impartially on the scales of pure justice balanced on the fulcrum of the healthy Woollyhead intellect,

depending on how closely they concerned the brilliant Skrofulowski. Thanks to the English principle of non-intervention to
which the intelligentsia adhered, the general agreement and
unanimity were only rarely disputed (by remarks about the
pox, rotting livers and the plague, exchanged *en passant* in the
form of wishes, not only by the rival parties, but by the judges
as well).

Also thanks to this priceless principle of non-intervention, I
presume, all the cases were resolved in such a way that both
the winning and the losing parties had to contribute a rather
high quota to 'village funds'. On the one hand this ensured the
independence of the Elder and the Clerk – so essential in com-
munal institutions – and on the other hand it discouraged people from pettyfogging and thereby helped to raise the moral
standards of the Woollyhead community to the level of which
the eighteenth-century *philosophes* dreamt in vain. Also worthy
of mention is the fact, and here I refrain from voicing approval
or disapproval, that Mr Skrofulowski always wrote down in
the books only half of the sum destined for 'village funds', the
other half being designated for 'unforeseen necessities' – in
which the Clerk, the Elder or Councillor Gomuła might find
themselves.

Finally, the court proceeded to the adjudication of criminal
cases. The constable was ordered to fetch the prisoners. I need
hardly say that the most modern system of cellular detention,
catering to all the demands of progress, was applied in Woollyhead. This cannot be denied by even the most vicious
tongues. Anyone can go and see for himself that there are no
less than four partitions in the Elder's pigsty. The prisoners
can sit in these in the exclusive company of those creatures of
which a certain *Zoology For Young People* writes: 'PIG – an
animal rightly so named on account of its filthiness,' etc . . .,
and to which Nature unconditionally refused horns, further
proof of her far-sightedness. The prisoners sit in their cells in
this company, which, as we know, could in no way hinder
them in their reflections, their consideration of the evil done
and their resolution to mend their ways.

The constable, who had gone to the prison immediately,
brought before the court not two but distinctly a couple of
prisoners, from which the reader can easily perceive the deli-

cate nature and the psychological intricacy of the cases which the Woollyhead court sometimes had to judge. This particular case was exceedingly delicate. A certain Romeo, otherwise known as Wach Rechnio, and a certain Juliet, or Baśka Żabianka, served a certain farmer together, he as plough-hand and she as maid, and, there is no point in hiding it, they loved each other so much that they could not be apart, just like Nevadendeh and Bezendeh. In short, they loved each other passionately, though just how platonically I would not venture to say. But jealousy soon crept in between Romeo and Juliet, as the latter once noticed Romeo spending some time with Jagna, a maid from the manor. From that moment, the unhappy Juliet awaited her chance. One day that Romeo came back from the fields too early, according to Juliet, and began insistently clamouring for food, there was a crisis, followed by reciprocal explanations, in the course of which a few dozen blows with fists and a ladle were exchanged. The trace of these was clearly visible on Juliet's sublime features, as well as on the gashed forehead of Romeo's ideal masculine countenance. The court now had to decide which party was in the right and who was to pay to whom the sum of seventy-five silver kopecks, as damages for the amorous betrayal as well as for the consequences of the dispute.

The corrupting wind from the West had as yet not begun to wither the healthy spiritual pith of this court, which, disgusted to the depths of its soul by the idea of female emancipation – a concept completely alien to the more bucolic Slav disposition – gave Romeo the first say. Clutching his gashed head, he spoke thus:

'Honourable court! That there bitch's had it in for me for a long time. I come back in for the evening meal, and she says to me: "You dog, you pig!" she says, "the farmer's still in the fields and you're back already. I bet you'll lie down by the stove and start winking at me!" she says. And I never winked at her, only she saw me with Jagna from the manor the time I was helping her pull the bucket out of the well, and ever since then she's been waiting to give it to me. She banged the bowl down on the table so my dinner nearly spilled out. And then she wouldn't even let me eat in peace, only started cursing: "You son of a pagan, you traitor, you surveyor! You Suffragan!" she says. So when she says "Suffragan", I bashed her, but just like that; out of anger. And then she clouted me on the head with the ladle . . .' Here the sublime Juliet could hold herself no longer, and, clenching her fist, which she held right up to Romeo's nose, she began screaming hideously:

'It's not true! You're lying! It's not true! You're yapping like a dog!' She then burst into tears, and launched into the following address:

'Honourable court! Oh help me, I'm only a poor orphan, for God's sake! It's not by the well I saw him with Jagna – the plague on them both – I saw them go into the rye together, and they stayed there for at least five long rosaries. "You rake!" I says, "how many times did you say you loved me? And now you just want to bash me in the ribs!" I hope he drops dead! I wish his tongue would stick in his throat! It's not a ladle he needs – it's a club! Just look at my misfortune! The sun's still high and he comes home from the fields and calls for food . . . I says to him kindly, just like any nice person: "You thieving bastard, why d'you come crawling home when the farmer's still in the fields?" But I never called him "Suffragan", as the Lord's my witness . . . I hope he . . .' At this point the Elder called her to order.

'Shut your ugly mug, you slut!'

There was silence for a moment. The court began to ruminate over the sentence, and – what a delicate assessment of the problem – did not award either party the seventy-five kopecks. Instead, both for the sake of its own dignity and also as a warning to all loving couples throughout Woollyhead, it condemned both plaintiffs to a further twenty-four hours in the cellular prison and the payment of a silver rouble each to 'village funds'.

'From Wach Rechnio and Baśka Żabianka, fifty silver kopecks each for village funds,' Skrofulowski wrote down.

The session was over. Mr Skrofulowski rose, and pulled his sand-coloured cords up and his violet waistcoat down. The councillors were already picking up their caps and whips on the way out, when the door, which had been carefully closed after the invasion by the piglets, suddenly flew open to reveal Turnip, grim as night, with his wife and Kruczek behind.

Turnip's wife was white as a sheet; her lovely delicate fea-

tures expressed sadness and humility, while tears gushed from
her great black eyes and flowed down her cheeks. Turnip
walked in boldly with his head up, but when he saw the whole
court, the Elder with his medal, the crucifix, and the goatee
beard and turned-up nose on the long legs, he lost all his
composure, and said quietly:

'May He be praised!'

'Forever and ever!' replied the councillors in unison.

'And what do you want here?' came the threatening voice of
the Elder, who had been taken aback at first, but quickly
regained his self-assurance. 'You got some case? Had a fight or
something?'

'Let them speak!' said the Clerk unexpectedly.

'Honourable court . . . oh hell . . .' began Turnip.

'Shut up! Shut up!' interrupted the woman. 'Let me talk –
you keep quiet.' Having said this, she wiped her eyes and nose
on her apron, and then started telling the whole story in a
quivering voice. But what was she doing? – she had come to
complain about the Elder and the Clerk to the Elder and the
Clerk! 'They took him,' she went on, 'they promised him the
forest if he signed, so he signed. They gave him fifty roubles,
but he was drunk and he didn't know he was selling himself
and me and the baby. He was drunk, Honourable Court,
drunker than any of God's creatures,' she continued, weeping
copiously. 'A man doesn't know what he's doing when he's
drunk – even in court when a drunkard gets up to something
they let him off, 'cause they say he didn't know what he was
doing. For God's sake! A sober man doesn't sell himself for
fifty roubles! Oh, take pity on him, and on me and the innocent child! What will become of me, all alone in the world
without him, without my darling? God will give you happiness
and reward you for us wretches!' Here sobbing interrupted the
speech. Turnip was weeping too, wiping his nose with his
fingers now and again. The councillors had grown sullen.
They began to look at each other and finally turned towards
the Elder and the Clerk, wondering what to do. Then the
woman pulled herself together and started off once more.

'The poor fellow's wandering about more dead than alive.
He says to me 'I'll kill you and the child, I'll burn the house,
but I won't go!' But what am I to blame for? What about the

poor child? And he can't do anything any more; he won't touch the scythe or the axe any more, and just sits at home sighing and sighing. But I waited for this session – you people have got the Lord in your hearts and you won't let this injustice fall on us! Jesus of Nazareth, Holy Mother of Częstochowa, take our side, help us! . . .' Again there was a moment when only her sobbing could be heard, but then one old councillor murmured:

'It ain't nice to get a man drunk and then sell him.'

'No, it ain't right,' repeated others.

'May the Lord and His most holy Mother bless you!' exclaimed the woman, kneeling on the threshold. The Elder was confused, Councillor Gomuła looked morose, and both stared at the Clerk, who was picking his nose. When she had finished, he stopped picking it and said to the murmuring councillors:

'You fools!'

There was dead silence. Then the Clerk went on:

'It is clearly written that whoever tries to intervene in a voluntary contract will be judged by Naval Law, and do you know, you cretins, what Naval Law is? No, you half-wits, you don't know. Naval Law is . . .' At this point he produced his handkerchief and blew his nose, in which a great deal of matter had obviously gathered during this time. Then, in cold and official tones, he continued his speech:

'Any one of you bunch of fools who doesn't know what Naval Law is, just try and poke your nose into this kind of business, and you'll find out exactly what Naval Law is, because your seventh skin will be smarting. If a volunteer takes the place of a conscript, then beware of butting in, you lot. The agreement's been signed, there are witnesses, and that's all there is to it! This is understood in the constitution, the jurisprudence and in the first pronouncements of the Supreme Commission for Peasant Affairs, and if you don't believe me, then look it up in the procedure and the footnotes. And so what if they do have a drink over it? Don't you drink too, you idiots, always and everywhere?'

Had Justice herself with her scales and her bared sword emerged from behind the Elder's back and appeared to the councillors, she could not have had a greater effect than this

Naval Law, these constitutions, jurisprudences, procedures and footnotes. A deathly hush reigned until Gomuła said quietly, while everyone stared in amazement at his boldness: 'True, you sell your horses, so you have a drink; you sell your oxen, and you have a drink; you sell your pigs, and you have a drink. It's just the custom in these parts.'

'Yes, we just had a drink then out of habit,' butted in the Elder.

Then the councillors turned to Turnip with more confidence.

'Well, you've made your bed, now lie on it!'

'You're not a baby any more – don't you know what you're doing?'

'They won't pull your head off, you know!'

'And when you go to the army, you can take a farm-hand; he'll keep your land in order and your wife warm.' Gaiety began to creep into the gathering. Suddenly, the Clerk opened his mouth once more, and everything quietened down.

'But you have no idea of what to leave alone and what to intervene in. You *can* look into the fact that Turnip threatened his wife and child and swore to burn his house, and it is your duty to do so. Since Mrs Turnip has come here to complain, we cannot let her leave without justice being done.'

'Not true! Not true!' screamed the woman in despair. 'I di'nt complain; he's never hurt me. Oh Jesus! Oh sweet Wounds of God! This must be the end of the World.'

Nevertheless, the court went into consultation, and the immediate result of this was that not only did the Turnips gain nothing, but the court, rightly concerned as much with the maintenance of public order as with the safety of the woman, decided to protect her by detaining Turnip in the pigsty for two days. So that similar thoughts should not enter his head in future, he was also ordered to pay the sum of two roubles and fifty kopecks in silver to village funds. But Turnip leapt forward, protesting that he would not go to the pigsty; as for the village funds, instead of the two roubles, he threw the fifty he had taken from the Elder to the floor, screaming:

'Anybody who wants it can have it!'

There was terrible confusion. The constable rushed in and started tugging at Turnip. Turnip punched him, but he grabbed Turnip by the head. The woman started screaming, whereupon one of the councillors seized her by the scruff of the neck and threw her out of the door, with a punch for good measure. Others helped the constable, and dragged Turnip off to the pigsty by the hair. The Clerk wrote down:

'From Wawrzon Turnip, one silver rouble and twenty-five kopecks for village funds.'

Turnip's wife made her way back home dazed with grief. She did not look where she was going and stumbled over every stone, wringing her hands and wailing as she went.

The Elder, who had a good heart, said to Gomuła as they slowly walked towards the inn:

'I feel a bit sorry for that woman. Maybe I'll give her a quarter of peas or something.'

Meanwhile, the old councillor who had taken Turnip's side was saying to the others:

'I say that if the gentlemen came to the meetings, things like this wouldn't happen.' Having said it, he climbed on to his cart, cracked his whip and drove off, for he was not from Woollyhead.

VI

Imogen.

I suspect that by now the reader must have understood and appreciated the ingenious plan of my amiable hero. You might say that Mr Skrofulowski had checkmated the Turnips. Merely putting Turnip down on the list would have led to nothing. But getting him drunk and then making him sign the agreement and take the money made the whole matter that much more intricate. It was a skilful manoeuvre, and it proved that, with the help of more favourable circumstances, Mr Skrofulowski could have played a remarkable role in the world of diplomacy, for instance. The Elder, who had been prepared to buy out his son for eight hundred roubles (which certainly represented his entire collection of coppers), agreed to this plan with joy, particularly as Mr Skrofulowski, who was reasonable as well as ingenious, demanded only twenty-five roubles for himself in this case. It wasn't out of greed that he took this money, just as it wasn't out of greed that he split the village funds with Beet. I need hardly disclose that Mr Skrofulowski was in constant debt to Srul, the Dunceford tailor, who fitted the entire district out with 'real Paris fashions'.

Now that I have started along the road of disclosures, I shall no longer hide the reason for which Mr Skrofulowski dressed with such care. It is of course true that his aesthetic sensitivity was largely responsible, but there was another reason as well. Mr Skrofulowski was in love.

Do not, however, make the mistake of assuming that he loved Turnip's wife. For her he felt 'a little whim', as he had once put it himself, and that was all. Mr Skrofulowski was capable of higher-reaching and more complex emotions. At least my female readers, if not the others, must surely have guessed by now that the object of these emotions could be none other than Miss Jadwiga Skorabiewska.

Betimes, when the silver moon rose in the sky, Mr Skrofulowski would take his accordion, an instrument he played fluently, sit down on a bench by the farm-hands' quarters, and gazing in the direction of the manor, he would sing to the accompaniment of melancholy and sometimes even wheezing harmonies:

> 'At break of day I rise,
> Till late at night I weep;
> Asleep, I breathe in sighs,
> I have abandoned hope.'

Through the poetic silence of summer nights his voice would waft towards the manor, and after a pause he would add:

> 'Oh people, cruel people,
> Why have you poison'd a poet's life?'

Were anyone to accuse Mr Skrofulowski of sentimentality, I should have to correct him. The mind of this great man was too keen to be sentimental. Thus in his dreams, Miss Jadwiga became Isabella and he Serrano or Marfori, and then the expression of their relationship assumed the form it would have taken in Spain; kissing of stockings and so on. But since reality refused to give body to his dreams, this man of steel eventually betrayed himself.

This occurred one evening when he was passing by the manorial wood-shed and saw some petticoats drying on the line. By the initials J. S. and the coronet embroidered beside the fly, he realised that they belonged to Miss Jadwiga. Tell me, please – who could have resisted at a moment like this? Nor did he resist. He approached and smothered one of the petticoats with passionate kisses. Seeing this, the manor maid Małgośka rushed into the house to report that 'Mister Clerk's blowin' his nose in our young lady's petticoat!' Luckily, this was not credited, particularly as no *corpus delicti* could be found on the garment, and so the Clerk's feelings remained hidden from everyone.

Did he entertain any hope? Please do not think ill of him for this, but – he did. Every time he went to the manor some voice inside him, weak but persistent, would whisper in his ear: 'Miss Jadwiga might just press your foot under the table during dinner today . . .'

'Hmmm . . . I wouldn't even mind about my patent leather shoes,' he would add, with that magnanimity peculiar to those passionately in love.

The reading of Mr Breslauer's publications kept alive his faith in the possibility of his foot being pressed in some way. However, not only did Miss Jadwiga not press his foot with her own, she would look at him – who can understand women? – as though she were looking at a fence, a cat, a plate or something of the sort. What torments did the poor man not go through in order to attract her attention! While trying on some new tie of unbelievable hue, or donning a new pair of cords with a fabulous stripe, he would say to himself: 'Well, now she just can't fail to notice!' Srul himself would say, when bringing him a new set of clothes: 'Now, with trousers like that you can go and visit a countess!'

But no. He would go to dinner, and Miss Jadwiga would come into the room proud, virginal and pure as a queen, the folds and creases of her dress rustling around the marble mysteries of her body. She would then sit down and take the spoon in her thin fingers without so much as a glance in his direction.

'Doesn't she realise that it's expensive, apart from anything else?' Skrofulowski would say to himself in despair. But he never gave up hope. 'If only I were made Sub-Inspector, then I wouldn't budge from the manor. And from Sub-Inspector to Inspector isn't far! I'd have a calash and a pair of horses, and then she'd have to squeeze my hand, under the table at least . . .' Mr Skrofulowski would then immerse his thoughts in the extremely far-reaching consequences of this hand-squeezing, but we shall not divulge them as they are rather too emotional and personal.

In order to appreciate what a subtle being this Mr Skrofulowski was, one only has to look at the ease with which he managed to juxtapose on the one hand his sublime feelings for Miss Jadwiga, which embodied all the aristocratic dispositions of his youth, and on the other hand his 'little whim' for Turnip's wife. Although Turnip's wife was a beautiful woman, the Woollyhead Don Juan would certainly never have wasted so much time over her had it not been for her strange stubbornness, which deserved to be punished. Resistance from a common woman – to him of all people! – seemed to Mr Skrofulowski so impudent and at the same time so stupendous, that not only did she acquire in his eyes all the charms of a forbidden fruit, but he also decided to give her the lesson she so greatly deserved. The incident with Kruczek only hardened him in his resolve. But he knew that the victim would defend herself, and that was why he had invented the voluntary agreement between Turnip and the Elder, which appeared to place Turnip and his whole family at his mercy.

Turnip's wife had not given up, despite the incident in court. The next day was a Sunday, and she decided to go as usual to high mass in Humbug, and to go to the priest for advice at the same time. There were two of them; one was the parish-priest, Canon Flawless, but he was so old that his eyes had come right out of his head, like those of a fish, and his head shook from side to side continuously. The woman decided to by-pass him, and go to the curate, Father Siskin, who was very holy and intelligent and could give advice and comfort. She had originally wanted to set off early and see Father Siskin before mass, but as her husband was in the pigsty, she had to do all his work as well as her own. By the time she had tidied the house, fed the horse, the pigs and the cow, cooked some breakfast and taken it to Turnip in the pigsty, the sun was already high, and she realised that she would not make it before mass.

The service had already begun when she arrived. Women in green coats were sitting in the graveyard, pulling on the shoes they had brought with them. She did the same and went inside to church. Father Siskin was just delivering his sermon, while the Canon in his biretta sat on a chair by the altar, his eyes popping out and his head shaking in the usual way. The Gospel was over, and Father Siskin was, for some unknown reason, preaching about the medieval heresy of the Catharists, explaining to his parishioners just how they ought to regard this heresy and the bull *ex stercore* aimed at it, in accordance with the principles of the Church. He then very eloquently warned his lambs, the poor little birds of the heavens so dear to God, with great anxiety, not to listen like simpletons to the various false sophists and to people blinded by Satan's pride in general, for they sow thorns instead of wheat and will reap tears and sin. *En passant* he mentioned Condillac, Voltaire, Rousseau and Ochorowicz, without bothering to draw any distinction between them, and then passed on to a graphic description of the various misfortunes to which all sinners would be exposed in the next world.

The woman felt fresh strength welling up inside her, for although she could not understand what Father Siskin was saying, she assumed that 'it must be very beautiful, because he's shouting so hard he's come out in a sweat, and the people are sighing as if they were going to die.'

The sermon came to an end and the mass continued. The poor woman prayed and prayed as she had never prayed before, and she could feel her heart getting lighter and lighter. At last the solemn moment arrived. The Canon, white as a dove, took the Most Holy Sacrament out of the ciborium and turned towards the people. For a moment his shaking hands held up the monstrance like a sun in front of his face. He seemed to be gathering his thoughts, his eyes half-shut and his head bowed, gripped by the holiness of the moment, and finally he intoned:

'Before this Great Sacrament . . .'

And a hundred voices boomed in answer:

'We fall to our knees.

Let the Old Testament make way for the New,

Where reason is confused our faith is enlightenment.'

The psalm sounded so loud that the windows shuddered. The organ roared, the bells rang and the drum rolled outside the church. Bluish smoke rose from the thuribles and caught the sun's rays, which came through the windows in a bright rainbow. The priest lifted and lowered the Holy Sacrament amidst the music, the voices, the light and the smoke. This white old man with the monstrance looked like some heavenly apparition, radiant through the smoke. He diffused bliss and comfort, which poured into every heart and every pious soul. This sensation of well-being and solace also embraced the troubled soul of Turnip's wife. 'Oh Jesus of the Blessed Sacrament! Jesus!' called out the unhappy woman. 'Don't forsake me, your poor creature!' And tears gushed from her eyes, but not the tears she had shed in front of the Elder, only good, sweet and even serene tears, large as Calcutta pears. The woman fell on her face before the Majesty of God, unconscious of what was happening. She imagined that heavenly angels were lifting her from the ground and carrying her upwards to eternal happiness, where there was no Skrofulowski, no Elder, no draft list, but merely one vast sunburst. In the heart of that sunburst stood God's throne, surrounded by hosts of angels with white wings, just like little birds, and its radiance made her screw up her eyes.

The woman lay like this for a long time. When she looked up, mass was over and the church had emptied. The smoke had risen right up to the vault, the last people were leaving through the door and an old man was putting out the candles on the altar. So the woman got up and went to see the curate.

Father Siskin was eating his lunch, but he came out immediately he was told that a tearful woman wished to see him. He was a young priest, with a pale but serene face; he had a tall white forehead and wore a kindly smile on his face.

'What do you want, my good woman?' he asked in a quiet but melodious voice. Touching his knees, she started telling him the whole story, crying and kissing his hand all the while, and finally, raising her black eyes at him, she said: 'If only you could give me some advice, your reverence; I've come for advice.'

'And you were right, my good woman,' replied Father Siskin gently. 'But I can only give you one recommendation; offer up all your troubles to God. The Lord tries out His faithful. He even tries them cruelly, like Job whose own dogs licked his festering wounds, or like Azarias whom He blinded. But the Lord knows what He is doing, and He can reward His faithful in time. Consider the misfortune which has befallen your husband as a punishment for his grave sin of drunkenness, and thank God that by punishing him on earth He may let him off after his death.'

The woman looked at the priest with her black eyes, then embraced his knees again and left quietly, without a word. She could feel something strangling her as she walked. She would have liked to cry, but no tears came.

VII

Imogen.

At about five o'clock in the afternoon a blue parasol, a yellowish russet hat with blue ribbons and a hazel dress also trimmed with blue appeared on the main road between the cottages. It was Miss Jadwiga going for a walk with her cousin, Master Wiktor.

Miss Jadwiga was what you might call a lovely young lady. She had black hair, blue eyes and a milky complexion, and her charm was enhanced by the surprisingly studied, tidy and blooming dress, which seemed to radiate around her. Her beautiful girlish figure, with its generous outlines, seemed to float through the air. With one hand Miss Jadwiga held her parasol, and with the other her dress, beneath which could be seen the crimped hem of a white petticoat and a pair of lovely feet encased in little Hungarian boots.

Master Wiktor, who was walking beside her, also looked like a figure from a painting, despite his enormous stack of curly fair hair and the barely perceptible moustache beginning to appear on his lip.

Health, youth, gaiety and happiness radiated from this couple. But also to be seen in them were the symptoms of a higher and more solemn existence; the life of winged escape into the realms of thought, of grander passions, of boundless ideals and the gilded, iridescent paths of fancy.

In the midst of these cottages, the village children, the peasants, and the simplicity of the environment as a whole, they stood out like a pair of beings from another planet. It was rather pleasant to think that no link existed between this gorgeous, cultivated, poetic couple and the prosaic, grim, semi-animal life of the village. No spiritual link, at least. They strolled side by side, talking of poetry and literature just like any normal young lady and gentleman. Those people in canvas clothes, those peasants and their women could never hope to understand their words or their language. What a nice thought – admit it, my gentle readers.

There was nothing one had not heard a hundred times before in the conversation of this lovely couple. They fluttered from book to book, like butterflies from flower to flower. But such conversation never seems empty or commonplace when one is talking to the love of one's heart, when conversation is no more than a canvas on which love embroiders the golden flowers of its thoughts and feelings, when it reveals its nature as a white rose reveals its blushing heart. Such conversation soars up into the blue spheres like a bird, reaches out for the spiritual world and climbs ever higher, like a plant along a stake. Over at the inn people were drinking and talking of common things in common words, but this couple were drifting towards a different land on a ship that had, as Gounod's song says, 'masts of ivory, a flag of lilac silk and a rudder of pure gold'.

It might also be worth mentioning the fact that Miss Jadwiga was turning her cousin's head, just for practice. In these circumstances, the conversation most often turns to poetry.

'Have you read Asnyk's latest book?' asked the young man.

'Do you know, Wiktor,' replied Miss Jadwiga, 'that I'm absolutely crazy about Asnyk? Whenever I read him, I seem to hear some kind of music, and I cannot help thinking of myself in terms of that poem by Ujejski:

'Melting into silence,
Upon a cloud I lie;
My breath I cannot hear,
Sleepy tears fill my eye.
With sweetest scent embalmed
Upon a sea of violets,
Clasping hand in hand
I float . . . I drift . . .'

'Oh!' she interrupted herself suddenly, 'If I knew him I'm sure I'd fall in love with him! I'm sure we should understand one another.'

'Luckily he's married!' observed Master Wiktor drily.

'Miss Jadwiga inclined her head slightly, pursed her lips into the semblance of a smile so that little dimples formed in her cheeks, and, glancing sideways at Master Wiktor, asked:

'Why do you say "Luckily"?'

'Luckily for all those for whom life would become unbearable.' As he said this, Master Wiktor looked very tragic.

'Oh, you flatter me too much!'

Master Wiktor waxed lyrical.

'You're an angel . . .'

'Well . . . all right . . . let's talk about something else. So you don't like Asnyk?'

'I began to loathe him a moment ago!'

'You're a nasty pedantic person. I really ought to smack you. Please uncloud your face and name your favourite poet.'

'Sowiński . . .' murmured Master Wiktor grimly.

'Oh, I'm simply terrified of him! Irony, blood, fire, wild outbursts . . . Brrrr . . .!'

'That sort of thing doesn't frighten me!' As he said this, Master Wiktor looked ahead so courageously that even a dog which had run out of a nearby house hid its tail between its legs and retreated in terror.

They walked up towards the farm-hands' quarters; a goatee beard, a turned-up nose and a pale green tie flashed past one of the windows. Then they stopped by a pretty house covered in wild vines, with a back window looking out over a lake.

'Look at that pretty little house; it's the only poetic spot in the whole of Woollyhead.'

'What is it?'

'It used to be a day-nursery. The village children used to learn to read there while their parents were in the fields. Papa had it built specially.'

'And what happens there now?'

'Now it's full of barrels of vodka. You see, times have changed. Now we are just the neighbours of our peasants, and we have to try to have as little to do with them as possible.'

'Hmmm . . .' mumbled Master Wiktor, 'but still . . .' He did not finish the phrase, for they had come to a great puddle in which lay several pigs, 'rightly so named for their filthiness'. In order to circumvent the puddle, they had to pass by Turnip's cottage, so they went towards it.

Turnip's wife was sitting on the stump by the gate with her elbows leaning on her knees and her face in her hands. Her countenance was pale and stone-like. Her eyes were red, and there was a dim look in them as they stared blankly into the distance. She did not notice them pass, but the young lady noticed her.

'Good evening, Mrs Turnip!' The woman got up, approached and putting her arms around the knees of Miss Jadwiga and Master Wiktor began to cry quietly.

'What's the matter?' asked the young lady.

'Oh, my golden little peach! Oh, my rosy dawn! Maybe the Lord has sent you to me – help me, dear comforter!' Here she started telling the whole story, kissing the young lady's hands, or rather her gloves, which she stained with her tears. The young lady grew very confused. Her pretty, serious face grew distinctly worried, as she had no idea what to do. In the end, she said:

'What can I say to you, my dear Mrs Turnip? Enfin! I feel terribly sorry for you, but we have no authority now . . . we cannot interfere in anything . . . really, what can I advise? Go and see Papa . . . maybe Papa . . . Well, goodbye my dear Mrs Turnip . . .' Having said this, Miss Jadwiga lifted her dress higher, so that a white stocking with blue stripes appeared above the little boots, and she moved on with Master Wiktor.

'May the Lord bless you, my lovely little flower!' the woman called after them.

But Miss Jadwiga grew sad, and Master Wiktor thought he

could even see a tear in her eye. In order to dispel this sadness, he started talking about Kraszewski and various smaller fishes of the literary sea. As the conversation became more animated they forgot about this unpleasant affair.

Meanwhile, Turnip's wife said to herself:

'The manor? But I should have gone there in the first place, before going to the Elder. Where can I find help, if not at the manor? Oh, what a stupid woman I am!'

VIII

Imogen.

The manor had a porch overgrown with vines which looked out on to the courtyard and the poplar alley beyond. The squire and his family took coffee here after dinner in summer. They were sitting there now, with Canon Flawless, Father Siskin and Stołbicki, the distillery inspector. Mr Skorabiewski, a rather stout and ruddy man with a great moustache, was sitting in a chair smoking a pipe. Mrs Skorabiewska was pouring out the tea, while the inspector, who fancied himself as a nihilist, was teasing the old Canon.

'Why doesn't your reverence tell us about that famous battle?' he asked.

The Canon put his hand to his ear and asked:

'Eh?'

'About the battle,' repeated the inspector very loud.

'Oh! About the battle, eh?' said the Canon. With great concentration he began to whisper to himself and look upwards, evidently trying to remember something. The inspector had already made a face, getting ready to laugh, and everyone else waited for the account, which they had all heard a hundred times before, as the poor old Canon was always being dragged into it.

'What?' began the Canon. 'I was only a curate then, and Father Bland was the parish priest . . . that's right – Father Bland. He's the one who rebuilt the sacristy – eternal light . . . So just after high mass I said to him: "Father?" and he said;

"What?" "I think something's going to happen," I said. And he said: "I think something's going to happen too." We looked, and they came from behind the windmill on horseback and on foot, with cannons and flags. So I thought to myself: "Well!" And then from the other side; I thought it was sheep, but it wasn't sheep, it was cavalry. When they saw them they halted, and the others halted too. And then from the woods came the cavalry, so these ones went to the right, and the others went to the left, and then these went to the left, and the others went after them. These ones saw there was nothing to be done, so they went for the others too. Then they started shooting, and something flashed behind the hill. "Do you see that, father?" I said, and the parish priest said: "I see, all right!" And then they banged away with their cannons and rifles. The others tried to get to the river, but these ones wouldn't let them, so these ones got the others, and the others got them . . . These ones were on top at first, but then the others were. Explosions and smoke everywhere! And then they went in with their bayonets. But I could immediately tell that these ones were weakening. "Father, I think the others are winning," I said, and he replied: "I think they're winning too." I had only just finished saying it when these ones took to their heels, and the others went after them. Then they started drowning, killing and taking them prisoner, and I thought it was all over, but not at all! . . . They . . . I said, well, exactly! . . ."

At this point the old man waved his hand, and settling himself deeper in his chair, seemed to fall into a reverie while his head shook more violently than usual and his eyes popped right out.

The inspector was laughing so much there were tears in his eyes.

'Reverend Father,' he asked, 'who was fighting who, where and when?'

The Canon put a hand to his ear and said:

'Eh?'

'I just can't keep a straight face!' said the inspector to Mr Skorabiewski.

'Have a cigar.'

'Some coffee, perhaps?'

'No, I'm laughing too much.'

The Skorabiewskis were also laughing out of politeness to the inspector, although they had to listen to this story every single Sunday. The gaiety was suddenly interrupted by a quiet, frightened voice coming from just beyond the porch.

'The Lord be praised!'

Mr Skorabiewski jumped up, walked up to the front of the porch and said:

'Who's there?'

'It's me, Turnip's wife.'

'Well, what is it?'

The woman bowed as low as she could with the child on her arms and embraced him round the knees.

'I've come for help, honourable squire, and for mercy.'

'My dear Mrs Turnip, can't you even leave me in peace on a Sunday?' answered Mr Skorabiewski as candidly as if the woman had disturbed him on every single day of the week. 'You see that I have guests now. I can't leave them to come and talk to you.'

'I can wait . . .'

'Yes, why don't you wait – I won't vanish into thin air.' Having said this Mr Skorabiewski once again slipped his bulk into the porch, while the woman retreated to the garden fence where she took up a humble stance. But she had a long time to wait. The gentry were passing the time in conversation, and gay laughter drifted over towards her, gripping her heart in a strange way, for she did not feel like laughing, the poor wretch. Then Master Wiktor returned with Miss Jadwiga, and everyone went inside. The sun slowly began to dip. Jasiek the footman, whom Mr Skorabiewski used to call 'you two', came out on to the porch and began laying the table for tea. He changed the table-cloth, set out the cups and threw the spoons into them noisily. The woman waited and waited. She thought of going home and coming back later, but she was afraid that might be too late. She sat down on the grass by the fence and gave the child her breast. The child sucked its fill and fell into an unhealthy sleep; it had been a little weak since morning. The woman felt hot and cold shivers running through her from head to foot. Once or twice she got the jitters, but she took no notice and waited patiently. Gradually it grew dark and the moon rose into the vault of the sky. The tea things were ready and lamps were burning on the porch, but the guests did not appear for some time, as the young lady was playing the piano. Turnip's wife started reciting the Angelus to herself by the fence. Then she began to wonder how Mr Skorabiewski was going to save her. She did not understand how it was all done, but she knew that the squire, being a gentleman, must be on good terms with the District Chief and the Governor. He would only have to explain how it had all come about, and then everything would be put right, with God's help. And she knew that if the Elder or Mr Skrofulowski objected, he would know where to go for justice.

'The squire's always been good and merciful to the people,' she thought, 'and he won't forsake me now.' She was not mistaken, for Mr Skorabiewski was indeed a compassionate person. She reflected on how kind he had always been to Turnip, and on the fact that her dead mother had weened Miss Jadwiga, and she felt greatly comforted. 'People can say what they want,' she said to herself, 'but when hard times come you just have to go to the manor, and nowhere else.' The fact that she had already waited a couple of hours seemed so natural to her that she did not even think about it.

The guests came back on to the porch. Through the vine-leaves the woman could see the young lady holding a silver pot and pouring out tea, or, as her dead mother used to call it, 'a sort of fragrant water that makes you thirsty'. They began to drink it, talking and laughing merrily. It was only then that she was struck by the thought of how much more happiness there was in the gentry's condition than in the peasants', and tears again started running down her face for no reason. But the tears soon gave way to another sensation. 'You two' had just appeared on the porch with steaming dishes, and the woman remembered that she was hungry; she had only drunk a little milk that morning and had been unable to eat lunch.

'Oh, if only they'd let me chew some bones!' she thought. She knew very well that they would have given her much more than bones, but she did not want to intrude before the squire and his guests, and she felt too shy to ask.

At last the dinner came to an end. The inspector drove off immediately, and half an hour later the two priests climbed into the manor cabriolet. The woman watched the squire help the Canon up and judged that the right moment had come, so she came up to the porch. The cabriolet rolled away, and the squire shouted to the coachman:

'And don't spill them on the dyke, or I'll break your neck!' He then looked up at the sky, trying to make out the next day's weather, and finally caught sight of the woman's white blouse in the darkness.

'Who's there?'

'Turnip's wife.'

'Oh, it's you. Tell me what you want quickly – it's late.'

The woman told him everything. The squire puffed away at his pipe as he listened, and finally said:

'My dear friends, I'd love to help you if I could, but I had to make a resolution to keep out of village affairs. In the old days things were different – yes sir! . . . But now I can't have anything to do with you, nor you with me. Now you're just my neighbours.'

'I know, your honour,' said the woman, her voice shaking, 'but I thought maybe your honour would take pity on me . . .' Her voice broke off suddenly.

'That's all very well,' said Mr Skorabiewski,' but what can I do? I cannot break my word for you; and I cannot go and disturb the Governor on your account – as it is he complains that I pester him too much with my own affairs . . . I mean to say. I repeat that I am nothing to you, and you are nothing to me nowadays. You have your village council, and if that can't help you, you know where to find the Governor as well as I do. I mean to say . . . Nowadays you've got a better chance with him than I have. The old days have gone, my dear Mrs Turnip . . . Well, you'd better be off now. The Lord be with you.'

'The Lord God thank you,' answered the woman dully, embracing the squire's knees.

IX

Imogen.

After being released from the pigsty, Turnip went not to his house, but straight to the inn. It is well known that in time of trouble, a peasant drinks. Inspired, just like his wife, by the thought that in adversity it is best to seek help from the manor, he then went to see Mr Skorabiewski. Here he made a great mistake.

A man who is not sober does not know what he is saying. He was, like his wife, told all about the principle of non-intervention. But he was a persistent fellow, and he completely failed to grasp this highly diplomatic concept, as a result of the mental obtuseness generic in simple people. Worse still, he replied, with the boorishness also peculiar to peasants, that 'all the lords only think of themselves nowadays', and got himself ejected.

When he got back home he said to his wife:

'I've been to the manor.'

'And what did you get?'

He banged his fist down on the table.

'I feel like burning the place down – the bastards!'

'Shut up, you drunkard. What did the squire say?'

'He told me to go and see the Governor. The Devil take . . .'

'I guess we'll have to go to Dunceford, then.'

'All right then, I'll go. I mean; ain't there anybody bigger than the squire in this world?'

The odd thing was that since his visit to the manor, Turnip stopped talking about the Elder and the Clerk with the same fury as he now directed at the squire. The Elder and the Clerk had put him in a very nasty position, but that was only to be expected of them. The manor was different; it was there to help him but had failed to do so.

'I'll go to Dunceford and I'll show him I can do without him!' he decided.

'No you won't, my poor darling – I'll go. You'll only have a drink and start getting tough, and that'll just bring more trouble.'

Turnip would not agree to this at first, but in the afternoon he went to drown his sorrows at the inn and did the same on the next day. So the woman did not bother about him any more. She took the child, entrusted everything to God and set off for Dunceford on the Wednesday.

The horse was needed for work in the fields, so she went on foot. She set out at dawn, for it was three long miles to Dunceford. She was hoping to meet some good people on the road who might give her a lift on a cart, but she met no one. At nine o'clock she sat down exhausted at the edge of the forest. She ate a crust of bread and a couple of eggs she had brought in her basket, after which she set off once more. The sun was scorching. She met Herszek, a factor from Humbug who was taking a cartload of caged geese to town, and she begged him for a lift.

'God be with you, Mrs Turnip,' answered Herszek, 'but the road's so sandy the horse can only just pull me. Give me a rouble and I'll take you.'

Then she remembered that she had a six-kopeck piece tied up in her kerchief. She offered it to the Jew, but he answered:

'Six kopecks? well, no . . . Though you don't find them lying around in the street – it's money too . . .' Saying this, he whipped up his horse and drove on. It was getting hotter and streams of sweat began to pour down the woman's face. But she marched on bravely, and an hour later she entered Dunceford.

Anyone who knows his geography can tell you that on entering Dunceford from the Woollyhead side one has to pass by the Conventual Church. It used to house a miraculous picture of the Mother of God, and even today swarms of beggars surround it every Sunday, screaming their heads off. As this was a weekday, there was only one beggar sitting by the fence, stretching out a naked toeless foot from beneath his rags and holding out the top of a boot-wax tin as he sang:

'Holy Mother of God, Queen of the angels . . .' Seeing somebody pass, he stopped singing and, stretching his foot out further still, started screaming as though he were being flayed alive: 'Merciful people! A poor cripple begs for mercy! May the Lord give you every benefit on earth!'

When she saw him, the woman untied her kerchief, produced the six-kopeck piece, came up to him and said:

'Have you got five kopecks?' She only wanted to give him one, but when the beggar felt the coin in his hand, he started screaming:

'You hold six kopecks back from God! God will withhold His help from you! Go and jump in the lake before I get angry!'

So the woman said to herself: 'Let it be to the glory of God', and she went on her way.

When she got to the market-place, she was overcome with awe. It was easy enough to get to Dunceford, but just as easy to get lost there. It was some town! Already in a strange village you have to start asking around to find out where anyone lives, but what about a place like Dunceford! 'This place is like a sea – I'll drown in it,' thought the woman. There was nothing for it but to start asking people. She managed to find out without too much trouble where the District Chief lived, but when she got to his house, she was told that he had gone to the provincial capital. They told her to go and look for the Governor at the District Office. But where was the District Office? Oh, silly, silly woman – in Dunceford, of course. So she started looking around for the District Office in Dunceford, and at last she found herself in front of a great palace painted green with an eagle over the gate. It was frighteningly big. In front of it stood countless cabriolets, carts and Jewish traps; she thought there must be some kind of fair going on.

'Where's the District Office around here?' she asked a man wearing a tail-coat, bowing to his knees.

'You're standing right in front of it, woman!'

She summoned up her courage and entered the palace. She looked around; she saw nothing but corridors with doors to the left, doors to the right, doors in front, and yet more doors, and each one had strange lettering on it. The woman crossed herself. She opened the first door, very quietly and shyly, and found herself in a huge room divided into two by a little balustrade like a church. A man in a tail-coat with gold buttons and a pen behind his ear sat beyond the balustrade, and in front of it there was a crowd of gentlemen. The gentlemen were paying and paying, while the one in the tail-coat smoked a cigarette and wrote out slips which he gave to them. They

left as soon as they had collected their slips. The woman
assumed that one had to pay here, and she was sorry to have
given away her six kopecks. She approached the balustrade
very shyly. But nobody so much as looked at her.

She waited and waited. An hour passed. People left and
others came in, the clock behind the balustrade ticked away,
and she just stood there. At last, the place emptied and there
was nobody left. The official sat down at a table and started
writing. The woman braced herself and said:

'Jesus Christ be praised!'

'What is it?'

'Honourable Governor . . .'

'This is the cash-desk.'

'Honourable Governor . . .'

'This is the cash-desk, I tell you!'

'Where's the Governor, then?'

'There!' Said the official, pointing to the door.

The woman went out into the corridor again. There? Yes,
but where? Doors all over the place. Which one should she
try? She caught sight of a peasant with a whip standing
amongst the people coming and going, so she went up to him.

'Father?'

'What d'you want?'

'Where you from?'

'From Porkington, why?'

'Where's the Governor?'

'How should I know?'

Then she asked another man with gold buttons. This one
was not wearing tails and he had holes at the elbows. He did
not even listen to her, and just snorted:

'I've got no time!'

Again she opened a door at random, not realising, poor
creature, that the notice on it read: 'private – staff only.' She
had not seen the notice, and even if she had she would not
have understood. She opened the door and looked in. The
room was empty; by the window someone was snoozing on a
bench. Beyond him was the door to another room, in which
men in tails and uniforms could be seen walking about.

She went up to the man sleeping on the bench. She did not
feel quite so shy with him as he looked common and the boots

on the legs stretched out in front of him had holes in them. She nudged him in the arm. He jumped up, looked at her and shouted:

'Not allowed! *Nielzya!* Get out!' The woman took to her heels. He cuffed her and slammed the door behind her.

For the third time she found herself in the same corridor. She sat down by the first door she could find and, with real peasant determination, decided to wait there to the end of the world if necessary. 'Maybe someone will come and ask me,' she thought. She was not crying, but she rubbed her eyes, which were watering. The whole corridor with all its doors was beginning to spin around her.

People rushed hither and thither, slamming doors and talking to each other, just as if it were market-day.

At last God took pity on her. A stately nobleman, whom she used often to see in church in Humbug, came out of the door by which she was sitting. He knocked into her and said:

'What are you sitting here for, woman!'

'For the Governor . . .'

'This is the bailiff's office, not the Governor's.'

The nobleman pointed to a door at the end of the corridor.

'Over there, where you can see the green notice, what? But don't go to him now, as he's busy, what? Wait here – He'll have to pass by here.'

The nobleman walked off. The woman gazed after him as though he were a guardian angel. She thought: 'It's always the gentry what takes pity on you first.' But she still had to wait quite a long time.

Eventually the door with the green plaque flew open, and a middle-aged military man hurried noisily down the corridor. It was not difficult to see that this was the Governor; several men were galloping along beside him, rushing up from right and left, with exclamations of:

'Mr Governor, sir!'

'Just a word, Mr Governor!'

'Worthy Governor!'

He paid no attention and just marched on. The woman's eyes clouded at the very sight of him.

'God's will be done,' she thought as she knelt down in the middle of the passage, barring his way with her outstretched arms. He saw her and stopped. The whole procession came to a halt before her.

'What is this?' he asked.

'Most holy Govern . . .' she could say no more. She was so terrified that her tongue knotted and her voice died.

'What?'

'Oh, oh, the . . . the . . . about that draft . . .'

'Are they trying to draft you? What?' asked the Governor. All the gentlemen burst into laughter simultaneously, trying to keep up the good spirits of the Governor, but he snapped at his courtiers:

'Please! Quiet! Please!' And then he turned to the woman impatiently: 'Quickly, what is it? I haven't got much time.' But the laughter of the men had completely disconcerted her, and she just mumbled incoherently:

'Beet . . . Turnip . . . Beet . . . Turnip, oh!'

'Must be drunk!' said one of the men.

'Left her tongue at home in the hovel,' added another.

'What do you want?' repeated the Governor with growing impatience. 'Are you drunk, or what?'

'Oh, Jesus, Mary!' the woman cried out, feeling the last straw of salvation slipping out of her grip. 'Most holy Governor . . .'

He really was extremely busy, for the conscription had started, there was a great deal of work, and on top of it all there was to be a ball in Dunceford, which it was his duty to organise. Anyway, he could not get anything out of the woman, so he finally waved his hand and exclaimed:

'There – Vodka! Vodka! And the woman's still young and pretty.' Then, in a voice which made her want to sink through the floor, he said to her: 'When you've sobered up, you can take your problem to your village council and they'll bring it to me.'

Having stung her to the quick with this remark, he hurried on, while the gentlemen behind him resumed their pleas:

'Mr Governor, sir!'

'Just a little word, Mr Governor!'

'Kind sir!'

The corridors emptied and there was silence, broken only by the crying of little Turnip. The woman woke from her trance, got up, lifted the child, and started humming to it in a strange voice.

Then she went out of the building. The sky had filled with clouds and thunder was audible in the distance. The air was sultry.

I do not undertake to describe what was going on in the woman's soul as she again passed by the Conventual Church on her way back to Woollyhead. If only Miss Jadwiga were to find herself in a similar situation! Then I should be able to write a sensational novel and convince all the most inveterate realists that sublime beings still walk this earth. With Miss Jadwiga, every reaction would find expression; the desperate impulses of her soul would be translated into equally desperate and highly dramatic thoughts and words. This vicious circle, this deep and painful sensation of helplessness, powerlessness and vulnerability, of being the leaf in the storm, and the dull realisation that there can be no help from heaven or earth, all this would certainly have inspired Miss Jadwiga with a poignant monologue, which I should only have to reproduce in order to gain a reputation. But the Turnip woman? When common people suffer, they just suffer. Caught in the hard grip of misfortune, this woman took on the look of a bird that is being teased by a child.

She walked on with sweat running down her face, the wind pushing her from behind. Whenever the sick child opened its mouth and started breathing heavily as though it were about to die, she would call to it:

'Jasiek! My darling Jasieńko!', pressing her maternal lips to its forehead.

She passed the Conventual Church and walked on far out into the country. Suddenly she halted, for she could see a drunken peasant reeling towards her.

The clouds in the sky were thickening, and a storm was evidently brewing inside them. From time to time there was a flash of lightning, but this did not seem to worry the peasant; he lurched to one side and then to the other, with his overcoat billowing in the wind and his cap cocked on one ear, and as he tottered along, he sang:

'Doda was in the garden today, trying to pick
   some parsnips,
But then I gave her arse a slap, and that was why she
   ran away!' . . .

Catching sight of the woman, he stopped, stretched out his
arms and called out:

'Come into the rye I say,
Oh, you're good enough to lay!'

He tried to grab her round the waist, but she was scared for
herself and the child, so she leapt aside. The peasant tried to
go after her, but he was so drunk he fell over. He jumped up
immediately, but instead of chasing her he merely picked up a
stone and threw it wildly. She could hear it whirring through
the air. Then she felt a sudden pain in her head. Everything
grew dim and she sank to her knees, but the thought of the
child flashed through her head and she ran on. It was only
when she had reached a roadside crucifix that she stopped.
Looking round, she saw that the peasant was about half a mile
away, tottering on towards the town.
   Her neck felt strangely warm, so she felt it with her hand.
She saw blood on her fingers. Her eyes grew dim and consciousness left her.
   She woke up leaning against the crucifix. In the distance she
could see a cabriolet approaching from Ościeszyn. It was
young Master Ościeszyński with the governess. Master
Ościeszyński did not know the Turnip woman, but she knew
him from church. She thought of running up to the cabriolet
and begging him at least to take the child away before the
storm. She got up, but could not walk.
   Meanwhile, the young gentleman had driven up, and, noticing an unfamiliar woman standing at the foot of the crucifix,
he called out:
   'Here, woman, take a seat.'
   'May the Lord bless y-'
   'On the ground, I mean!'
   Oh, this young Master Ościeszyński was a joker renowned
throughout the neighbourhood, and he would play jokes on
everyone he met. Having played this one on the Turnip

woman, he drove on. She could hear him laughing with the governess, and as the cabriolet disappeared into the gloomy distance, she could see them kissing.

The woman was alone once more. But it is no empty saying that 'you can't kill a peasant woman with an axe'. After about an hour she pulled herself together and walked on, even though her legs were giving way beneath her. 'What's this poor child guilty of, the little innocent fish, my good Lord?' she repeated, pressing the sick Jasiek to her breast. Then fever must have clouded her mind, for she started murmuring drunkenly: 'My man's taken his gun and gone to war, the cradle's empty in the house . . .'

The wind blew the bonnet off her head; the beautiful hair cascaded on to her shoulders and fluttered about. Suddenly there was a flash. The lightning struck so close that she was overpowered by the smell of sulphur and had to crouch down for a while. This brought her back to her senses.

'And the Word was made flesh! . . .' she called out. She looked up at the sky, turbulent, unmerciful and livid, and in a trembling voice began to chant the hymn: 'When under His protection . . .'

The clouds were shedding a sort of evil coppery glare. The woman entered the forest, but it was darker and even more frightening there. From time to time a great murmur would start up. It was as though the terrified pines were whispering to each other: 'What's going to happen now? Oh God!' Then again there would be silence. Sometimes a voice seemed to call out from the depths of the forest. The woman's skin crept – she thought it might be 'the Evil' laughing in the swamps, or that at any moment the Gomon might wind by in a horrific procession. 'Just get through the forest, just get out of it,' she thought, 'after the forest there's Miller Jagodziński's cottage.' She struggled on with the rest of her strength, her parched lips gasping for air.

Meanwhile, the heavens opened up over her head and rain mixed with hail poured down in torrents. The wind bore down with such force that even the pines bowed towards the ground. The forest was filled with mist, steam and driving rain. It was impossible to make out the road. The trees were sweeping the ground with creaks and groans, and branches could be heard splintering in the darkness.

The woman felt herself weaken. 'Help! Someone!' she called out in a pathetic voice, but nobody heard. The wind forced the sound back down her throat and stifled her breath. She understood that she would get no further.

She took off her kerchief, jacket and apron; she stripped down almost to her blouse and swathed the child. Then, catching sight of a weeping birch nearby, she dragged herself towards it on all fours. Laying the child under the thicket, she collapsed beside it. 'God receive my soul!' she whispered quietly, and shut her eyes.

The storm raged on for some time before abating. Then it grew dark and stars began to twinkle in the gaps between the clouds. The woman's still figure showed up white under the birch-tree.

'Gee-up!' suddenly resounded in the darkness. This was followed by the rumble of a cart and the sloshing of hooves through puddles. It was Herszek, the factor from Humbug, going home for the night, having sold all his geese in Dunceford. When he saw the woman, he climbed down from his cart.

X

The triumph of genius.

Herszek of Humbug picked the woman up from under the birch-tree. As he was driving her to Woollyhead, he came across Turnip who had driven out with his cart to meet his wife when he saw the storm brewing.

She lay through all of that night and the next day, but on the second day she got up, for the child was ill. The old women came and fumigated it with blessed garlands, while Old Cicowa the blacksmith's wife tried to charm away the illness with a sieve and a black hen. The child got better immediately, but now Turnip himself was becoming more and more of a problem. He was imbibing vast quantities of vodka, which there was no way at all of preventing.

It was strange that when the woman first regained consciousness and immediately asked about the child, Turnip answered grimly, showing no concern for her:

'You go running off to town – of course the child gets ill. I would've really bashed you if you'd lost him.' Bitterness welled up inside the woman at such ungratefulness, but she could not express it. She called out in a voice fraught with pain, coming from the depths of her heart:

'Wawrzon!' and looked at him through her tears. The man almost fell off the case he was sitting on. There was silence for a moment, and then he said in a changed tone:

'My Maryśka, forgive me – I've wronged you.' He burst into loud sobs and started kissing her feet, while she answered him with tears. He felt that he was unworthy of such a woman. But the peace did not last. Sadness, rankling like a wound, began to set one against the other. Whenever Turnip came back home, whether drunk or sober, he would just sit down on the chest without saying a word to his wife and stare at the floor. Thus he would sit for hours on end, as though he had been turned to stone. The woman would move about the room working as usual, but she also said nothing. Eventually they began to feel estranged, even when they wanted to say something to one another. So a deathly silence hovered over the house, although they were both full of reproach. What were they to talk about, when they both knew that their fate had already been settled?

After a few days, the man began to have bad thoughts. He went to confess to Father Siskin. The priest would not give him absolution and told him to come back the next day, but on the next day the man went to the inn instead of the church. People heard him say drunkenly that since God refused to help him, he would sell his soul to the Devil, and they began to steer clear of him. It was as though a curse were hanging over the house. People began to wag their tongues, saying that the Elder and the Clerk had been right, as such a rake would only bring the wrath of God down on the whole of Woolly-head. The old women started telling the most unbelievable stories about Turnip's wife too.

One day the Turnips' well dried up, so the woman had to fetch water from in front of the inn. On her way, she overheard some boys talking to each other:

'There goes the soljer's woman!' While another said:

'She's not the soljer's woman – she's the Devil's wife!' The woman walked on without a word, but she saw the boys cross themselves. She filled her can with water and started back. Szmul was standing in front of the inn. When he saw her, he pulled out the porcelain pipe which as usual hung down his beard and called:

'Mrs Turnip!'

The woman stopped and asked:

'What d'you want?'

'You been to the village court?'

'Yes.'

'You been to the priest?'

'Yes.'

'Been to the manor?'

'Yes.'

'And you haven't got anywhere?'

The woman only sighed, so Szmul went on:

'Well, how stupid you are! There can't be anyone stupider in the whole of Woollyhead! Why did you go to them?'

'Where else was I to go?'

'Where?' answered the Jew, 'and what does the agreement rest on? On paper; no paper – no agreement. Tear up the paper and there's an end to it.'

'Oh, that's clever, that is,' said the woman, 'if I had that paper I would have torn it up long ago.'

'Well, don't you know the Clerk's got the paper? Well, I know, Mrs Turnip, you can get anything out of him. He told me himself: "If that woman comes to me," he says, "and asks me, I'll tear up the paper just like that".'

The woman did not reply. She picked up the can and went home. Outside it grew dark.

Later that evening, having undressed, the Clerk lay on his bed, goatee upwards, wearing only his linen. He was reading *The Secrets of the Court of the Tuileries*, also published by Mr Breslauer. He was just reading the scene in which Olozaga, the new Spanish Ambassador, starts kissing Eugenie's stockings.

The scene was so beautifully described that the Clerk was bouncing up and down on his bed with excitement. The candle was burning and the fly crackled in the wax. Suddenly he heard someone knock on the door, but so softly that he could only just catch the sound.

'Who's there?' he called out, annoyed at being disturbed.

'Me,' answered a whisper.

'Who's me?'

'Turnip's wife . . .' whispered the voice.

The Clerk leapt to his feet and opened the door. The woman came in, so terrified that she could not speak, although she wanted to say something. But he was a good man, Skrofulowski, and he immediately put her at her ease. As he was not dressed, he grabbed her round the waist and exclaimed:

'Aha! The donkey's come to the cart! You've come for the contract, eh, Marysia?'

'Yes.'

Then he drew her to himself and held her tight, pressing his mouth to her trembling lips.

'And what now, eh?' he asked gaily. The woman went white as a sheet.

'God's will be done!' she whispered.

The Clerk blew out the candle.

XI

An end to the misery.

The Lesser Bear had already sunk in the sky when the door of Turnip's cottage creaked, and the woman quietly slipped in. When she got inside, she froze. She had been expecting Turnip to spend the night at the inn as usual, but Turnip was sitting on the chest, with his fists leaning on his knees and his eyes fixed on the floor. The embers in the fireplace were shedding their last.

'Where you been?' asked Turnip grimly.

Instead of answering, she threw herself to the floor at his feet with sobs and tears.

'Wawrzon! Wawrzon! It was for you I did it! It was for you I covered myself with shame! He cheated me, cursed me and then threw me out. Wawrzon! Won't you take pity on me? My darling, Wawrzon!'

Turnip took his axe from behind the chest.

'No,' he said calmly, 'you've come to your end, you poor creature. Say goodbye to this world; you won't be seeing it again. You won't sit in the house no more, my darling, you'll be lying out in the graveyard . . . you won't . . .'

It was only then that she looked up at him, in terror.

'What? D'you mean to murder me?'

He just went on:

'Now, Maryśka, don't waste time. Cross yourself and then it'll all be over. You won't even feel anything, you poor wretch.'

'Wawrzon – you're only pretending . . . ?'

'Lay your head on the chest . . .'

'Wawrzon, mercy!'

'Lay your head on the chest!' he shouted, foaming at the mouth now.

'Oh God! Help! People, hel-'

There was a dull blow, followed by a moan and the thud of the head on the floor. Then came a second blow and a weaker moan; then a third blow, a fourth, a fifth and a sixth. A stream of blood gushed over the floor. The embers in the fireplace died away. The woman's body twitched convulsively from head to foot, then the corpse strained and became motionless.

A little later, the darkness of the night was pierced by a broad, bloody glow. The manor buildings were on fire.

EPILOGUE

And now, my readers, I shall tell you a little secret: they would never have accepted Turnip for the army. An agreement such as that signed at the inn was not sufficient. But, you see, the peasants know nothing about these things, and the intelligentsia not much either, thanks to its neutrality, so . . . Mr Skrofulowski, who did know something about it, calculated that fear would throw the woman into his arms while the matter dragged on.

And this man had not miscalculated.

You will probably be wondering what happened to him. What was there to happen? Having set the manor on fire, Turnip went in search of vengeance on him too, but as the entire village was woken by cries of 'Fire!', Mr Skrofulowski was able to survive.

And so he reigns on in the position of Clerk at Woollyhead, but now he has hopes of being made a Judge. He has just finished reading *Barbara Ubrich*, and expects Miss Jadwiga to squeeze his hand under the table any day now.

Whether these high hopes of judgeships and squeezings will ever come true, only time will tell.

BARTEK THE CONQUEROR

I

My hero's name was Bartek Słowik, but as his eyes had a habit of bulging right out of his head when he was being spoken to, his neighbours called him Bulging Bartek. It is true that he had very little in common with a nightingale,* while his mental capacities and his Homeric simplicity had earned him yet another name; Bartek the Idiot. This last was the most popular, and probably that one alone will go down in history, although Bartek had a fourth, official name. Since the words Słowik and Człowiek† sound very similar to a German ear, and as the Germans are wont, in the name of civilisation, to translate barbaric Slavic names into a more cultivated language, the following conversation took place during the military registration:

'What's your name?' the officer asked Bartek.

'Słowik.'

'*Schloik? Ah, ja! Gut!*' and the officer wrote down '*Mensch*'.

Bartek came from the village of Pognembin, a name not uncommon in the Duchy of Poznań, or, for that matter, throughout the areas of the former Polish Commonwealth. Apart from some land, a cottage and couple of cows, he was the proud owner of a piebald horse and a wife called Magda. Thanks to this happy combination of circumstances, he was able to live his little life quietly, according to the sagacity contained in this peasant rhyme:

> 'I've got a wife, and a nag to ride,
> As for the rest, the Lord will provide.'

Somehow, his whole life had seemed to work out just as the Lord had provided, and it was only when the Lord provided war that Bartek felt his world upset. He was called up. He would have to abandon the house and the land, entrusting it all to the woman's care. Most of the inhabitants of Pognembin

* 'Słowik' is the Polish for 'nightingale'.
† 'Człowiek' is the Polish for 'man'.

were rather poor, and sometimes in winter Bartek would go to
work in the local factory, which helped him to make ends
meet, but now what? Who could tell when the war with the
French would end? Having read the conscription order,
Magda began to curse:

'I hope they all go blind from it, curse them! I'm sorry to
see you go, even though you're an idiot. And those Frenchmen
won't let you off lightly, either; they'll cut your head off, as
like as not . . .'

Bartek appreciated the wisdom of his wife's words. Besides,
he was scared stiff of these Frenchmen, so he too was very
sorry to go. What had the French done to him, anyway? Why
should he have to go off to those terrible faraway lands where
there is no kindred soul? When you sit around in Pognembin,
well, it's not too good and it's not too bad, the way it's always
been, but when they tell you to go, you realise that it's better
there than anywhere else.

There was nothing for it; he had to resign himself to fate.
Bartek gave his wife a hug, embraced his ten-year-old Franek,
then spat on the floor, crossed himself and left the house, followed by Magda. Their farewells were not excessively emotional. The woman and the boy sobbed, while he merely
repeated:

'Quiet now, quiet!' and so they found themselves in the
street. It was only then that they realised the same was happening all over Pognembin. The entire village had turned out,
and the street was filled with conscripts going to the station,
followed by the women, the children, the old men and the
dogs. The conscripts were gloomy, except for a few of the
younger ones jaunting along with pipes hanging out of their
mouths, and a few others who were already drunk. Some were
croaking out a Polish marching song, while here and there the
odd German colonist from Pognembin was singing the *Wacht
am Rhein* to assert himself.

This colourful crowd, hemmed in here and there by the
glinting bayonet of a policeman, moved along the village street
and out onto the road, amidst chatter, hubbub and shouting.
The womenfolk hung on to their soldiers, lamenting bitterly.
Some old hag, displaying one yellow tooth, was threatening
the distance with her fist, while another muttered: 'May the

Lord put our tears down on your consciences!'

Farewells could be heard everywhere, while the dogs barked and the church bell tolled.

The parish priest was already saying prayers for the dead, for out of all those who were now leaving, many would never return; the war was taking them all, but it would not give them all back. Now the ploughs would rust in the fields, for the village of Pognembin had declared war on France. Pognembin could never bring itself to sanction the pre-eminence of Napoleon III, and had taken to heart the affair of the Spanish Succession.

The procession left the village to the sound of the tolling bell. Heads were bared as it passed the road-side sanctuary.

A golden dust rose from the road, as the day was dry and fine. On both sides of the road the ripening corn rustled its heavy ears as it swayed to and fro in the gentle breeze. Larks were poised high up in the blue sky, singing loudly.

At the station, the crowd was even greater. The conscripts from Upper Krzywda, Lower Krzywda, Wywłaszczyńce, Niedola and Mizerów had arrived, creating noise and confusion. The walls of the station were plastered with manifestoes. Apparently the war was in the name of 'God and the Fatherland', and the *Landwehr* was marching out in defence of its families, wives, children, houses and fields, which had been threatened. It was clear the French were particularly interested in Upper and Lower Krzywda, Niedola, Mizerów and Pognembin, or so it seemed to those reading the posters. More and more people kept arriving at the station. The tobacco-smoke filling the waiting-room was so thick that it even obscured the posters. It was impossible for anyone to make himself understood in the commotion, as everybody was walking about, calling and shouting. The commands of the German officials could be heard on the platform; they sounded brisk, harsh and decisive.

A bell rang, followed by a distant whistle and the evil breathing of a locomotive. As it came nearer, the sound became more and more distinct, and it seemed as though this were war itself approaching.

A second bell rang, and a shiver ran down every spine. Some woman squealed: 'Here they come!' while another

added, shrieking with terror: 'Here come the French!' For a
split second, panic seized not only the women, but also the
future heroes of Sedan. The crowd swayed as the train pulled
in and stopped. At every window appeared uniforms and caps
with red piping. There seemed to be a tremendous number of
soldiers. The open carriages bristled with bayonets, and on the
coal-wagons lay the long, black, morose bodies of cannons.
Evidently, the soldiers had been told to sing, for the whole
train vibrated with the sound of strong, masculine voices, and
a strange force and power emanated from this monster, whose
long tail stretched right out of sight.

The conscripts were being formed up on the platform.
Those who could were saying goodbye. Bartek waved his
paws, like the sails of some windmill, and his eyes bulged right
out of his head.

'Well, Magda, farewell.'

'Oh, my poor boy!'

'You'll never see me again.'

'I'll never see you again!'

'There's nothing for it.'

'The Mother of God guard and protect you . . .'

'Farewell, and take good care of the house!'

The woman flung her arms round his neck, weeping bitterly:
'May the Lord guide you!'

The last moment had come. For a few minutes the sobs,
shrieks and laments of the women drowned everything.
Farewells could be heard on all sides. By now, however, the
soldiers had been separated from the disorderly crowd. They
were being formed up into a compact black mass, gradually
taking on the shapes of squares and rectangles, and were
beginning to move with that accuracy and regularity peculiar
to machines. At the command: 'All aboard!', the squares and
rectangles split up and stretched out into long files, which
began to disappear inside the carriages.

The locomotive whistled and belched forth clouds of pale
grey smoke, puffing like some dreadful dragon, its loins steaming. The wailing of the women had reached its peak. Some
covered their faces with their aprons, others stretched their
arms out towards the carriages. Sobbing voices repeated the
names of husbands and sons.

'Farewell, Bartek!' shouted Magda from down below. 'And don't you go running where they don't send you! May the Mother of God . . . Farewell! . . . Oh Lord!'

'Take care of the house,' answered Bartek.

The chain of carriages suddenly shuddered; they knocked against each other and started to move off.

'And remember you've got a wife and child!' squealed Magda, traipsing alongside the train. 'Farewell! In the name of the Father, the Son and the Holy Spirit . . . Farewell! . . .'

The train was now moving faster and faster, bearing its load of warriors from both Krzywdas, Niedola, Mizerów and Pognembin.

II

While Magda and the other women made their sorrowful way back to Pognembin, the train, bristling with bayonets, was carrying Bartek in the opposite direction, into the grey distance. He could see no end to this grey distance. Pognembin was only just visible now; only the lime-tree and the church spire, its golden cross catching the sunlight, could be seen. Soon even the lime had faded away, and the cross was no more than a sparkling dot. While this dot still shone, Bartek gazed at it intently, but when that disappeared as well, the poor peasant's unhappiness know no bounds. An intense feeling of helplessness overcame him, and he felt that he was lost forever. He then transferred his gaze to the non-commissioned officer; apart from God, he was the only person to turn to now. What was to happen to them was the corporal's headache; Bartek himself no longer knew or understood anything. The corporal sat on a bench smoking a pipe, gripping his rifle between his knees. Now and again, the smoke from his pipe would hide his serious sad face, like a passing cloud. Bartek's were not the only eyes fixed on this face; it was being gaped at from every corner of the carriage. In Pognembin or Mizerów, every Bartek or Wojtek was his own master; everyone had to think of himself and for himself, but now that was the corporal's job. If he told them to look to the right, they would all look to the right; if he told them to look to the left, they would look to the left. All eyes asked the same question; what was to happen to them next? In fact, the corporal knew no more than they did, and would have been very glad himself if someone had given him some orders or explanations. The peasants were afraid of asking any questions, for, now that there was a real war on, the whole apparatus of military law and regulations loomed up before their eyes. One could never tell what was allowed and what was forbidden, and they were terrified of expressions such as 'Court-martial', the more so as they had not the faintest idea of what they really meant.

At the same time, they felt that this corporal was even more essential to them now than during the field days near Poznań because he, and only he, knew everything. He thought for everyone, and without him there was just nothing doing. Meanwhile, he must have found his rifle cumbersome, for he threw it to Bartek to hold. Bartek took the weapon eagerly, and, holding his breath, stared at the corporal with his bulging eyes, but this proved unenlightening.

The situation was plainly anything but good, since even the corporal looked grim. At every station there was singing and shouting. The corporal would bustle about, commanding and scolding, but as soon as the train moved on, he would quieten down like everyone else. For him too, the world now had two sides, the one clear and understandable – the cottage, the wife and the feather-bed; the other dark, very dark – France and the war. His morale, and the morale of this whole army, would gladly have borrowed some spirit from a tortoise. The Pognembin warriors were in effect animated by feelings which only burdened their hearts, and, since every soldier was already weighed down by his knapsack, overcoat and other military gear, this helped to make the going extremely heavy.

The train snorted, clattered and tore on into the distance. Carriages and locomotives were added on at every station. At every station one could see yet more spiked helmets, cannon, horses, infantrymen's bayonets and lancers' pennants.

A fine evening was drawing in, and the sun spilled out into a vast red sunset. Flocks of little wispy clouds raced along high up in the sky. At last the train ceased taking on carriages and men, and merely trundled on towards the red sunset, as though it were about to plunge into a sea of blood. From the open carriage occupied by Bartek and the Pognembin peasants, one could see villages, hamlets and towns, church spires, hunched cranes standing on one leg in their nests, single cottages and cherry-orchards. All of this flashed past, and all of it was red. The soldiers had begun to whisper among themselves, all the more freely as the corporal, using his pack as a pillow, had fallen asleep, with the clay pipe still stuck in his teeth. Wojtek Gwizdała, a peasant from Pognembin sitting next to Bartek, nudged him with his elbow.

'Bartek, listen!'

Bartek turned his pensive face towards him, his eyes bulging.

'You look like a calf on its way to the slaughterhouse,' whispered Wojtek. 'You'll get butchered all right . . .'

Bartek moaned.

'You scared?' asked Wojtek.

'You bet I'm scared . . .'

The sunset had gone a deeper red, so Wojtek pointed to it and went on:

'D'you see that light? Know what it is, stupid? It's blood! This is Poland, see, our country; understand? And way over there, where it's so light, that's France . . .'

'Will we get there soon?'

'You in a hurry, then?' 'They say it's devilish far. But don't you worry; the Frenchmen will come out to meet us!'

With visible effort, Bartek set his Pognembinian head to work, and after a moment he asked:

'Wojtek?'

'What?'

'What sort of a people are these Frenchmen, exactly?'

Here, Wojtek's knowledge found itself at the edge of an abyss. He knew that the Frenchmen were French. He had heard something about them from the old people, who used to say that they always beat everyone. One thing he was sure of; they were some kind of very foreign people, but how on earth was he to set about explaining this to Bartek, so that he too should know just how foreign they were? So he repeated the question:

'What sort of a people?'

'Yes.'

Wojtek knew of three nations; in the middle were the Poles, with the Russians on one side, and the Germans on the other. But then there were various different types of Germans. So, attempting to be clear rather than precise, he said:

'What sort of a people, the French? Well, how should I say, they're some kind of Germans, only worse . . .'

'The dogs!'

Until that moment, Bartek had nourished only one feeling towards the French: indescribable terror. It was only now that this Prussian *Landwehrmann* began to feel a sort of patriotic ill-will towards them. But he had still not quite understood, so he asked again:

'So the Germans are going to fight other Germans?'

Here Wojtek, like a second Socrates, decided to use the method of comparison, and answered:

'Well, don't my dog Burek fight your Łysek!'

Bartek's mouth fell wide open, and for a moment he stared at his master.

'Aye, you're right . . .'

'Even the Austrians are Germans,' carried on Wojtek, 'and didn't our Germans fight them? Old Świerszcz used to tell us about when he fought in that war: Steinmetz used to shout to them: "Come on lads, go for the Germans!" But then it ain't that easy with the French . . .'

'Oh Lord!'

'The French have never lost a war. When one of them gets hold of you, you'll never get away, don't worry! Each one of them is about twice or three times as big as one of our peasants, and they have beards like Jews. Some of them are black, like devils; when you see one of those, start praying to the Lord!'

'Why are we going there, then?' asked Bartek in despair.

This philosophical question was perhaps not quite as stupid as it seemed to Wojtek, who, under the influence of official propaganda, answered quickly:

'I'd prefer not to go either, but if we don't go to them, they'll come to us, see? There's nothing for it; you read what the posters said. You see, they're specially keen on our peasants. People say they're greedy for these lands, because they wanted to smuggle vodka out of the Kingdom, but the government wouldn't let them, so that's why there's a war, understand?'

'I understand,' said Bartek with resignation.

Wojtek went on:

'They're greedy for women, too; like dogs for a bitch . . .'

'D'you mean they wouldn't leave Magda alone?'

'They don't even let the old ones off!'

'Ah!' exclaimed Bartek, in a tone that meant: 'If that's the way it is, I don't mind if I do have a go at them!'

Somehow, it seemed to him that this was too much. He did not really object to their smuggling vodka out of the Kingdom, but if they were after his Magda! Now Bartek began to see this whole war from a personal point of view. He even felt a certain warmth in his heart at the sight of this whole army marching out with all those cannons, just to defend his Magda against the lechery of the French. His fists clenched unconsciously, and fear of the French was now tempered in his mind by hatred of them. He came to the conclusion that there was nothing for it but to go and fight. Meanwhile, the light faded from the sky, and it grew dark. Running on uneven rails, the carriage had begun to jolt, and all the helmet-spikes and bayonets swayed from side to side in unison as it went.

An hour passed, then another. The locomotive showered millions of sparks into the darkness, and they raced through the air in confusion, like so many gleaming snakes. For some time Bartek was unable to sleep. Thoughts about Magda, Pognembin, the French and the Germans flew about in his head, just like those sparks in the night. It seemed to him that he was chained to the bench on which he was sitting.

At last he fell into an unhealthy half-sleep and started dreaming. First, he saw his Łysek fighting with Wojtek's Burek, so fiercely that one could see the hairs fly. He was about to separate them with a stick, when he suddenly saw something else; a Frenchman, black as holy mother earth, was sitting next to Magda, and she was baring her teeth in a contented grin. Other Frenchmen were pointing at Bartek and laughing. The locomotive must have started rattling violently at that moment, for he could hear all the Frenchmen calling: 'Magda! Magda! Magda!' Łysek and Burek were barking, and the whole of Pognembin was shouting: 'Don't let them take your woman!' Bartek could not move; it was as though he were tied up. He tugged and threw himself forward, and the shackles gave way. He seized the Frenchman by the beard, and suddenly . . .

Suddenly he was conscious of great pain from a violent blow. Bartek woke up and leapt to his feet. The whole carriage had woken up, and everyone was asking what had happened. Bartek had seized the corporal's beard in his sleep. Now he was standing to attention, with two fingers to his forehead, while the corporal waved his arms about and shouted like a lunatic:

'*Ach! Sie dummes Vieh aus der Polackei!* Just you wait till I clout one of you in the mug – I'll knock all his teeth out!'

The corporal was hoarse with rage. Bartek stood motionless, still saluting. The other soldiers were biting their lips not to laugh, while the parting shots were still being fired by the corporal:

'*Ein polnischer Ochse!* Podolian cattle!'

At last everything quietened down. Bartek sat down again in his place. He could feel his cheeks swelling up a little. As though on purpose, the locomotive continued to call: 'Magda! Magda! Magda!'

He felt very sorry for himself . . .

III

Morning came. A diffuse, pale light fell on the sleepy faces, exhausted from lack of rest. The soldiers slept in disorder on the benches, some with their heads bent forward, others leaning right back. The dawn had filled the world with a rosy light. The air was fresh and bracing, and the soldiers began to wake. The radiant morning dispelled the shadows and the mist, unveiling a completely new countryside. Where was Pognembin, where the two Krzywdas, where was Mizerów now? This was already a foreign land, and everything was quite different. All around, there were little hills covered in oak-woods. In the valleys stood houses covered with climbing vines, with white walls, black cross-beams and red tiled roofs, all as fine as manors. Pointed church spires and factory chimneys topped with plumes of pink smoke could be seen here and there. But it was somehow rather cramped; there was no flat land, and no expanses of cornfields. The villages and towns that kept flying past were crawling with people. The train did not stop, but clattered on, passing through quantities of minor stations. Obviously something had happened, as there were crowds everywhere.

The sun rose slowly above the hill-tops, so some of the men began to recite their morning prayer. The others followed their example, and the sun's first rays lit up the serious faces of the praying peasants.

The train stopped at a major station. It was immediately surrounded by a throng of people, for news had arrived from the front. A victory! Cables had brought the tidings a few hours before. Everyone had been expecting defeat, so joy was boundless when they awoke to good news. People left their homes and their beds only half-dressed to hurry to the station. Flags fluttered on rooftops and handkerchiefs waved in every hand. Beer, tobacco and cigars were brought to the carriages. The enthusiasm was indescribable, and the faces radiant. The *Wacht am Rhein* was booming out from every quarter. Some were crying, others were falling into each other's arms. '*Unser Fritz*' had won easily, taking cannons and standards from the enemy. In their noble enthusiasm, the people were giving the soldiers whatever they had. A new sensation of well-being crept into the hearts of the men, and they started singing. The carriages shuddered under the strain of the powerful male voices, as the crowd listened in astonishment to the unintelligible words of the song; the peasants were singing a Polish Insurrection song.

'*Die Polen! Die Polen!*' repeated the onlookers, by way of explanation. They gathered around the carriages to admire the martial bearing of the men, and nourished each other's exuberance by telling fantastic anecdotes about the fierce courage of these Polish regiments.

Bartek's cheeks were still swollen, a fact which, together with his yellow moustache, bulging eyes, and his gigantic frame, really did give him a fearsome aspect, and people admired him as they might some peculiar animal. What splendid defenders Germany had! He would show the Frenchmen! Bartek was smiling with satisfaction, for he was greatly relieved that the French had been beaten. At least now they

would not go to Pognembin, or muck about with Magda, or
take away his land. So he was smiling, but as his face still gave
him pain, this smile was more of a grimace, which helped to
make him look monstrous. Nevertheless, he was tucking in
with the appetite of a hero of mythology. Sausages and mugs
of beer vanished down his throat as though it were an abyss.
People gave him cigars and pennies, and he accepted it all.

'They're not such a bad lot, these Germans,' he remarked
to Wojtek, and added after a pause: 'You see, they did beat the
French.'

But the sceptical Wojtek cast a shadow over his friend's jollity. Cassandra-like, he prophesied:

'The French always let themselves get beaten first, just so
as to lead you on, and then, when they get going, you can see
the chips fly!'

What Wojtek did not know was that the majority of Europe
shared his opinion, and what he realised even less was that the
majority of Europe, just like him, was quite wrong.

The train moved on. Every house in sight was now draped
with flags. At some stations, the halts were long, as the junc-
tions were crammed with trains. Troops from every corner of
Germany were hurrying to reinforce their victorious brothers-
in-arms. Some of the trains were decked with green garlands,
and many of the lancers had adorned their spearheads with
bunches of flowers they had been given on the way. Amongst
the lancers, the majority were Poles, so now and again calls
and remarks would be exchanged between trains standing
alongside each other:

'How are things with you?'

'Where d'you think the Lord will take us now?'

Occasionally, as a train trundled past on the neighbouring
track, a familiar song would be heard:

> 'In a place near Sandomierz,
> Says a maiden to the soldiers . . .'

Then Bartek and his companions would pick it up and join
in:

> 'Mister soldier, come and kiss me.'
> 'Thanks a lot, but first I'll feed me!'

In contrast to their dejected departure from Pognembin, everyone was now filled with enthusiasm and bravado. These high spirits were spoiled somewhat by the sight of the first convoy of wounded being brought back from France. It stopped at Deutz, and stood there for some time, so as to let by those hurrying to the front. A good few hours passed before they could all cross the bridge into Cologne. Bartek and his friends ran up to look at the sick and wounded. Some of them were in closed carriages, but others, for lack of space, were laid out in open wagons, and these could be seen perfectly. After the first glance, Bartek's heroic spirit began to sink down into his boots.

'Come here, Wojtek!' he shouted in horror. 'Just take a look at all these people the French have mucked up!'

It really was quite a sight. Nothing but pale, tired faces, blackened by smoke, distorted with pain and spattered with blood. To the general manifestations of joy, these men replied only with moans, cursing the war, France and Germany. Blackened and parched lips kept calling for water. Their eyes were haggard, like madmen's. Here and there amongst the wounded, the stiffened face of a dying man stood out by its serenity and the bluish shadows round the eyes, or sometimes by the convulsions, the bared teeth and the glare of terror in the eyes. This was Bartek's first glimpse of the bloodier fruits of war. Confusion once more arose in his mind, and he stood in the crowd with his mouth wide open and his eyes gaping like a drunkard's, being jostled from all sides, until he caught a policeman's rifle-butt in the neck. He searched out Wojtek in the crowd, and said:

'Wojtek! My God, Oh!'

'The same'll happen to you, for sure.'

'Jesus, Mary! And to think people can murder each other like this! When you or me clouts another peasant, the police come and then the court punishes you . . .'

'Now the best man's the one that murders most people. You ass! You didn't think you was coming here to shoot blanks, or aim at targets, like on field-days, did you?'

The difference between theory and practice suddenly became very apparent. After all, Bartek was a soldier; he had been on drills and field-days, and he was used to shooting. Moreover, he knew very well that war was for killing people, but now that he had seen the blood of the wounded and the misery of war, he felt his stomach turning inside out, and he only just managed to stay on his feet.

Once more, a feeling of awe crept over him, and he only lost it when the train pulled out of Deutz and halted in Cologne. At the central station they saw the first prisoners, surrounded by a throng of soldiers and civilians gazing at them in wonder, but still without hatred. Bartek elbowed his way through the crowd, peeped into one of the carriages, and was struck with amazement.

A selection of small, wretched, dirty French infantrymen in tattered greatcoats were crammed inside the carriage, like herrings in a barrel. Where the guards made no objection, they were stretching out their arms to receive the miserable gifts some of the onlookers were offering. From what he had heard Wojtek say, Bartek had imagined the French to be completely different. His courage came flooding back into his heart, and he turned to Wojtek, who was standing beside him.

'What were you going on about?' asked Bartek. 'They're just a measly lot of little wretches – if I took a swipe at one, I bet four would fall over!'

'They must have wasted away, or something . . .' answered Wojtek, equally disillusioned.

'What language are they yapping in?'

'It certainly ain't Polish, anyway!'

Reassured by all this, Bartek walked on along the carriages.

'Terrible bunch of cripples,' he commented, having passed in review all the troops of the line.

However, the next few carriages were occupied by Zouaves, and these gave Bartek more to think about. As they were huddled into closed carriages, it was impossible to ascertain whether each one really was twice or three times the size of a normal man, but through the windows one could see long beards, menacingly sparkling eyes, and the tanned, serious, martial faces of veteran soldiers. Bartek's courage once more began to ebb away from his heart.

'These are worse,' he whispered, as though fearing they might overhear him.

'You still haven't seen them that didn't get caught!' retorted Wojtek.

'Oh, Lord!'

'You'll see!'

Having inspected the Zouaves, they went on, but by the next carriage Bartek jumped back as if he had been stung by something.

'Oh, Wojtek! Help! Save me!'

Through the open window appeared the dark, almost black face of an Algerian. He must have been wounded, as his face was distorted with pain, and the whites of his eyes shone fiercely.

'What's up?' asked Wojtek.

'That's an evil spirit, not a soldier . . . God be merciful to me, a poor sinner!'

'Take a look at them teeth of his!'

'May the devils take it away . . . I'm not going to look at it.'

'. . . Wojtek?' Bartek asked after a short silence.

'What?'

'Would it help if I made the sign of the cross at him?'

'These pagans don't have no understanding of the faith.'

They were ordered back into their train. After a while it moved off.

When it had got dark, Bartek could still see the black face of the Algerian before him, with its gleaming eyes.

From the feelings animating the mind of this Pognembinian brave at that moment, it would have been impossible to foretell his future deeds.

IV

His participation in the battle of Gravelotte at first only convinced Bartek of the fact that in war there was a great deal to gape at and very little to do. He and his regiment were told to stand at ease at the foot of a hill covered in vineyards, while cannons thundered in the distance. Now and again, cavalry regiments galloped past, with pennants fluttering or sabres flashing, making the ground vibrate with the pounding of hoofs. Grenades flew hissing through the blue sky above the hill, like little clouds, and finally smoke filled the air and blotted out the horizon. The battle seemed to

be passing them by like a storm. But this illusion was soon
dispelled.

After some time, an unusual animation could be felt around
Bartek's regiment. Other regiments began taking up positions
beside it, and soon artillery teams galloped up, hastily unlim-
bered their guns in the gaps between the regiments, and
turned them to face the hill. The whole valley gradually filled
with troops. Aides were dashing about on horseback, and
orders were being given on every side. Our wretched rankers
were whispering to each other:

'We're in for it now, we're in for it!' or asking anxiously:

'Is it going to start now?'

'Must be now . . .'

Uncertainty, doubt, maybe even death were closing in . . .

There was tremendous ferment and activity in the dense
smoke covering the hill. The deep booming of cannons and the
thudding of machine-guns drew closer, and the dull crash of
grapeshot could be heard in the distance. Suddenly, the
newly-arrived guns opened fire, and it seemed as though the
earth and heavens had been shaken. Then there was a fearful
hiss in front of Bartek's regiment; they looked up, and saw
something like a white rose or a little cloud, and inside that
cloud something was hissing, cackling, grinding and howling.

'Grenade! Grenade!' shouted the peasants. This bird of war
rushed on like the wind, came closer, hurtled to the ground,
and exploded. A formidable bang, a crash that could have been
the world splitting in two, and a rush of wind hit their ears.
There was confusion in the ranks standing by the cannons,
and then an order was barked out:

'Close up!'

Bartek stood in the front rank, with his head up, his rifle
shouldered and his chin-strap fastened, as a result of which his
teeth could not chatter. There was to be no moving and shooting; the ranks just had to stand and wait. Now came a second
grenade, followed by a third, a fourth, and a tenth. The wind
slowly cleared the smoke from the hill. The French had
already thrown the Prussian batteries off it, and installed their
own, which now breathed fire into the valley. One after another, columns of white smoke came bursting out from amongst
the vines. Under cover of their guns, the infantry were slowly

advancing down the hill to engage with small-arms. They could be seen perfectly, now that the wind had blown away the rest of the smoke. The red caps of the infantry turned the vineyard into a poppyfield in bloom. Soon, however, they had disappeared among the tall vines, and only here and there a tricolour standard revealed their whereabouts. A rapid, feverish and irregular rapping of machine-guns burst forth from different places. The cannon still thundered above this noise, their shells crossing in the air. From time to time a shout would go up on the hill, to be answered from below by the German 'Hurrah!' The cannon in the valley boomed on tirelessly, while the regiment stood still.

It was gradually coming into the field of fire, and bullets began to fly, buzzing like flies or bees from afar, but whining ominously as they flew past heads, noses, eyes and shoulders, in thousands, in millions it seemed. It was a miracle anyone was left standing. Suddenly, Bartek heard a moaning voice just behind him:

'Jesus! . . .' followed by the harsh command: 'Close up!' Again he heard: 'Jesus . . .' and again the order came: 'Close up!'

Now the moans were almost uninterrupted, the words of command were rapped out faster, the ranks closed up, and the whine became more frequent, unremitting and horrible. The dead were being pulled away by the legs. It was like Judgement Day.

'You scared?' asked Wojtek.

'Terrified!' replied our hero, his teeth chattering.

However, both Bartek and Wojtek stood firm, and the thought had not even entered their heads that they could run. They had been told to stand there, so they stood there. Bartek was lying; he was not nearly as scared as thousands of others would be in his position. Discipline reigned over his imagination, and he did not realise a fraction of the atrocity of the situation. Nevertheless, he had come to the conclusion that he would be killed, and he communicated this to Wojtek.

'Well, the grass won't turn blue just because one idiot gets killed,' answered the latter irritably.

These words had a comforting effect on Bartek. It was as though his only worry at that moment had been to prevent the

grass from turning blue. Reassured by all this, he stood
patiently, but he began to feel terribly hot; in fact, sweat was
pouring down his face. Meanwhile, the enemy fire had become
so withering that the ranks were melting away visibly. There
was nobody left to haul the dead and wounded away. The rat-
tle of the dying blended in with the whine of bullets and the
crash of discharges. From the movements of the tricolour standards it was evident that the infantry hidden in the vineyards
were approaching. Volleys of grapeshot continued to decimate
the ranks, which were beginning to give way to despair. But a
trace of anger and impatience could be sensed even in this
despair. They would have gone like a hurricane, if they had
been ordered to advance then. It was the standing still that was
so unbearable. One soldier suddenly tore the helmet off his
head and, hurling it to the ground, said:

'Come on! A man can only die once!'

The enormous sense of relief that Bartek felt from hearing
these words almost made him forget his fear, for, if a man can
only die once, then there was really nothing to it. That is peasant philosophy, far superior to any other, as it brings consolation. In fact, Bartek was perfectly well aware of the fact that a
man can only die once, but it was nice to hear it said, so as to
be quite sure, particularly as the battle was beginning to turn
into something of a butchery. The regiment was already half
destroyed, without having fired a single shot. Streams of soldiers from other broken units were running past in disorder,
and only the peasants from Pognembin, Greater Krzywda,
Lesser Krzywda, Niedola and Mizerów stood their ground,
held in the iron grip of Prussian discipline. But even in their
ranks a certain amount of hesitation could now be felt. The
chains of discipline might give way soon. The ground beneath
their feet was getting soft and slushy from the blood, whose
raw smell blended in with that of the smoke. They could no
longer close up in some places, as there were stacks of corpses
in the way. At the feet of those left standing, the other half lay
in their blood, with moans, convulsions, in the throes or the
silence of death. There seemed to be no clean air left to
breathe. Murmuring had now started up in the ranks:

'They've brought us to the slaughterhouse!'

'We're all done for!'

'*Still, polnisches Vieh!*' shouted an officer.

'You're all right, you are; hiding behind my back . . .'

'*Steht, der Kerl da!*'

Suddenly, a voice began to recite:

'Under Your protection . . .' and Bartek immediately joined in the prayer: '. . . we place ourselves, Holy Mother of God!' Soon, a whole choir of Polish voices on this field of death and destruction was calling on the Holy Virgin of Częstochowa:

'Do not remain unheedful of our entreaties . . .' was answered by moans of 'O, Mary, Mary . . .' from the ground.

Evidently, She must have taken heed of their prayer, for at that moment an aide galloped up on a foaming horse, and shouted the order:

'To the attack! Hurrah! Forward!'

A comb of bayonets leant forward; the ranks stretched into a long line, which surged forward at the hill to ferret out with its steel the hidden foe. But a good two hundred paces separated the peasants from the foot of the hill, and that had to be crossed under a murderous fire. Would they survive? Would they retreat? They might be mown down, but they would never have retreated, for the Prussian command knew which tune to play to make these Polish peasants move. Amidst the thunder of cannon, the rapping of machine-guns, amid the smoke, the confusion and the cries, louder than all the bugle-calls, they struck up to the heavens with the anthem that sets Polish blood on fire.

'Hurrah!' answered the Wojteks, 'While still we live! . . .'

Their spirit had been unleashed, and their faces were on fire. They rushed on like the wind, over dead men and horses, over broken cannon. They fell, but swept on, with their shouts and their hymn. They reached the edge of the vineyard and disappeared into the vegetation, but still the singing rang out, and here and there a bayonet glinted in the sun. The fire from the hill was becoming more and more fierce, while the bugles played on from down below. The French salvoes began to succeed each other more rapidly, still more rapidly, feverishly, and suddenly . . . suddenly they ceased.

Down below, the old warrior Steinmetz lit his porcelain pipe, and commented with satisfaction:

'You just have to lay on the right music for them. Good

lads! They've made it!'

A moment later, one of the proudly waving tricolour standards leant forward, swung sideways, and fell.

'They're not joking, either!' said Steinmetz.

The bugles struck up the same anthem, and a second
Poznań regiment went in to help the first. A bayonet fight was
raging in the vineyard.

And now, o muse, you must sing of my Bartek, that poster-
ity should know of his deeds. In his heart, the feelings of fear,
impatience and despair had all fused into a single emotion –
rage. When he heard the music, every vein in his body braced
like wire, his hair stood on end and sparks flew from his eyes.
He forgot about the world, he forgot all about a man dying
once, and, gripping the rifle in his powerful paws, he leapt forward with the others. By the time he reached the foot of the
hill he had fallen on the ground about ten times, banged his
nose, and covered himself with earth and blood, but he surged
on, furious and panting, catching his breath through his open
mouth. His eyes were bulging in the effort to spot some
Frenchman in the thicket, and at last he saw three of them,
defending a standard. They were Algerians; but does my reader think that Bartek would be intimidated? At this stage, he
was quite prepared to take Lucifer himself by the horns. He
ran towards them, and they moved forward with a howl to
meet him. Two bayonets, like a couple of stings, seemed ready
to tear into his breast, but when my Bartek had taken his rifle
by the thin end like a club, when he had taken his swing . . .
Only a scream followed by a ghastly groan answered him, and
two black bodies started twitching convulsively on the ground.

At this point, about a dozen comrades came to the rescue of
the third, who was still holding the standard. Like some fury,
Bartek hurled himself at them all at once. They fired; there
was a flash, a bang, and from the cloud of smoke came Bartek's
hoarse shriek:

'Missed!'

Once more, the rifle performed a horrific circle in his hands,
and again his blow was answered by moans. The Algerians
retreated in terror at the sight of this giant, blind with rage,
and, it might have been Bartek's imagination, or they really
might have been shouting something in their native tongue,

suffice it to say that he was convinced their wide lips were calling out:

'Magda! Magda!'

'Oh, so you want my Magda, do you?' bellowed Bartek, and
with one leap he was in their midst. Luckily, the Wojteks,
Macieks and other Barteks came to his assistance at the
moment. A fight at extremely close quarters ensued in the
vineyard, dominated by the sound of splintering rifles, the
wheezing of nostrils and the heavy breathing of the combat-
ants. Bartek was raging like a storm. Black from smoke, covered with blood, more of an animal than a man, oblivious of
everything, he sent men flying, shattered rifles and stove in
heads with every blow. His hands moved with terrible speed,
like the limbs of some machine built for destruction. Having
reached the ensign, he seized him by the throat in an iron grip.
The ensign's eyes popped out of their sockets, his face turned
livid, he made a choking sound, and his hands let go of the
standard.

'Hurrah!' yelled Bartek, picking up the standard and waving
it in the air.

This was the very standard General Steinmetz, watching
from below, had seen waver and fall. But he could only have
seen it for a split second, for in the next Bartek had used it to
smash in some head wearing a red kepi with a golden tassel on
it. Meanwhile, his companions had rushed on ahead. Bartek
was alone for a moment. He tore away the flag, put it away in
his tunic, and, clutching the pole with both hands, rushed
after his friends.

Groups of Algerians, howling like beasts, were now running
for the shelter of the guns at the top of the hill, followed closely by the Poles, who were shouting and hitting out with both
ends of their rifles. The Zouaves standing by the guns greeted
them both with volleys of rifle-fire.

'Hurrah!' roared Bartek.

The peasants had now reached the cannons, where a new
struggle with sabres and bayonets had begun. At this moment
the second Poznań regiment came up to the aid of the first.
The standard pole had now turned into a sort of infernal flail
in Bartek's hands. Its every sweep opened up a clear path
through the serried French ranks. Terror began to take hold

of the Zouaves as well as the Algerians, and they began to give
way before Bartek, who was soon sitting astride one of the cannons, as though it had been some old Pognembin nag. Before
anyone had taken in the fact, he was already sitting on another,
beside which he sent another ensign to the ground.

'Hurrah! Bartek!' yelled the peasants.

The victory was complete: all the cannons were taken. The
retreating infantry came up against another Prussian regiment
on the flank of the hill, and laid down their arms. But Bartek
had managed to take yet another standard during the pursuit.

He was quite a sight as he strode back down the hill with
the others, covered in sweat and blood, puffing like a bellows,
and lugging three standards on his shoulders. The French
indeed! Well, he knew what he could do with them now! A
scratched and somewhat mangled Wojtek was walking along
beside him, so Bartek said:

'What were you going on about? They're like worms – no
strength in their bones. Just scratched us about a bit, like kit-
tens; that's all. And whenever I took a swipe at one, he was on
the ground before . . .'

'Well, who'd have thought you'd be getting so worked up?'
replied Wojtek, who was beginning to look at Bartek in an
entirely new light, having witnessed his exploits. And who had
not witnessed them? History, the entire regiment and most of
the officers had seen, and everyone began to feel a measure of
admiration for this enormous peasant with his scraggy yellow
moustache and bulging eyes.

'Ach! Sie verfluchter Polacke!' the Major even said to him,
giving his ear a tug, while Bartek beamed so wide you could
see his back teeth. When the regiment had once more drawn
up at the foot of the hill, the Major showed him to the
Colonel, and the Colonel showed him to Steinmetz himself.
The latter inspected the standards, then had them taken away
and began to inspect Bartek. Bartek was standing up straight,
presenting arms, while the old General looked at him, shaking
his head with contentment. He then said something to the
Colonel, and only the word *'Unteroffizier'* was distinctly audible.

'Zu dumm, Excellenz!' answered the Major.

'Let's try him,' said His Excellency, and, turning his horse, he came up to Bartek. Bartek no longer knew what was happening to him; that a general should speak to a simple private was unheard of in the Prussian army. His Excellency would find this all the easier as he spoke Polish. Besides, this particular private had captured three standards and two guns.

'Where are you from?' asked the General.

'From Pognembin,' answered Bartek.

'Good. What's your name?'

'Bartek Słowik.'

'Mensch . . .' explained the Major.

'Mens!' affirmed Bartek.

'Do you know why you are fighting the French?'

'Yes, Xellency!'

'Tell me why, then.'

Bartek began to stammer:

'Well, because . . .' Luckily, he remembered Wojtek's wise words at this moment, and he rattled them off quickly, so as not to forget.

'Because they're Germans too, only much worse pigs!'

The face of the old Excellency started to twitch uncontrollably, as though he were about to burst out laughing. After a moment, he turned to the Major and said:

'You were quite right.'

Bartek, very pleased with himself, was standing motionless.

'Who won the battle today?' the General asked again.

'I did, Xellency!' replied Bartek, without a moment's hesitation.

His Excellency's face started twitching again.

'Yes, yes, you did. And here's your reward . . .'

Saying this, the old warrior took the Iron Cross off his own chest, and, leaning down, pinned it onto Bartek's.

The good humour of the General was naturally reflected in the faces of the Colonel, the Majors, the Captains, and so on down to the corporals. After the General's departure, the Colonel gave Bartek ten thalers, the Major five, and so on. Everyone kept repeating laughingly that he had won the battle, and Bartek was in his seventh heaven.

Only Wojtek was not too pleased with our hero. In the evening, when they had both sat down by the camp fire, when Bartek's chivalrous face was as stuffed with hog's gut as the gut itself was with pudding, Wojtek remarked with resignation:

'Oh, Bartek! You're stupid, so stupid . . .'

'What's wrong?' asked Bartek through the pudding.

'Why d'you have to tell the General that the French are Germans too?'

'But you said . . .'

'But you should have taken into account that the General and the officers are Germans.'

'What's that got to do with it?'

Wojtek began to hesitate:

'Well, even if they are Germans, you shouldn't say so; it's not nice . . .'

'But I said it about the French, not about them . . .'

'Yes, but then . . .' Wojtek stopped suddenly. He obviously wanted to say something else himself; he would have liked to explain to Bartek that one cannot call Germans Germans to their faces, but his tongue failed him . . .

V

Some time later, the Royal Prussian Post delivered the following letter to Pognembin:

May the Lord Jesus Christ be praised! And His Holy Mother too! My beloved Magda! How are you? You must be all right at home, under the eiderdown, while I'm fighting so hard over here. We were near the great fortress Metz, and there was a great battle, and I let the French have it so well that all the infantries and artilleries wondered. The General was so pleased that he said I won the battle, and gave me a cross. And now the officers and corporals have respect for me and don't clout me so often. Then we marched further and there was another battle, but I've forgotten what the place was called, and again I let them have it, and I took a fourth standard, and I knocked down one of the greatest Colonels of the Dragoons, and made him a prisoner. When they start sending our regiments back home, the corporal told me to write an appeal to stay on, because in war you don't always have a place to sleep, but there's more to eat than you can hold, and there's wine everywhere, because the people in this country are very rich. When we were burning down one village, we didn't even let the women and kids off, and I joined in. We burnt the church down to the ground, because they're Catholics, and a lot of people got baked inside. We're marching on the Emperor himself now, and that will be the end of the war, so you look after the house and Franek, and if you don't, I'll come and clout you good and proper, to show you what I mean. I entrust you to God.

Bartłomiej Słowik

Evidently Bartek had acquired a taste for war, and he was beginning to see it as his rightful profession. He had gained great self-assurance, and now went into battle in the same way as he might go out to do a job of work in Pognembin. More medals and crosses appeared on his breast after every action, and, although he was never promoted to corporal, he was universally recognised as the best private in the regiment. He was still as obedient as ever, and he possessed the blind courage of a man who fails to see the danger. This courage was no longer inspired by rage, as on the first occasions; now its source was self-assurance and military experience.

Besides this, his enormous strength carried him through all the most difficult conditions, the most arduous marches and the longest actions. Others could be seen to wither away beside him, while he survived intact, except for the fact that he was becoming more brutal and more of a Prussian soldier every day. He not only fought the French, he loathed them as well. Many of his ideas changed. He became a solder-patriot, and started worshipping his commanders blindly. In his next letter, he wrote to Magda:

'Wojtek got shot in half, but that's what the war's all about, see? Anyway, he was a fool, because he used to say that the Frenchmen were Germans, but they're French, and the Germans are us.'

In reply to both letters, Magda let fly at him in every way she could think of:

Most beloved Bartek, married to me before the altar of
God! May the Lord punish you! You're a fool yourself, you
pagan, since you go along with the Prussian pigs and murder Catholic people. You don't understand that the Prussians are Lutherans, and you, a Catholic, are helping them.
You like war, you loafer, because you can do nothing except
brawl, drink and hurt other people, and burn Churches and
forget about fasting! It would be better if they were roasting
you in hell for swanking about it and showing no understanding for old people and children. Remember, you goat,
what is written in gold letters in the Holy Faith, from the
beginning of the world to the final day of judgement of our
people, on which the Lord won't have no understanding for
blockheads like you, so take a hold on yourself, you Turk,
unless you want me to smash that head of yours in! I am
sending you five thalers, although we're in great poverty
here, as I cannot manage alone, and the homestead is falling
apart. I embrace you, my most beloved Bartek,

Magda

The morals enclosed in this letter had little effect on Bartek,
who merely muttered: 'The woman doesn't understand soldiering and shouldn't butt in.'

So he carried on fighting as before. He distinguished himself in almost every battle, so that in the end even more ele-
vated eyes than Steinmetz's fell upon him. When the
decimated Poznań regiments were being sent back to Germany, he followed the corporal's advice, wrote an appeal and
stayed on. As a result, he found himself before Paris.

His letters were now full of disdain for the French.

'In every battle, they run like a lot of hares,' he wrote to
Magda, and it was true.

However, he did not find the siege greatly to his taste. They
had to dig defence works, and often got drenched, lying for
days on end in the trenches, listening to the booming of heavy
guns. Besides, he began to regret not having his old regiment
with him. The new one, into which he had been moved as a
volunteer, was made up mostly of Germans. He had learnt a
little German working in the factory back home, but hardly
enough; now he began to pick it up quickly. He was neverthe-

less called *'ein polnischer Ochse'* in the regiment, and only his row of crosses and his gigantic fists forestalled more personal jokes. After a few battles, he had gained a little more respect from his comrades, and he gradually began to get along with them. In the end, since he brought fame to the regiment, they accepted him as one of themselves. Bartek would previously always have considered it a great insult if anyone had ever called him a German, but he now styled himself as *'ein Deutscher'*, to distinguish himself from the French. It seemed to him that there was a subtle difference in the terminology, and at the same time he did not wish to feel inferior to the others.

Eventually something occurred that might have given him much to think about, had thinking not been out of the question for his heroic mentality. One day, several companies from his regiment were ordered to march out against some Franc-Tireurs. They set an ambush, into which the Franc-Tireurs fell. This time, however, Bartek did not see any red caps running after the first shots, for the detachment was made up of veterans, the remains of some Foreign Legion regiment. Surrounded as they were, they fought on fiercely, and eventually surged forward to cut their way through the ring of Prussians with bayonets. Their attack was so determined that some of them managed to break through. They were particularly reluctant to let themselves be taken alive, well knowing the fate reserved for captured Franc-Tireurs, and Bartek's company took only two prisoners. In the evening, these were put in a forester's cottage: the next day they were to be shot. A guard of several soldiers was posted outside the door, while Bartek was placed by the broken window, in the same room as the prisoners. One of them was an elderly man with a greying moustache and a look of complete indifference to everything in his eyes. The other looked as though he might be twenty years old. A fair moustache was just beginning to appear on his face which was more like a young girl's than a soldier's.

'Well, this is the end,' said the younger of the two after a while, 'a bullet in the head, and that's it!'

Bartek jumped and nearly dropped his rifle; the young man was speaking Polish.

'I don't care any more,' replied the other in a tone of dis-

couragement. 'It's all the same to me now. I've knocked about
so much in my life, I've had enough now . . .'

Bartek's heart was pounding violently under his uniform.

'Listen,' went on the elder, 'there's nothing to be done; if
you're scared, think of something else, or else lie down and go
to sleep. Life is worthless. As God is my witness, I really don't
care any more . . .'

'I feel sorry for my mother,' answered the boy dully. Evidently trying to stem his emotion or delude himself, he started
to whistle. Suddenly he broke off, and exclaimed in despair:

'Dammit, I didn't even say goodbye!'

'So you ran away from home?'

'Yes; I thought they'd beat the Germans, and then things
would be better in Poznań.'

'I thought so too, but now . . .' The man waved his hand
and added something quietly, but the rest of his words were
drowned by the sound of the wind. The night was cold. Light
drizzle came over in waves now and again; the forest outside
was black as coal. The wind whistled round the corners of the
room and howled like a dog in the chimney. The lamp was
hung high above the window, so that the wind should not
extinguish it, and threw plenty of twinkling light into the room,
leaving Bartek, who was standing just beneath it, shrouded in
darkness. It was perhaps better that the prisoners could not see
his face. Strange things were happening to the peasant. He was
struck with amazement, and his eyes bulged out at them as he
tried to understand what they were talking about.

So they had come here to fight the Germans and make
things better in Poznań, while he was fighting the French for
the same reason. And these two were going to be shot next
day. What was the poor man to think of it all? Should he speak
to them? What if he told them that he was one of them, that
he felt sorry for them? Suddenly, something seemed to be
strangling him. What could he say to them, anyway? Would it
save them? He'd only be shot too. So what was wrong with
him? Sadness was choking him, and he could not contain his
emotions. Terrible nostalgia seized him; it came from somewhere far away, somewhere in Pognembin. Compassion, that
unwelcome guest in a soldier's heart, wailed in his ear:

'Bartek, save your kin! They're your people!' His heart flew towards Magda and Pognembin, and he felt such home-sickness as never before. He was suddenly sick of this wretched war, of France and of all the fighting.

'Bartek, save your people!' sounded the voice, more and more distinctly. At that moment he wished that the whole war could just be swallowed up by the earth. Through the broken window he could see the black forest and hear it soughing, just like the pines in Pognembin, and in that soughing, something again called out:

'Bartek, save your people!' What was he to do? Should he run away with them, into the forest? Everything that Prussian discipline had managed to instil into him shuddered at the thought. In the name of the Father and of the Son . . . he mentally crossed himself. He, a soldier, desert? Never! Meanwhile, the trees soughed louder and the wind whistled still more plaintively. Suddenly, the elder prisoner said:

'That wind . . . It's like autumn at home . . .'

'Oh, spare me . . .' moaned the younger despondently, but after a pause he repeated: 'At home, at home! Oh, my God, my God . . .'

His deep sigh blended into the whistle of the wind, and then both prisoners lay silent. Bartek was beginning to shake with fever. There is nothing worse than not knowing what is wrong. Bartek had not stolen anything, yet he felt as though he had and he was afraid of being caught. Nothing threatened him, and yet he was terrified. His knees were shaking, the rifle weighed in his hands, and he felt great sobs stifling him. Was it for Magda or for Pognembin? For both, but he also felt such pity for the young prisoner that he was completely at a loss. There were moments when he thought he must be dreaming.

Outside, the wind was getting stronger, and strange voices could be distinguished in its howling. All of a sudden, every hair stood on end under Bartek's helmet. It now seemed to him that out there, somewhere in the dark wet depths of the forest, someone was moaning repeatedly:

'At home! At home! At home!'

Bartek flinched and banged his rifle-butt against the floor to wake himself up. This made him feel more alert. He looked round. The prisoners were lying in the corner, the lamp was twinkling, the wind was howling; everything was in order. The light fell on the face of the young prisoner. It really was the face of a child or a maiden. His eyes were half-shut, his head rested on the straw, and he looked as though he were already dead. Never in all Bartek's life had grief tormented him so. Something was distinctly squeezing his throat, and he could feel suppressed sobbing inside his chest.

The older prisoner moved over onto his side with difficulty, and said:

'Good night, Władzio . . .'

Silence followed. An hour passed. Bartek was in a bad way. The wind was playing in his ear like the Pognembin church organ. The prisoners lay still, but suddenly the younger one raised himself wearily and called:

'Karol!'

'What?'

'You asleep?'

'No . . .'

'Listen, I'm frightened . . . Say what you like, but I'm going to pray.'

'Well, pray then.'

'Our Father, who art in heaven, hallowed be Thy name, Thy kingdom come . . .'; sobbing interrupted the boy's words, but he went on. 'Thy will . . . be done . . .'

'Oh, Jesus! Jesus!' something screamed inside Bartek. He could hold himself no longer. In a moment, he would call out: 'Little squire! I'm one of our peasants!' Then through the window, out into the forest and . . . come what would!

Suddenly, from the porch, came the sound of measured steps. It was the patrol with a non-commissioned officer come to change the guard.

The next day, Bartek was drunk from the early morning. The day after that as well.

In the days that followed, however, there were further marches, drills and fighting, and I am happy to be able to inform my reader that our hero returned to normal. The only difference was that after that night he acquired a certain consideration for the bottle, in which one can always find pleasure and sometimes oblivion. In battle he became fiercer than ever, and victory followed in his footsteps.

VI

A few more months passed. It was already well into spring. In Pognembin the cherry-trees were in full leaf, and the fields were green with rich young shoots of corn. Magda was sitting in front of her cottage, peeling some miserable sprouting potatoes, more fit for swine than humans. It was the lean period before the harvest, and poverty had visited Pognembin. This could be seen from Magda's face as well; it was gloomy and full of sorrow. Perhaps it was in order to dispel this that the woman was singing to herself in a thin, strained voice, with her eyes half-shut.

The sparrows in the cherry-trees twittered as though they wanted to drown her voice, but she sang on, gazing pensively at the dog sleeping in the sun, at the road running past the house, or at the path leading from the road through the garden and out into the fields. Perhaps she gazed at the path because it was a short cut to the station, and on that day God granted that she did not look out in vain. A figure appeared in the distance. The woman shielded her eyes from the sun, but could make out nothing. Łysek woke up, lifted his head, barked once or twice and began to sniff, pricking up his ears and tilting his head this way and that. At the same moment, the indistinct words of a song reached Magda's ears. Łysek jumped up, and made off at full tilt towards the approaching man. Magda grew pale. Was it Bartek? She got up so suddenly that the basin fell to the ground. There was no doubting it. Łysek was leaping up at the newcomer's chest. The woman rushed forward, calling joyfully:

'Bartek! Bartek!'

'Magda, it's me!' shouted Bartek, cupping his hands to his mouth, and quickening his pace. He opened the gate, nearly tripped over the bolt, and they fell into each other's arms.

The woman started to talk very fast:

'And I thought you'd never come back . . . I thought: they've killed him. What's wrong with you? Show yourself to me. Let me have a good look at you. You're all withered. Oh, Jesus! Oh, you idiot! Oh, my dearest, sweetest! He's come back. He's back! . . .' From time to time she would step back from him to take a good look, and then wrap her arms round his neck again.

'He's back! Praise be to the Lord . . . My darling Bartek! . . . How are you? Come inside . . . Franek's at school. The German pig pushes him around a bit, but the boy's in good health. Except that he's got great big bulging eyes like you. Oh, it's high time you were back. I can't help it; poverty, real poverty. The house is falling apart. The barn roof is caving in . . . How are you? Oh, Bartek, Bartek! That I should look on you again! The trouble I had with the hay! The Cmiernickis helped me, but it wasn't any use . . . And how's your health? Oh, I'm so happy to see you, so happy! The Lord must have protected you. Come inside. It's so strange – you're still Bartek, but not quite Bartek . . . Hey! What's wrong with you? Help! . . .'

Only at that moment had Magda noticed a long scar running from his left temple, along the cheek and down to his chin.

'Oh, nothing – dragoon took a poke at me, but I got him too. I've been in hospital.'

'Oh Jesus!'

'Ah, it's nothing.'

'And you're as skinny as death.'

'*Ruhig,*' answered Bartek.

He was, true enough, skinny, tanned and bedraggled. A real conqueror! He was also swaying on his legs.

'You drunk?'

'No, I'm still a little weak.'

He was still a little weak, it is true, but he was also drunk. In his condition one measure of vodka was ample, and he had had four at the station. Nevertheless, he had the spirit and expression of a real conqueror. He never used to have such an expression.

'*Ruhig,*' he repeated. 'We've finished the *Krieg,* and now I'm a gentleman, understand? And see this?' Here he pointed to the row of crosses and medals on his breast. 'See what sort of a fellow I am? Eh? *Links, rechts! Heu, Stroh!* Right, Left! Hay, Straw, Straw, Hay, *Halt!*'

This last word was roared out so violently that the woman jumped back a few paces.

'Have you gone off your head?'

'How are you, Magda? Can you understand French, stupid?

Monsoo, Monsoo! Who's Monsoo? I'm Monsoo! See?'

'What's come over you, man?'

'What's that got to do with you? *Was?* Donney dinner! Understand?'

A storm was brewing on Magda's face.

'What language are you gurgling in? What? Don't you speak Polish any more? What a Prussian pig! Really! What have they turned you into?'

'Give me something to eat.'

'Get inside!'

Any command made such an impression on Bartek that he could not resist it. Hearing this imperative tone, he straightened up, stretched his arms out by his sides, and, with a half-about turn, marched off in the indicated direction. It was only when he reached the threshold that he came to, and turned to stare at Magda in amazement.

'Well, what the hell, Magda! What are you . . .'

'At the double – move!'

He went in, but came to grief on the doorstep. Now the vodka had really gone to his head. He started singing, and looked around for Franek. He even said: *'Morgen, Kerl!'* though Franek was not there. Then he burst out laughing, took one immense stride, followed by two short ones, yelled *'Hurrah!'* and collapsed headlong on to the bed.

In the evening, he woke up fresh and sober, and, having greeted Franek and wheedled a few pennies out of Magda, made a triumphal march to the inn.

The fame of his exploits had preceded him to Pognembin, as several soldiers from other companies of his regiment had returned sooner and recounted his glorious deeds at Gravelotte and Sedan. As soon as news got about that the conqueror was at the inn, all his old comrades hurried over to see him.

Nobody would have recognised our Bartek now as he sat at the table. He who used to be so meek was banging the table with his fist, swaggering and gobbling like a turkey.

'D'you remember, lads, what Steinmetz said to me when I gave the French such a beating?'

'We remember, all right!'

'They talked an awful lot of rubbish about them Frenchmen and tried to scare us, but they're a creepy people, *was?* They

eat salad like rabbits, and they run like rabbits. And they don't
drink beer, only wine.'

'Aye.'

'When we was burning one village, they clasped their hands
and screamed: "Pitcher! Pitcher!", meaning that if we spared
them they'd give us a drink, but we took no notice.'*

'How can you understand their jabbering?' asked a young
farmhand.

'You don't understand, 'cause you're stupid, but I understand. Donney du pan! Understand?'

'What on earth are you talking about?'

'Have you ever seen Paris? There was battles there, one
after another. But we beat them every time. They don't have
a good command. That's what people said. The fence is good,
but the joints are feeble. Their officers are useless and their
generals are useless, but on our side they're good!'

Maciej Kierz, a clever old Pognembin farmer, started shaking his head.

'Oh, the Germans have won a terrible war, they have, and
we helped them, but what will come of it for us now, God
only knows.'

Bartek's eyes bulged out at him.

'What's that you're saying?'

'The Germans have never respected us; now they've stuck
their noses up as though there was no God above them. And
they'll despise us even more – they're already beginning to.'

'Rubbish!' said Bartek.

Old Kierz had such standing in Pognembin that the whole
village thought through his head, and it was impertinent to
contradict him. But Bartek was now a conqueror, and he too
had standing. Nevertheless, everyone looked at him with surprise, and a certain amount of indignation.

'You can't argue with Maciej, you can't . . .'

'What do I care for Maciej? I've talked to better than him,
see? Didn't I talk to Steinmetz, lads, *was?* Maciej can think
what he likes. Now things'll be better!'

Maciej looked at the conqueror for a moment.

'You fool!' he said.

* *'Pitié'* (mercy) is similar in sound to the Polish *'picie'* (drink).

Bartek banged his fist on the table so hard that all the mugs and glasses jumped.

'*Still der Kerl da! Heu, Stroh!* . . .'

'Quiet, don't scream. Ask his reverence or the squire, you idiot.'

'Did his reverence fight in the war? Did the squire? I did! Don't believe it, lads – now they'll start respecting us. Who won the battles? We did. I did! Now they'll give whatever I ask for. I can be a squire in France if I want. The government knows who clouted the French hardest. Our regiments were the best. That's what was written in the despatches. Now Poles are tops, see?'

Kierz waved his hand, got up and left. Bartek had won a victory in the field of politics as well. The younger ones, who had stayed behind, began to look at him as though he were an oracle.

And they'll give me whatever I want,' he went on: 'If it hadn't been for me, well! Old Kierz is a simpleton, see? The government told us to thump them, so we thumped them. Who's going to despise me? A German? And what about this?' He again pointed to his crosses. 'And who did I clout the French for, if not for the Germans, eh? I'm better than any German; no German's got as many of these as me. Bring more beer! I've talked to Steinmetz and Podbielski. Bring more beer!'

A drinking-bout was developing, and Bartek started singing:

> '*Trink, trink, trink!*
> *Wenn in meiner Tasche*
> *Noch ein Thaler klingt* . . .'

He suddenly produced a handful of coppers from his pocket.

'Take this! I'm a gentleman now . . . Don't you want it? Oh, we took better stuff than this in France, except it all got spent. We didn't half burn a lot, kill a lot of people. God knows, all sorts . . . Frantirors . . .'

The moods of drunken people have a tendency to change unexpectedly. Bartek scooped the money off the table, and began to call out pathetically: 'God be merciful to my sinful soul!' He then put his elbows on the table, hid his face in his paws and remained silent.

'What's wrong with you?' asked one of the drunkards.

'It wasn't my fault,' mumbled Bartek in dismay. 'Who asked them to get caught? It's just that I was sorry for them, 'cause they was ours. God be merciful! One of them was like the rosy dawn. The next day he was white as snow. And when we started shovelling earth on them, they was still alive . . . Vodka!'

There was a moment of gloomy silence. The peasants looked at each other in astonishment.

'What's he going on about?' asked one.

'He's talking to his conscience.'

'It's because of this war you have to drink,' grumbled Bartek. He took a couple of draughts of vodka. For a while he sat in silence, then spat on the floor and his good spirits returned unexpectedly.

'You've never talked to Steinmetz, have you? I have. Hurrah! Come on, drink! Who's paying? I am!'

'You're paying, you drunkard,' came Magda's voice, 'but just you wait and see how I pay you back!'

Bartek looked through glazed eyes at the woman who had just come in.

'Have you ever talked to Steinmetz? What are you . . .'

Instead of replying, Magda turned to the sympathetic audience and started lamenting:

'Oh, people, people, look at my shame and my misfortune. He came back and I greeted him with joy, but he was drunk. He's forgotten God and he's forgotten Polish. He went to sleep to sober up, and now he's drinking again, and he's paying with my work and the sweat of my brow. Where did you get that money from? Wasn't it my effort and my toil? Oh, people, people, he's not a Catholic, not a man any more. He's a cursed German – he jabbers in German and laughs at human sorrow. He's a disgrace, he's . . .'

The woman burst into tears at this point, and then went on, raising her voice by an octave:

'He was stupid, but he was good. And now what have they made of him? I waited in the mornings, I waited at night, and he came back . . . No comfort, no mercy from anywhere. God Almighty, God the patient! . . . I hope you get the staggers, and go all German . . .'

These last words were so tearful that she almost intoned them.

'Shut up, or I'll thump you!' retorted Bartek.

'Come on, beat me, cut off my head, cut it off now, kill me, murder me!' screamed the woman insistently, and, stretching out her neck, she turned to the peasants:

'And you, good people, watch him!'

But the peasants began to leave, and the inn was soon quite empty; only Bartek and the woman craning her neck remained.

'Why are you sticking your breather out like a goose?' muttered Bartek. 'Come on home.'

'Cut it off!' insisted Magda.

'No I won't cut it off!' said Bartek, thrusting his hands into his pockets. At this point, wishing to put an end to the scene, the innkeeper blew out the only candle. It was dark and quiet. After a moment, Magda's squealing voice pierced the silence.

'Cut it off!'

'No I won't!' retorted Bartek triumphantly.

By the light of the moon, two figures could be seen walking back from the inn towards the cottages. The one walking in front was lamenting volubly; that was Magda. Behind her, with his head bowed, the victor of Gravelotte and Sedan followed sheepishly.

VII

Bartek had come back so exhausted that he could do no work for several days. This was a misfortune for the holding, which urgently needed a man's hand. Magda did all she could, working from dawn till dusk, and their neighbours the Cmiernickis helped a little, but all this was insufficient and the place was slowly drifting towards ruin. There were also a few debts, run up with a German colonist, Just. He had bought a few acres of wasteland from the Pognembin estate, and now had the best holding in the village, as well as ready money which he lent out at quite high rates of interest. He mainly lent money to Squire Jarzyński, whose name was knocking about somewhere in the *Golden Book of the Gentry*, and who, for that very reason, felt obliged to maintain the splendour of his household at an appropriate level. But Just also lent money to the peasants. For six months now Magda had owed him a few dozen thalers, part of which had been used to keep the holding afloat and part of which she had sent to Bartek while he was still at war. This would have been of little consequence in itself. The Lord had granted promising crops and the debt could have been paid off with the future grain, if only an extra pair of hands and a little hard work had been put into it. Unfortunately, Bartek could not work. Magda refused to believe this, and she went to take council of the parish priest on how to wake the peasant up. But he was in fact genuinely unfit for work. He would run out of breath and his back would ache whenever he got down to a job. So he spent whole days sitting in front of the cottage, smoking a porcelain pipe adorned with a miniature of Bismarck in white uniform and dragoon's helmet, looking at the world with the tired dreamy eyes of a man whose bones are full of weariness. He would think a little about the war, a little about the victories, a little about Magda, a little about everything, and a little about nothing.

One day, as he was sitting like this, he heard Franek crying in the distance. Franek was on his way back from school, and was blubbering so loud that it carried over the neighbourhood. Bartek took the pipe from his mouth.

'What's the matter, Franz?'

'What's the matter? . . .' repeated Franek, sobbing.

'Well, what are you blubbering about?'

'Why shouldn't I, when I've been clouted in the mug . . .'

'Who clouted you?'

'Mister Boege, who else!'

Herr Boege fulfilled the duties of schoolmaster in Pognembin.

'And what right's he got to clout you?'

'He must have, 'cause he did . . .'

Magda, who was digging in the garden, crossed over the fence, and came up to the boy, hoe in hand.

'What did you do?' she asked.

'I didn't do nothing, only Mister Boege called me a Polish swine and clouted me and said that now they've beaten the French, they're going to kick us around, because they're the strongest now. And I didn't do nothing, only he asked me who was the greatest man on earth, and I said the Holy Father was, and he clouted me and I began to howl, and he called me a Polish swine and said that now they've beaten the French . . .' Franek started repeating over and over again: 'And he said . . . And I said . . . and then he said . . .' At last, Magda put her hand over his mouth and, turning to Bartek, called out:

'Hear that? Hear it? You go off and fight the French, so that a German can kick your son around like a dog, insult him . . . You go off and fight so that the Kraut can kill your child – that's your reward! That low swine . . .'

Touched by her own words, Magda started crying with Franek, while Bartek's eyes bulged and his mouth fell open in amazement. He was so taken aback that he could not say a word or take in what had happened. What about all his victories? . . . He sat in silence for a while, but all of a sudden something flashed in his eyes and blood rushed to his face.

Amazement, as well as fear, often turns to rage in the minds of simpletons. Bartek jumped to his feet and hissed through clenched teeth:

'I'll talk to him!' And off he went.

It was not far; the school lay just beyond the church. Herr Boege was standing in front of his porch, surrounded by a crowd of piglets, which he was feeding with pieces of bread. He was a solid man of about fifty, still as strong as an oak. He was not fat, and only his face was podgy. In that face swam a pair of fish-like eyes which expressed daring and energy. Bartek came up very close to him.

'What are you kicking my kid about for, you German – *Was?*' he asked. Herr Boege drew back a few paces, and, looking him up and down without a trace of fear, said:

'Clear out, you Polish fool!'

'What are you clouting my kid for?' persisted Bartek.

'I will clout you also, Polish scum! Now we will show you who is master here! Go to the devil! Complain in court, if you dare . . . Get out!'

Bartek seized the teacher by the shoulder and began to shake him, shouting in a croaking voice:

'D'you know who I am? D'you know who beat the French? D'you know who talked to Steinmetz? Why are you kicking the boy around, you German filth?'

Herr Boege's fishy eyes popped out in competition with
Bartek's, but he was a strong man, and he decided to liberate
himself from the assailant with one movement. This took the
form of a powerful slap across the face of the victor of Gravelotte and Sedan. At this, the peasant lost all restraint. Herr
Boege's head was shaken by two sudden movements
reminiscent of the action of a pendulum, with the only difference that these were breathtakingly quick. The terrible flail of
Algerians and Zouaves awoke once more inside Bartek. In vain
did the twenty-year-old Oskar, every bit as tough as his father,
come to Boege's aid. A short but fierce struggle ensued, during
which the son was hurled to the ground while the father felt
himself being picked up and lifted high into the air. With his
arms stretched out above him, Bartek carried his adversary he
knew not where himself. Unfortunately, just by the house
stood a barrel full of slops, thriftily saved for the swine by
Frau Boege. A dull splash resounded in it now, and after a
moment Boege's legs could be seen sticking out of it, kicking
violently. Frau Boege rushed out of the house screaming:

'Help! Help!'

The sensible woman immediately tipped the barrel over,
spilling her husband out onto the ground with the slops.

Other colonists came running from nearby cottages to the
rescue of their neighbour. Nearly twenty Germans made for
Bartek and started laying into him with fists and sticks. It was
impossible to distinguish him from his adversaries in the ensu-
ing commotion, as all the bodies had fused into one convulsive
mass. All of a sudden, Bartek shot out of the mêlée and started
running towards the fence for all he was worth. The Germans
surged after him, but at that moment the fence gave a horrific
crash, and a hefty stake began to wave in Bartek's mighty
paws. He wheeled round, foaming and livid, and raised the
stake in his hands. Everyone ran. Bartek went after them.
Luckily, he did not catch any up. The pursuit cooled him
down, and he started drawing back in the direction of his cottage. Oh, if only there had been Frenchmen before him now!
History would have immortalised this retreat.

The attackers, nearly twenty of them, had rallied and were
on his heels once more. He was stepping back slowly, like a

wild boar cornered by a pack of hounds. Now and again, he would stop and face them, and then the pursuers would halt as well. The stake filled them with the greatest respect. They began throwing stones, and one of these wounded Bartek in the forehead. Blood flooded his eyes and he could feel himself weakening. He swayed on his legs, dropped the stake, and fell.

'Hurrah!' yelled the colonists. But before they had managed to reach him, he was on his feet again. This wounded wolf could still be dangerous. Besides, they were not far from the first cottages now, and a few farmhands were making for the scene of the skirmish as fast as their legs would carry them. The colonists beat a retreat towards their own houses.

'What happened?' asked the newcomers.

'I had a bit of a go at the Germans,' answered Bartek.

VIII

The affair took a serious turn. The German newspapers printed touching articles about the persecutions suffered by the peaceful German population at the hands of the primitive dark masses, goaded on by anarchist agitators and religious fanaticism. Boege became a hero. He, a quiet, benign teacher spreading enlightenment at the distant limits of the country, a real missionary of culture amongst barbarians, had been the first victim. Luckily, a hundred million Germans stood behind him, and they would not allow, etc . . .

Bartek had no idea of the proportions of the storm that was gathering over his head. In fact, he was quite cheerful. He was convinced that he would win the case in court. It was Boege who had beaten his child, Boege who had hit him first, and later, he had been attacked by so many. They had even cut his head open with a stone. And whose head? His, who had been mentioned in despatches as an example, who had won the Battle of Gravelotte, who had talked to Steinmetz himself, who had won so many crosses! He failed to see how the Germans could possibly not be aware of all this, and how they could do him injustice. Moreover, he could not understand how it was that Boege could threaten the peasants, saying that the Germans were going to kick them about, since they, the peasants,

had fought the French so bravely whenever the opportunity
arose. He was quite certain that the magistrates and the government would take his side. They would know who he was
and what he had done during the war. Even if nobody else did,
Steinmetz would take his side. Bartek had even grown poor
and run up debts on the holding because of this war. They
simply could not refuse him justice.

Meanwhile, the police came to Pognembin to fetch Bartek.
They must have been expecting determined resistance, since
there were five of them, with rifles loaded. They were quite
wrong – Bartek had not the slightest intention of resisting.
They told him to get into the carriage, and he got in. But
Magda was in despair, and kept repeating:

'Oh, why did you have to fight those Frenchmen so well?
That's where it's got you, you poor thing, look!'

'Shut up, you idiot!' answered Bartek. Along the road, he
smiled gaily at the passers-by.

'I'll show them who they've insulted!' he called from the
carriage. With his medals and crosses on his breast, he drove
to court like a triumphant conqueror.

It so happened that the magistrates were very lenient
towards him. The existence of attenuating circumstances was
admitted. Bartek was sentenced to only three months' impris-
onment. Apart from this, he was also ordered to pay an indem-
nity of a hundred and fifty marks to the Boege family, and
other 'bodily insulted colonists'.

'However, not only was the criminal not a bit abashed by
the sentence when it was read to him,' wrote the *Posener
Zeitung* in its report, 'he exploded into such coarse language
and began to recite his so-called services to the state so impudently, that one can only be surprised at the present magistrate
for not drawing up a new case against him for contempt of
court and insult to the German race . . .'

Meanwhile in jail, Bartek was peacefully reminiscing on his
deeds at Gravelotte, Sedan and the siege of Paris.

But we should be committing an injustice if we said that
Herr Boege's behaviour had provoked no public outcry. It did
indeed. One drizzly morning, a certain Polish delegate very
eloquently brought to the Reichstag's notice how the attitude
towards the Poles had changed in the Duchy of Poznań, how

in return for the sacrifices made by the Poznań regiments and
their bravery during the recent war, the Germans ought to be
more respectful of the human rights of the people of that
province, and how, finally, Herr Boege of Pognembin abused
his position of teacher, beating Polish children, calling them
Polish swine and promising that after this war the colonists
would crush the aborigines under their boots.

The rain kept falling while the delegate spoke, and, as
drowsiness always takes hold of people on such a morning, the
Conservatives yawned, the National-Liberals yawned, the
Socialists yawned, and so did the Zentrum, for the Kulturkampf had not started yet. At last, after this 'Polish com-
plaint', the house passed on to the order of the day.

Meanwhile, Bartek sat in jail, or rather, lay in the prison
hospital, for the stone had opened up an old war wound.
When he had no temperature, he would think and think, like
that famous turkey which thought so much that it died. But
Bartek did not die – he simply never thought anything up.
Sometimes, however, in those moments science calls *lucida
intervalla*, a vague suspicion would begin to gnaw at him that
perhaps all his beating up of Frenchmen had got him nowhere.

Magda, on the other hand, began to know hard times. The
fine had to be paid, and there was nowhere to get the money
from. The priest of Pognembin wanted to help, but he had less
than forty marks in his chest. It was a poor parish, this
Pognembin, and anyway, the poor old man never knew where
the money was spent. Squire Jarzyński was not at home. People said he had gone off to court some rich young lady in the
Kingdom.

Magda was at a loss as to what to do. There was no use
even trying to have the term prolonged. What was she to do?
Sell the horses or the cows? It was just before the harvest, the
time of greatest hardship. The harvests were drawing near and
the holding badly needed money, but there was no way of getting any. The woman was in despair. She made several appeals
for mercy to the magistrates, mentioning Bartek's services, but
she never even received an answer. The deadline and, with it,
the sequestration drew near.

She prayed and prayed, remembering with bitterness the
old days before the war, when they had been well off, when

Bartek even used to earn extra money at the factory in winter. She went to borrow money from the neighbours, but they had none – the war had left its mark everywhere. She dared not go to Just, as she was already heavily in his debt and had not even paid him the interest. But Just unexpectedly came to see her.

One afternoon, she was sitting on the doorstep of her cottage doing nothing, for despair had sapped her energy. She was contemplating the gnats chasing each other about in the air, and she thought how lucky all those little insects were, just flying around and never having to pay anything. From time to time she would sigh deeply and her pale lips would quietly utter a supplication:

'Oh, my God, my God! . . .'

Suddenly, the hooked nose of Herr Just, with a hooked pipe just beneath it, appeared in front of the gate. The woman turned pale. Just said:

'*Morgen!*'

'How are you, Mister Just?'

'What about my money?'

'Oh, my darling Mister Just, please be patient. I'm poor; what can I do? They've taken my husband and now I've got to pay a fine for him, and I can't do anything. It would be so much better if I could die, instead of having to wear myself out like this every day. Please wait, my dearest Mister Just!'

She burst into tears and, bending down, humbly kissed Herr Just's plump red hand.

'The squire will come back, and I'll borrow some money from him to pay you back.'

'And what are you going to pay the fine with, eh?'

'God knows; I suppose I'll have to sell a cow.'

'Well, I'll lend you some more.'

'May the Lord thank you, sir. Though you're a Lutheran, you're a good man. If all the Germans were like you, then we'd bless them all, truly!'

'But I won't lend without a percentage . . .'

'I know, I know!'

'Well then, you can write me out one receipt for the lot.'

'Yes, dear sir. God bless you for it!'

'I'll go to town, so we can draw up the deed.'

He went to town and drew up the deed, but first Magda

went to take council of the parish priest. There was very little to advise. The priest said that the term was too short and the interest too high, and he moaned about Squire Jarzyński being away, as he would have helped had he been at home. Magda could not wait, on account of the impending sequestration, and she had to accept Just's conditions. She borrowed three hundred marks, twice the amount due, as she needed some money to keep the farmstead going. Bartek had to sign the deed himself, to make it valid, and Magda paid him a special visit in jail.

The conqueror was very dejected, crushed and sick. He had tried writing an appeal representing his injuries, but this had been rejected. The attitude of the administrative circles had been forcefully swayed against him by the articles in the *Posener Zeitung;* should these authorities not provide greater protection for the peace-loving German population, 'which had made such great sacrifices and proved its love for the Fatherland in the recent war'? So, quite rightly, Bartek's appeal was rejected. Little wonder that he felt crushed.

'Now we're completely done for,' he said to his wife.

'Completely,' she repeated.

Bartek began to ponder something.

'A terrible injustice is being done to me,' he said finally.

'Boege's persecuting the boy,' said Magda. 'I went to beg him to stop, but he just insulted me. Oh, the Germans are tops in Pognembin now. Now they're not scared of anyone.'

'That's for sure; they're the strongest,' said Bartek sadly.

'I'm only a simple woman, but I'll tell you something; the Lord's stronger still.'

'He's our refuge,' said Bartek. There was a pause. Then Bartek asked:

'What about Just?'

'If Almighty God gives us a good harvest, then we might just be able to pay him off. Maybe the squire can help us, though he's got debts with the Germans too. Even before the war, people were saying that he'd have to sell Pognembin, unless he finds a rich lady.'

'Will he be back soon?'

'Who knows? At the manor they say he'll be back with a wife soon. The Germans will squeeze him when he turns up.

Always these Germans! They crawl in everywhere, just like
maggots. Wherever you look, all around you, in the town and
in the country; Germans! It must be a punishment for our
sins. And no help from anywhere!'

'Maybe you'll think up something – you're a clever woman.'

'What can I think up? Did I take money from Just of my
own free will? You see, our house and the land – it's already
his. Just is better than the rest of the Germans, but he knows
which side his bread is buttered. He won't let us off, just as he
never let others off. I'm not stupid! D'you think I don't know
why he's throwing money at us? But what else can we do? You
give some advice, since you're so clever. You know how to
beat up Frenchmen, but what'll you do when you don't have
a roof over your head or a spoonful of food to eat?'

The victor of Gravelotte took his head in his hands, and
cried out:

'Oh, Jesus! Jesus!'

Magda had a good heart, and she was touched by his grief,
so she said:

'Quiet, man, quiet! Don't touch your loaf before it's healed
up. As long as the Lord grants a good harvest. The rye is so
beautiful you want to get down and kiss the earth, the wheat
too. The earth isn't German, it won't hurt us! You and your
war didn't do the farm any good, still, it's growing so beautifully that . . .' The kind Magda smiled through her tears.

'The earth isn't German,' she repeated once more.

'Magda!' said Bartek, looking at her through his bulging
eyes: 'Magda!'

'What?'

'Well, you're so . . . well . . .'

A feeling of deep gratitude welled up in Bartek's heart, but
he just could not find a way of expressing it.

IX

Magda really was worth ten other women. She kept her Bartek
on a tight rein, but was genuinely attached to him. In
moments of anger, like the scene at the inn, she would tell him
to his face that he was stupid, but on the whole she preferred

to make people believe otherwise.

'My Bartek always pretends he's an idiot, but he's cunning all right!' she would say. In fact, Bartek was about as cunning as his horse, and without Magda he would never have managed, either in farming or in anything else.

Now everything rested on her honest shoulders, and she started running about, traipsing to and fro, paying calls and begging so tirelessly that she managed to get some help. A week after her last visit to the prison hospital, she rushed in to see Bartek again, radiant, happy and out of breath.

'How are you, Bartek, darling?' she cried out joyfully. 'You know, the squire's back! He got married in the Kingdom – the young lady's a perfect little peach! And he got an awful lot of all kinds of riches with her . . .'

The master of Pognembin had indeed got married, he had come back to the manor with his wife, and really had acquired 'an awful lot of all kinds of riches'.

'Well, what of it?' asked Bartek.

'Quiet, you idiot!' answered Magda. 'God, I'm out of breath! Oh, Jesus! . . . Well, I went over to pay my respects to the new lady, and you should have seen her! She came out to me like a princess – fresh as a flower, beautiful as the sunrise . . . It's really hot! . . . I'm all out of breath . . .'

Magda began to wipe the perspiration from her face with her apron. Then she went on.

'She had a lovely, beautiful blue dress, just like cornflowers . . . I took her round the knees, and she gave me her hand to kiss . . . She's got little hands, all scented and lovely, like a baby's. Just like a Saint in a picture, and she's so kind and understanding of human unhappiness. I started begging her to rescue us, may the Lord give her health, and she says: "Whatever is in my power, I will do," she says. And she's got such a lovely voice, that when she speaks, you feel sweetness all around you! Then I started saying how unhappy the people are in Pognembin, and she says: "Aye, and not only in Pognembin . . ." and so I started blubbering and so did she. Then the master came up and saw her crying, and you should have seen it when he started kissing her; on the eyes, on the mug . . . the masters aren't like you lot! Then she said to him: "Do what you can for this woman." So he answered: "Anything on earth for your sake." May the Mother of God bless her, that dear little peach! May She bless her with children and with health! And then the master said to me: "You've done badly to let yourselves fall into the hands of the Germans, but I'll help you pay off Just", he says.'

Bartek started scratching the back of his neck.

'But the Germans have the master in their hands too.'

'Never mind! The lady's rich. Now he can buy all the Germans in Pognembin, so he can say what he likes. He said: "There will be elections soon, so make sure that nobody votes for a German, and I'll pay off Just and deal with Boege." And then the lady put her arms round his neck, and then the master asked about you and said: "If he's weak, then I'll persuade the doctor to write a report saying he cannot stay in now. If they don't let him off altogether, then at least he can go back and finish off his spell in winter, but now he can be useful for the harvests." See? Yesterday the master came to town, and today the doctor's going out to Pognembin, to visit the master. He's not a German, he'll write a report. In the winter you can sit around in jug, like a king – you'll be warm and fed for nothing – and now you'll come home to work, and we'll pay off Just, and maybe the master won't ask for any interest, and if we don't manage to give it all back by the autumn, then I'll go and beg the lady again. May the Mother of God bless her! . . . D'you understand?'

'A good lady, sure enough!' said Bartek with enthusiasm.

'You'll go and fall at her feet . . . you'd better go, or I'll pull that yellow head of yours off. If only the Lord would give a good harvest! And you see who saved us? Not the Germans! They never gave you a groschen for those medals of yours – all they gave you was a blow on the head, that's all! You'll go and fall on your knees to the lady . . .'

'I'll go and fall on my knees all right!' said Bartek with resolution. Fate seemed to be smiling at the conqueror once again. A few days later, he was informed that he was being temporarily let out of jail until the winter, on account of his health. First, however, he was to report to the Landrat. Bartek turned up with his heart in his mouth. This peasant who, bayonet in hand, had captured cannons and standards, now feared any uniform more than death itself. He carried in his soul a sort of deaf, uncontrollable feeling that they were persecuting him, that they could do with him whatever they liked, that there hung over him some immense force, hostile and evil, which would crush him completely were he to object. So he stood before the Landrat as he had once stood before Steinmetz; straight as a broomstick, with his stomach in, his chest forward and no breath in his lungs. There were several officers with the Landrat, so the whole war and military discipline loomed up before Bartek's eyes. The officers looked down at him through gold-rimmed pince-nez with all the pride and contempt due from Prussian officers towards a simple soldier and a Polish peasant at that. He stood breathless, while the Landrat started to say something in a tone of command. He was not asking or persuading; he was ordering and threatening.

The delegate in Berlin had died, and new elections had been announced. 'You Polish ox! Just you try to vote for Mr Jarzyński. Just you try!'

The brows of the officers creased into threatening leonine attitudes. One of them bit off the end of his cigar and repeated the Landrat's words: 'Just you try!'

Bartek's victorious spirit died within him. When he heard the command 'Get out!', he made a half-about turn to the left, marched out and took a deep breath. He had been ordered to vote for Herr Schulberg of Greater Krzywda.

He did not give these instructions much thought, and soon calmed down, because he was on his way to Pognembin, because he could be at home for the harvests, and because the master had promised to pay off Just.

He left the town. Jostled by the wind, the ears of the corn brushed against each other with a sound dear to every peasant. Bartek still felt weak, but the sun warmed him. 'Oh, how beautiful the world is!' thought the exhausted soldier. It was not far to Pognembin now.

X

The elections, the elections! Mrs Maria Jarzyńska's little head was full of them – she could talk, think and dream of nothing else.

'The good lady is a great politician,' said the neighbouring squire, kissing her little hands like a dragon, while the great politician blushed deeply, and replied with a charming smile:

'Oh, we agitate in every way we can.'

'Józef will be the next delegate,' replied the neighbour with conviction, to which the great politician answered:

'I would love that, of course, but it isn't only for Józio's sake,' and here the great politician turned crimson once again, 'but also for the general cause . . .'

'A real Bismarck, I must say!' exclaimed the neighbour, kissing the little hands once again, and then they began to discuss the best methods of campaigning. The neighbour took on Lesser Krzywda and Mizerów (Greater Krzywda was already lost, as the landowner was Herr Schulberg). Mrs Jarzyńska was to look after Pognembin. Her head was on fire with the feeling of importance this gave her. Every day she was to be seen in the road between the cottages, her dress lifted in one hand, her parasol in the other. Beneath the hem of her dress a pair of tiny feet could be seen enthusiastically traipsing towards great political goals. She visited the houses, and to those who were hard at work she would say: 'May the Lord help you!' as she passed.

She visited the sick, charmed everyone, and helped wherever she could. She used to do this anyway, even without the political motive, for she had a good heart, but the political element added considerably to her enthusiasm. What would she not have done for the sake of those politics? One thing that she did not tell her husband was that she felt an irresistible desire to assist at the peasant gathering. She had even vaguely composed a short speech which she would be expected to make at the gathering. And what a speech! In fact, she would probably have been too shy to make it, but if she had, well . . . However, news reached Pognembin that the authorities had abolished the peasant gatherings, whereupon the great politician burst into tears of rage in her room, tore one handkerchief to shreds, and had red eyes for the rest of the day. In vain did her husband beg her not to get so excited.

The next day the agitation was carried on in Pognembin with even greater fervour. Mrs Jarzyńska retreated before nothing now. She visited near on twenty houses a day and began to insult the Germans so vehemently that her husband had to restrain her. But there was no danger, for the peasants received her with joy, kissing her hands and smiling at her, as she was so fresh and pretty that whenever she came in the whole room would brighten.

Eventually she came to Bartek's cottage. Łysek tried to stop her, but Magda gave him a hefty blow on the muzzle with a stick.

'My lady! My dearest, most lovely lady, my little peach!' squealed Magda, covering her hands with kisses.

Bartek fell at her feet, as was to be expected, while little Franek kissed her hand, then put his thumb in his mouth, and sank into a reverie of profound admiration.

'I expect,' said the young lady after the greetings, 'that you, my dear Bartek, will vote for my husband, and not for Mr Schulberg.'

'Oh, my little sunrise!' exclaimed Magda. 'Who'd vote for that Schulberg fellow anyway! May the devil take him!' (She again kissed the lady's hands) 'Don't be angry, my lady, but when I get talking about them Germans, I just can't keep my tongue still.'

'My husband was just saying that he'd pay off Just.'

'May the Lord bless him!' She turned to Bartek.

'Why are you standing like a post? He's a very quiet fellow, my lady.'

'You'll vote for my husband, won't you?' asked the lady. 'We're Polish and you're Polish – we must stick together.'

'I'd screw his head off if he didn't,' said Magda. 'Why are you standing there like an ass? He's terribly shy, you know. Come on, move yourself!'

Bartek kissed the lady's hand once more, but said nothing, and he looked as gloomy as night. The Landrat was on his mind.

The day of the elections drew near, and at last arrived. Mr Jarzyński was sure of his success. All the neighbours came to Pognembin. The gentlemen had been to town to cast their votes and now awaited the news, which the priest would bring to Pognembin. Then there was to be a lunch, after which the couple would leave for Poznań, and then Berlin. Some of the constituency's villages had only finished voting the day before, so the results would be announced that day. Those assembled at the manor were full of optimism. The young lady was a little uneasy, but she was cheerful and smiling, as becomes a good hostess, and everyone agreed that Mr Jarzyński had discovered a real treasure in the Kingdom. This treasure simply could not sit still, and kept moving from guest to guest, to be assured a hundred times over by each one that 'Józio' would be elected. She was not in fact ambitious, and it was not out of vanity that she wanted to become a delegate's wife. She had dreamt up in her little golden head that both her husband and herself had a great mission to accomplish.

So her heart was beating as feverishly as on her wedding-day, and joy lit up her pretty face. Moving about gracefully between the guests, she came up to her husband, and whispered in his ear like a child: 'Mr Delegate!'

He smiled; they were both inexpressibly happy. They felt a wild urge to kiss each other properly, but this would hardly have been fitting in front of the guests. Actually, everyone kept looking out of the window, as the affair was really very serious. The old delegate had been a Pole, and this was the first time that the Germans had proposed their own candidate in this constituency.

Their victorious war had evidently given them courage, and it was for this very reason that those gathered together in Pognembin Manor wanted their own candidate to win. There was no lack of patriotic speeches before lunch, and these particularly moved the young hostess who was not used to them. Anxiety preyed on her. What if they were to fix the counting of the votes? But the committee was not made up solely of Germans. The older guests explained to the young lady how the votes were counted. She had already heard this a hundred times before, but insisted on hearing it all again. After all, it was the deciding factor in whether the local population was to have a defender or an enemy in the Reichstag. The whole question would be resolved very soon.

Extremely soon, in fact, as a cloud of dust could now be seen on the road.

'The priest's coming! The priest's coming!' repeated the guests. The hostess grew pale. Emotion was visible on every face. They were confident of the outcome, but their hearts beat faster all the same. In fact it was not the priest but the steward returning from town. Perhaps he knew something. He tethered his horse and started walking towards the house, while all the guests, led by the hostess, spilled out onto the porch.

'Is there any news? Has your master been elected? What? Come here! Do you know for sure? Have the results been announced?' The questions crossed each other and fell like rockets, while the peasant threw his cap into the air and shouted:

'Our master's been elected!'

The lady sank onto a bench and pressed her heaving breast with her hands.

'*Vivat! Vivat!*' shouted the neighbours.

'What about the priest?' asked someone.

'He's on his way – should be here soon. They were still counting the last votes,' replied the steward.

The servants came running out of the kitchen and started shouting:

'*Vivat!* We've beaten the Germans! Long live the delegate and his lady!'

'Serve lunch!' called out the master.

'*Vivat!*' repeated everyone.

The guests went back into the house. The congratulations were now flowing more soberly. Only the hostess could not restrain herself, and, notwithstanding the presence of others, wrapped her arms round her husband's neck. Nobody censured this, as everyone was extremely moved.

'Well, we're still alive,' said the neighbour from Mizerów.

The rumble of a cart was heard outside, and the priest came into the room with old Maciej of Pognembin.

'Greetings! Greetings!' shouted the company. 'Well, what was the final majority?'

The priest was silent for a moment, then he threw two short and sharp words into the face of the universal jollity:

'Schulberg's elected.'

There followed a moment of amazement and then a shower of hurried and anxious questions, to which the priest replied again:

'Schulberg's been elected.'

'How? What happened? The steward said . . . What happened?'

At that point Mrs Jarzyńska, biting her kerchief so as not to burst into tears or faint, had to be escorted from the room by her husband.

'What a disaster! What a catastrophe!' everybody repeated.

From the village came the muffled sounds of voices and shouts of joy; the Pognembin Germans were celebrating their victory.

The Jarzyńskis came back into the room. By the door, the young man said to his wife:

'Il faut faire bonne mine!' The young lady was no longer crying; her eyes were dry and very red.

'Now you must tell us how it happened,' said the host calmly.

'How could it have been otherwise, your honour,' replied old Maciej, 'when even some of the Pognembin Poles voted for Schulberg.'

'Who? What, from Pognembin?'

'Yes, I saw myself, and so did everyone – Bartek Słowik voted for Schulberg . . .'

'Bartek Słowik?' said the lady.

'Indeed. Now the others are all cursing him, his wife's cursing him, and he's writhing about on the floor, weeping. I saw it myself.'

'A fellow like that ought to be hounded out of the village,' said the neighbour from Mizerów.

'But your honour,' went on Maciej, 'the others who went to war, they voted the same. They say they were forced . . .'

'Abuse! Clear-cut abuse! Invalid election! Blackmail! Trickery!' shouted various voices.

Lunch was not very jolly that day at Pognembin Manor. In the evening, the couple left, but not for Berlin – for Dresden.

The wretched, cursed, insulted and reviled Bartek sat in his cottage, a stranger even to his wife, for she too refused to speak to him now.

In the autumn the Lord granted a good harvest, and Herr Just, who had just taken possession of Bartek's holding, was very pleased, as he had done rather well out of the deal.

One day, three people could be seen walking along the road from Pognembin to the town – a peasant, a woman and a child. The peasant was hunched up, and looked more like an old beggar than anything else. They were on their way to town, as they could find no work in Pognembin. It was raining, and the woman was bitterly lamenting her house and her village, both lost forever. The peasant was silent. The road was empty; not a cart, not a soul. Only the crucifix by the roadside held up its dripping arms over them. The rain was getting thicker and heavier, and the sky was growing dark.

Bartek, Magda and Franek were off to town, for the hero of Gravelotte and Sedan still had to spend some time in jail for the Boege affair.

The Jarzyńskis were still in Dresden.

ON THE
BRIGHT SHORE

The artist was sitting beside Mrs Elzen in the open carriage, with her twin sons Romulus and Remus facing him. His attention was divided between the conversation, the consideration of his position, which required decisive action, and the contemplation of the sea. It was certainly a view worth contemplating. They were driving from the direction of Nice towards Monte Carlo along the Vieille Corniche, the road which hugs the overhanging rocks, high above the sea. The view on their left was hemmed in by a mass of naked rock, grey with a rosy tinge, like mother of pearl, while on their right stretched the depths of the Mediterranean sea, which seemed immensely far below them, a deep and boundless chasm. From this height, the small fishing boats looked like tiny white specks, and it was even difficult to distinguish a distant sail from a gull circling above the water.

With the enraptured expression of a woman oblivious of her actions, Mrs Elzen rested her shoulder against Swirski's arm as her dreamy eyes floated across the mirror of the sea.

A shudder of delight ran through Swirski as he felt the pressure, and he mused that were it not for the presence of Romulus and Remus, he might have placed his arm around the young woman and pressed her to his bosom.

A twinge of alarm rapidly succeeded this thought, for if he did that, the hesitation would have come to an end and the situation would have been decided. But Mrs Elzen interrupted his thoughts.

'Let us stop the carriage!' she said.

Swirski stopped the carriage, and for a moment they sat in silence.

'How quiet it is here after the hubbub of Monte Carlo!' said the young widow.

'I hear only music,' answered the painter. 'They must be playing on the ironclads in Villefranche.'

Muffled strains wafted up to them from time to time, borne on the same breeze that brought them the scent of orange blossom and heliotrope. The roofs of seaside villas below, hidden in thickets of eucalyptus splashed here and there with the white of flowering almonds and the pink of peach-trees, over-looked the deep-blue sunlit bay of Villefranche, which was crowded with great ships.

The bustle below contrasted strangely with the lifelessness of the barren mountains, over which stretched a sky so cloud-less, so clear, that it seemed glassy, almost implacable. Up there, everything seemed small and insignificant amid the placid greatness, and the carriage with its passengers seemed no more than a beetle clinging to the rocks, impudently crawl-ing up these noble heights.

'Life itself seems to end here,' said Swirski, looking at the nakedness of the rocks.

Mrs Elzen leant even more heavily on his arm. 'To me it seems that life begins here,' she said in a slow, drowsy voice.

'Perhaps you are right,' answered Swirski after a while, his voice betraying emotion.

He cast an enquiring glance at her. Mrs Elzen lifted her eyes to him, but quickly lowered her lids, in apparent confu-sion. Almost in denial of her two sons sitting on the front ban-quette, she looked at this moment like a young girl whose eyes cannot stand up to the first gleam of love. They both fell silent, while the wind-borne snatches of music drifted up from below.

Meanwhile, a plume of smoke had appeared in the distance, at the very entrance to the bay, and the solemn atmosphere was shattered by Remus, who jumped up from his seat shouted:

'Tiens! Le Fohmidable!'

Mrs Elzen cast a glance of displeasure at the younger of her twins. She was sorry to have lost that magic moment, in which every word was so full of fateful import.

'Remus,' she snapped; *'Veux-tu te taire?'*

'Mais Maman, c'est le Fohmidable!'

'What an unbearable child!'

'Pouhquoi?'

'He's a fool, but he's right,' piped up Romulus. 'Yesterday we were in Villefranche – you saw us set off on our bicyclettes – and they told us that the whole squadron had arrived, except for the *Fohmidable*, which was to come the next day.'

'Fool yourself!' replied Remus, accenting the last letter of every word in the French manner.

The boys began digging each other in the ribs with their elbows. Knowing how much Swirski disliked her sons' manner of speaking and their upbringing in general, Mrs Elzen told them to be quiet, and said: 'I have already told you, and Mr Kresowicz, that you must speak only Polish amongst yourselves.'

Kresowicz was a student from Zurich with the beginnings of tuberculosis whom Mrs Elzen had encountered on the Riviera. After making the acquaintance of Swirski, and particularly after a declaration from the malicious but immensely rich Mr Wiadrowski to the effect that respectable homes no longer reared their children in the manner of travelling salesmen, she had taken him on as their tutor.

The wretched *Formidable* had completely spoiled the sensitive painter's mood. After a while, the carriage lurched forward with a crunching of gravel.

'It was you who insisted that we should bring them along,' said Mrs Elzen in a sugary voice, 'you are much too kind to them. But we must return here at night, by moonlight. Would you like to do that, tonight, perhaps!'

'I should be delighted to, but tonight there will be no moon, and your dinner will probably end too late,' answered Swirski.

'That's true,' Mrs Elzen said. 'But you must tell me when there will be a full moon. It is a pity that I asked other people to this dinner . . . It must be beautiful here with a full moon, although I confess that I always get palpitations of the heart at such a height. If only you knew how it is beating at this moment . . . but look at my pulse; you can see it through the glove.'

With these words, she turned over her hand, which was rolled up tightly in a kid glove, and proffered it to Swirski. He took it in both hands and looked at it.

'No,' he said, 'I cannot see, but perhaps I might hear it.' Leaning over, he put his ear to the buttons of the glove and pressed it to his face, then he brushed it with his lips and said: 'When as a boy I caught a little bird, I could hear the heart beat inside it just like this; it is just like the heart of a captured bird.'

She gave an almost melancholy smile, and repeated: 'Just like the heart of a captured bird . . .'

After a moment she asked: 'And what did you do with your captured birds?'

'I would get immensely attached to them, but they always flew away . . .'

'Wicked little birds . . .'

'And so it has always been in my life,' the painter went on, with a trace of emotion. 'In vain have I sought someone who would stay by my side, and at last I have lost all hope.'

'No! You must have hope,' replied Mrs Elzen.

Swirski suddenly felt that the time had come to conclude this business which had started so long before, and come what may. He felt a little like a man shielding his eyes and ears to plunge into the water, but he felt that this was no time for hesitation.

'Perhaps you would like to walk a little,' he said, 'the carriage can follow, and then we can converse more easily.'

'Very well,' replied Mrs Elzen, in a tone of resignation.

Swirski prodded the coachman with his cane, the carriage stopped, and they alighted. Romulus and Remus immediately ran ahead to where they could look down on the houses of Eze and roll stones down into the olive-groves below. Swirski and Mrs Elzen were left alone, but clearly fate was dogging him that day, for before they could take advantage of the moment of solitude, they saw a horseman followed by a groom dressed in the English fashion ride up from the direction of Monte Carlo and stop next to Romulus and Remus.

'It's de Sinten,' said Mrs Elzen, her voice betraying vexation.

'Yes, I recognise him.'

A moment later, they had before them a horse's head, and above it, the horselike head of the young de Sinten. He hesitated for a moment. He might have merely greeted them and ridden on, but he probably judged that if they had wished to be alone they would not have brought the boys. He therefore jumped down from his horse, tossed the reins to the groom, and bade them good day.

'Good day,' replied Mrs Elzen a little drily. 'Is this your hour?'

'Yes. In the mornings I shoot pigeons with Wilkisbey, so I do not ride lest I disturb my pulse. I am seven birds ahead of him already. Did you know that the *Formidable* is arriving at Villefranche today, and that the admiral is giving a ball on board the day after tomorrow?'

'We saw it sail in.'

'I was on my way to Villefranche to see one of the officers who is an acquaintance, but I see it is getting late. If you have nothing against it, I will return with you to Monte Carlo.'

Mrs Elzen gave a nod, and they went on together. A passionate horseman, de Sinten immediately began to talk of the hunter he had just been riding.

'I bought him from Waxdorf,' he said. 'Waxdorf lost at *trente et quarante* and needed money. He placed on *inverse* and hit on a series of six, but then his luck changed.' Here he turned to his horse. 'Pure Irish stock. I'll wager anything that there isn't a finer hunter on the whole Corniche. He's just a little tricky to mount.'

'Is he vicious?' inquired Swirski.

'Once you're in the saddle, he's like a child. He's got used to me now, but if, for instance, you were to try, he'd never let you get on.'

'What do you mean?' retorted Swirski, who in matters of sport was childishly vain.

'Don't try, at least not here, at the edge of the precipice,' cried Mrs Elzen.

But Swirski already had his hand on the horse's neck, and a moment later he was in the saddle. The horse had put up no resistance, perhaps because it was not in fact vicious at all, or because it realised that this rocky ledge was not the place for a struggle. Horse and rider then disappeared at a canter round a bend in the road.

'He has quite a good seat,' said de Sinten, 'but he'll lame my horse. There's really nowhere good to ride around here.'

'Your horse turned out to be quite docile,' said Mrs Elzen.

'I'm very glad of it, because there could have been a nasty accident in this spot – I was a little anxious.'

His face betrayed irritation. What he had said regarding the horse's fierceness now looked like a lie, and this only brought out the dislike he felt for Swirski. It is true that de Sinten did

not entertain any serious intentions where Mrs Elzen was concerned, but he would have preferred it if there had been
nobody about to hinder him in his less serious ambitions.
Besides, only a few weeks before, the two had exchanged sharp
words. In the course of a luncheon given by Mrs Elzen, de
Sinten, who was an intransigent aristocrat, had declared that in
his opinion Man begins at the level of a barony. Swirski, who
was in a bad mood, had enquired whether he meant upwards
or downwards. The young man had been so piqued by this
reply that he began to confer with Mr Wiadrowski and councillor Kładzki on what course he should take and it was then
that he learned, to his astonishment, that Swirski came from a
princely family. Further intelligence on Swirski's remarkable
physical fitness and his skill at shooting contributed a calming
influence on the nerves of the baron, with the result that this
exchange did not have any consequences. But it nevertheless
left a trace of ill-will in the hearts of the two men. And when
it had become clear that Mrs Elzen was inclining more
definitely towards Swirski, this ill-will became purely platonic.

But the painter felt it more acutely. It is true that nobody
had suggested the affair could lead to marriage, but already
members of their acquaintance were beginning to talk about
his attachment to Mrs Elzen, and he suspected that de Sinten
and his friends were attempting to ridicule him. Although they
did not speak a word of it, Swirski was convinced that he was
right, and it pained him, mainly out of consideration for Mrs
Elzen.

He was therefore delighted that, thanks to the docility of
the horse, de Sinten had been made to look like a man who
tells gratuitous untruths, and to make a point of this, he
announced on his return: 'A good horse, and gentle as a lamb.'

He dismounted, and they walked on, the three of them, or
rather the five of them, for Romulus and Remus now stayed
close. In order to spite de Sinten, or perhaps in an effort to get
rid of him, Mrs Elzen now began to speak of paintings and of
art in general, of which the young sportsman had not the
slightest notion. But he responded with gossip from the gam-
ing tables, and congratulated the young lady on her previous
night's luck. She listened to this with displeasure, ashamed
that Swirski should hear of her gambling. Her embarrassment

only increased when Romulus piped up.

'*Maman!* You told us that you never gamble! You'll have to give us a Louis each for that!'

'I was looking for Councillor Kładzki in order to invite him to dinner, and then we amused ourselves for a moment,' she said to nobody in particular.

'Give us a Louis each!' repeated Romulus.

'Or buy us a miniature roulette!' added Remus.

'Don't bother me, and get into the carriage. Good day to you, Monsieur de Sinten.'

'Till seven, then?'

'Till seven.'

They parted, and Swirski once more found himself beside the beautiful widow, but this time they sat on the front banquette, wishing to gaze at the setting sun.

'They say that Monte Carlo is more sheltered than Menton,' said the widow, 'but oh! how it sometimes tires me! That endless noise, the movement, those acquaintances one has to make, willy-nilly. I sometimes wish I could escape from there and spend the rest of the winter in some quiet place, where I would be able to see only people whom I wish to see. Which is the place that you like best in these parts?'

'I very much like St Raphael: the pine-trees there reach right down to the water's edge.'

'Yes, but it is so far from Nice,' she answered in a low voice, 'and Nice is where you have your studio.' There was a moment's silence, after which Mrs Elzen again asked:

'What about Antibes?'

'True, I had forgotten Antibes.'

'And it's so close to Nice! You must stay behind after dinner, so we can talk about where one could escape from people.'

'Is it really your wish to escape from people?' He looked deep into her eyes.

'May I speak openly?' she rejoined. 'I detect doubt in your question. You suspect me of talking in this way in order to appear a better, or at least a less shallow person that I really am . . . And you have every right to think of me in this way, seeing me continually in a social whirl. But one sometimes carries on in a certain direction simply because one was once impelled in that direction . . . and one accepts without willing them the consequences of a former way of life. In my case, perhaps, it is the weakness of a woman who lacks the will to break free without the help of another, I admit. But this does not prevent me from yearning sincerely for some quiet corner and a quiet life. People may say what they like, but we are like climbing plants, and if we cannot find the support to climb upwards, we crawl along the ground . . . People often mistakenly think that we do this out of choice. By crawling I mean leading a futile, worldly life, with no higher thoughts. But how am I, for instance, to defend myself against this? Someone asks one of my friends to present him to me, and then he pays a call, followed by a second, a third, a tenth . . . What am I supposed to do? Not invite him? Why? . . . Indeed! I invite him, partly because the more people I have around me, the more indifferent they all grow, and the more difficult it is for anyone to assume an exclusive position.'

'You are right there,' said Swirski.

'You see? And from this there springs that current of social life from which I cannot tear myself away by my own strength alone, and which wearies and tortures me so that sometimes I feel like crying with exhaustion.'

'I believe you.'

'You should believe me, and you should believe me when I say that I am better and less vain than I appear. If you are ever assailed by doubts, or if you ever hear people speaking ill of me, you must say to yourself: 'After all, she must have some good sides'. If you do not think that, I shall be very unhappy.'

'I give you my word that I always prefer to think of you in the very best light.'

'And that is how it should be,' she answered softly, 'because if the good in me were even more stifled than it is, it would revive by your side . . . So much depends on whom one is close to . . . I would like to say something more, but I am afraid . . .'

'Please say it . . .'

'You will not think me fanciful, or perhaps worse? . . . No, I am not being carried away; I speak as a sober-minded woman who sees things only as they really are and feels a little surprised herself. For by your side I seem to recover my real soul, as calm and serene as it was when I was a girl . . . And yet I am an old woman now . . . I am thirty-five years old . . .'

Swirski looked at her, his face radiant and loving, and, slowly raising her hand to his lips, he said:

'Oh, but next to me, you are still a child: I am forty-five – and that is me!' He gestured at the setting sun.

She gazed at the brightness, which was reflected in her eyes, and spoke softly, as if to herself:

'Oh, great, beautiful, beloved sun! . . .'

Silence fell. The serene red light illuminated the faces of both. The sun that was setting was indeed great and beautiful. The slender wisps of cloud beneath it took the shape of open lilies, glowing golden. The sea was cast into darkness by the shore, but further out, it shone with brilliance. Below, the immobile cypresses stood out against the lilac tint of the air.

II

Mrs Elzen's guests assembled at the Hôtel de Paris at seven o'clock. They were shown into a separate dining-room, next to which was a small withdrawing room in which coffee was to be served afterwards. Although Mrs Elzen had announced that it was to be an 'informal' dinner, the gentlemen knew what to make of this and turned up in dress coats and white neckties. Mrs Elzen herself appeared in a pale pink low-cut dress with a great fold falling from the back of the bodice to the floor. She looked fresh and youthful. She had a delicate face and a small head, which was what had most charmed Swirski at the beginning of their closer acquaintance. Her ample shoulders had the tone and transparency of mother-of-pearl, particularly that part of them which overflowed the dress, while her arms, from the elbow upwards, were slightly red and looked almost chapped. But this only enhanced the impression of their nakedness. Her whole person radiated gaiety, good humour, and that sort of radiance possessed by women at moments when they feel themselves to be happy.

Apart from Swirski and de Sinten, the guests included old Councillor Kładzki, with his nephew Zygmunt, a young gen- tleman of little polish but pronounced arrogance, whose eyes shone a little too obviously at Mrs Elzen, and who did not know how to hide it; Prince Walery Porzecki, a man in his forties, bald, with the huge face and pointed skull of an Aztec; Mr Wiadrowski, rich and malicious, the owner of an oil-well in Galicia, an art-lover and dilettante artist; and finally Kresowicz, a student and temporary tutor to Romulus and Remus, whom Mrs Elzen had invited because she knew that Swirski liked his impassioned look.

The young hostess's chief desire always, and particularly now, was to have what she called an 'intellectual salon'. She nevertheless found it difficult at first to turn the conversation away from local gossip and the happenings at the Casino, which Mr Wiadrowski always referred to as 'the Slav world', claiming that one heard more Slavic languages spoken there than any others. Wiadrowski's life in Monte Carlo seemed to centre round ridiculing his fellow-countrymen and cousins from the younger Slav nations. It was his hobby-horse, and once he was in the saddle he would gallop along without respite. He now started to recount how a few days previously there had been only seven people left at the tables in the Cercle de la Méditerranée by six o'clock in the morning, all of them Slavs.

'That is unfortunately our nature,' he concluded, turning to his hostess. 'In other countries, people count: nine, ten, eleven, twelve, and so on, but every true Slav cannot help counting: nine, ten, knave, queen, king . . . Yes! . . . The cream of our society comes to the Corniche, and here it is turned into cheese.'

Prince Walery, with his pointed crown, responded to this in the tone of a man who reveals unknown truths. He declared that every passion carried to excess can be fatal, but that the membership of the Cercle de la Méditerranée included many distinguished foreigners, with whom it was both pleasant and useful to strike up an acquaintance. It was possible to serve the cause of one's country in a variety of ways. Only three days ago, for instance, he himself had met there an Englishman, a friend of Chamberlain's. This Englishman had asked him about conditions in Poland, to which he had responded by writing out, on a visiting-card, a summary of the economic and political situation, the general position, and particularly the social aspirations of the masses. This visiting-card would undoubtedly reach the hands, if not of Chamberlain himself, who was not here, then certainly of Salisbury, which would in fact be even better. In all probability, he would be meeting Salisbury at the ball to be given by the French admiral – a ball during which the entire *Formidable* was to be lit up *a giorno* by electricity.

Kresowicz, who was not only a consumptive, but also a man from another camp who detested the society in which he had to move as the tutor of Romulus and Remus, began to snort at the bit about the visiting-card with the ironic and malicious laughter of a hyena. Mrs Elzen wished to divert attention away from him.

'They really are performing miracles here,' she said; 'I have heard that the whole road from Nice to Marseille is to be lit up with electricity.'

'Ducloz, the engineer, was working on the plan,' said Swirski, 'but he died a couple of months ago. He was such a passionate electrician that he apparently left instructions for his grave to be lit by electricity.'

'In that case,' said Wiadrowski, 'the inscription on his grave ought to read: "Eternal rest give unto him, O lord, and may electric light shine upon him for ever and ever, Amen!"'

But old Councillor Kładzki attacked him for making jests of such serious matters, after which he began attacking the whole Riviera. Everything, beginning with the people, was just make-believe and sham. All around, there were only 'marquis, comtes and vicomtes', but given half a chance, they would steal even your handkerchief. As for the amenities, you could fit the hole they had given him in the hotel five times into the estate office at Wieprzkowiski. The doctors sent him to Nice for the fresh air, but the Promenade des Anglais stank like a Kraków back-yard. He assured the company that it stank. His nephew Zygmunt would confirm this. But Zygmunt's eyes were riveted to Mrs Elzen's shoulders, and he did not hear any of this.

'Why do you not move to Bordighera, Councillor,' said Swirski. 'Italian dirt is at least artistic, while the French is merely vile.'

'You say this, but you live in Nice!'

'Because I would not find a suitable studio the other side of Ventimilia. Besides, if I do move, it will be in the other direction – to Antibes.' Saying this, he looked at Mrs Elzen, who smiled faintly and lowered her eyes. After a while, wishing to steer the conversation on to more artistic lines, she began to speak of the exhibition at Rumpelmayer's and of the new pictures which she had viewed two days before, pictures that had been described as impressionistic-decadent by the French journalist Krauss, who had accompanied her. At this, Wiadrowski raised his fork and asked, in the tones of a Pyrrho: 'Who are these decadents, anyway?'

'They are people,' answered Swirski, 'who really prefer to art itself the sauces with which art is flavoured.'

Prince Porzecki, who had felt slighted by what old Kładzki had said about 'marquis, comtes and vicomtes', observed that even the scoundrels here belonged to a higher order of scoundrels, and would not content themselves with a pocket handkerchief. Here one met *corsaires* in the grandest style. But besides these, everything that was most wealthy and everything that was most sophisticated also came here, and the fact that high birth came into contact with high finance was an excellent thing, for thus the world would continue to refine itself. Mr Kładzki should read, for instance, the *Idylle Tragique*, and he would then realise that besides the adventurers, one also met here the highest social spheres – 'the sort of people whom we shall meet aboard the *Formidable*, which for the occasion will be lit up *a giorno* by electricity.'

Porzecki had evidently forgotten that he had already communicated to the company the information about the illumination of the *Formidable*. But this time it did not take over the main current of the conversation, which moved to the subject of the *Idylle Tragique*. Speaking of the hero of this novel, young Kładzki observed that 'it served him right' – the man was a fool to give up a woman for a friend; he, Kładzki, would not do it for ten friends, not even for his brother, because 'well, this is one thing, and that's another.' But Wiadrowski interrupted him, for French novels, which he devoured, were his second hobby-horse, on which he practised the higher art of galloping over authors and their works.

'What drives me absolutely mad,' he said, 'is this passing off of dyed fox as sable. If these gentlemen are realists, then they should write the truth. Yet have you noticed their heroines?

The tragedy begins, the lady struggles within herself, thrashes about in the most frightening way for half a volume, while I know very well from the first page what will happen and how it will all end. It's so boring, and I've seen it all so many times before! I don't mind these hussies, and I don't deny them their right to literature either, but what I cannot abide is the way these wantons are passed off as tragic vestals. Where's the tragedy, when I know that this anguished soul had had lovers before the tragedy and will have many more after . . . She will again struggle with her conscience, and everything will end the same way every time. What humbug, what a perversion of the sense of morality, of truth, and what a bad example! To think that one reads this, that this rubbish is accepted as literature, these boudoir farces as drama – that it is taken seriously! In this way the difference between a respectable woman and a slut is effaced, and birds of passage are given the right to live in society. This French "polish" is taken on by our own young ones, and they behave as they like with the full authority of these authors! No principles, no character, no sense of duty, no decency – nothing, only false aspirations and the pretence of psychological depth.'

Wiadrowski was too intelligent not to realise that speaking thus he was casting aspersions on Mrs Elzen, but he was naturally spiteful and he meant what he said. Mrs Elzen listened to his words with a vexation which was all the greater for their obvious truthfulness. Swirski was burning to reply sharply, but he knew that in so doing he would be showing that Wiadrowski's words had real import, so he tackled the matter from a different angle.

'I have always been struck by something quite different in French novels,' he said. 'Namely, that they are populated by barren women. Elsewhere, whenever two people love each other, whether licitly or illicitly, the consequence of the union appears in the shape of a child, but here nobody ever has children. Is it not strange? I think it is because it has never entered the minds of these gentlemen who write the novels that love cannot always evade consequences.'

'As in society, so in literature,' said old Kładzki. 'It is well known that the population of France is shrinking. In higher circles, a child is a rarity!'

'*Mais c'est plus commode et plus élégant,*' put in de Sinten.

But Kresowicz, who had been snorting for some moments, said: 'It is the literature of bloated idlers, and it will perish along with them.'

'What did you say?' asked de Sinten.

The student turned a fierce face on the baron. 'I said, the literature of bloated idlers!'

Meanwhile, Porzecki had once again tumbled on a discovery: 'Every estate has its duties and its pleasures,' he said. 'I have two passions: politics and photography.'

The dinner was nearing its end. A quarter of an hour later everyone passed into the adjacent drawing-room for coffee. Mrs Elzen lit the thinnest imaginable cigarette and, leaning comfortably against the arm of her chair, crossed her legs. She felt that a certain nonchalance should be attractive to Swirski as an artist and something of a bohemian. But as she was of small stature and a little wide in the hips, her dress rode up a touch too far when she crossed her legs. Young Kładzki immediately dropped his match and began hunting for it on the floor until his uncle the councillor eventually gave him a slight prod with his foot and whispered: 'What are you about?'

'I really do not know,' answered the young nobleman in a whisper, straightening up.

Mrs Elzen knew from experience that even well-bred men become crude beasts at the slightest opportunity, particularly with women who have no male protection. She had not noticed young Kładzki's movements, but the nonchalant and almost insolent smirk with which he answered his uncle told her that he was speaking of her. She felt a wave of contempt for this whole company, with the exception of Swirski and young Kresowicz, whom she suspected of being in love with her, for all his avowed social hatred for women of her circle. But the one who almost brought on an attack of nerves in her that evening was Wiadrowski. It was as though he had vowed to repay all he had eaten and drunk by poisoning every spoonful of her coffee and every moment of her evening. He spoke generally and as it were objectively of women, without transgressing the bounds of propriety, but his words were underlain by cynicism and a thousand allusions to the character of Mrs Elzen and her social position, which were quite simply offen-

sive. They were particularly disagreeable to her in the presence of Swirski, who suffered with ill-concealed impatience.
She was therefore not a little relieved when at length the
guests dispersed and only the artist remained.

'Aah!' she exclaimed, 'I can feel the beginning of a
migraine, and I hardly know what is happening to me.'

'They exhausted you?'

'Yes, they more than exhausted me . . .'

'Why do you invite them?'

She came up close to him, as though overcome by nerves,
and spoke feverishly: 'Sit down, and do not move! I do not
know . . . Perhaps I shall lose respect forever in your eyes, but
I need this like medicine . . . Just for a moment to be able to
be close to an honest man . . . Like this!' She sat down beside
him and, resting her head on his shoulder, closed her eyes. 'A
moment! Just one moment! . . .'

Her eyelashes were moist with tears, but she placed a finger
over her lips as a sign that he should say nothing and allow her
to sit quietly.

He felt moved, for the sight of women's tears always made
him melt like wax. Her trust charmed him and filled him with
tender feelings. He could see that the decisive moment had
come, and, placing his arm round her, he said:

'Stay with me forever, be rightfully mine.' Mrs Elzen did
not reply, but large silent tears flowed from her eyes.

'Be mine,' repeated Swirski.

She put her hand on his other shoulder and nestled up to
him like a child. Leaning over, Swirski kissed her on the forehead, and then began kissing away her tears, and gradually fire
flamed up inside him. After a moment, he caught her in his
athletic arms, pressed her with all his might to his breast, and
his lips sought her lips. But she began to defend herself.

'No! No!' she said, panting, 'You aren't like the others . . .
Later! . . . No! . . . No! Have pity on me!'

Swirski held her close, with her head tilted back. At this
moment he was exactly like all the others, but happily for Mrs
Elzen her words had hardly died away when a light knocking
could be heard on the door. They sprang apart instantly.

'Who is there?' asked Mrs Elzen, somewhat impatiently.

The gloomy face of Kresowicz appeared at the door. 'For-

give me,' he said, in a halting voice, 'Romulus has a cough and
may be feverish . . . I felt I should let you know.'

'Should I go for the doctor?' said Swirski, springing up.

But Mrs Elzen had regained her usual composure. 'Thank
you,' she said, 'we can send from the hotel if necessary, but
first I must see the child . . . Thank you. I must go now – so
till tomorrow! . . . Thank you.' She held out her hand, which
Swirski raised to his lips.

'Till tomorrow, and every day after that. Goodbye!'

When they had been left alone, Mrs Elzen looked at Kresowicz questioningly.

'What is wrong with Romulus?'

He grew paler still, and replied, almost curtly:

'Nothing.'

'What is the meaning of this?' she enquired, frowning.

'It means that . . . please do not throw me out, or, or I shall
go mad!' Having said this, he turned about and left the room.
Mrs Elzen remained perfectly still awhile, her eyes flashing
with anger and her brow furrowed, but this regained its
smoothness by degrees. She might be thirty-five years old, yet
here was further proof that nobody could resist her charms.
She went up to the looking-glass, as though seeking confirma-
tion of this thought.

Meanwhile Swirski was returning to Nice in an empty carriage, periodically raising to his face two hands that smelt of
heliotrope. He felt agitated, but also happy, and the blood
rushed to his head every time he breathed in the smell of Mrs
Elzen's favourite scent.

III

The next day, however, he awoke with a heavy head, as
though after a night of drunkenness, and with deep uneasiness
in his heart. When the raw light of day falls on theatrical decorations, that which seemed enchanted at night appears no
better than tinsel and daub. It is often the same with life.
Swirski had not met with anything untoward. He had known
which way he was going and to what it led. But now that the
die was cast, he was seized with inexplicable alarm. Yesterday

it had still been possible to retreat, he reflected, and he was overwhelmed by self-pity. It was in vain that he told himself the time for reasoning had passed. All sorts of objections which he had in the past raised against Mrs Elzen, and above all against any idea of a union with her, now assailed him with redoubled vigour. The voice that had repeatedly breathed 'Don't be an idiot!' in his ear now began to cry 'You are an idiot!' And he could silence it neither by arguments nor by telling himself that 'what is done is done': his reason told him that what had been done was a folly, whose cause lay in his own weakness.

This thought filled him with shame. If he had been a young man, he could have blamed it all on inexperience. If he had only just met the lady on the Riviera, having heard nothing about her before, he could have justified himself with his ignorance of her character and her past. But he had met her long before. It is true that he had seen her only rarely, but he had heard more than enough about her, since in Warsaw she had been more talked about than anyone else. She was known as 'the wife-prodigy' and the local wits used her to sharpen their tongues as though she were a whetstone – which did not prevent all the men from thronging her drawing-room. Women, who were less well-disposed to her, also received her in consideration of her more or less close relationship to members of society. Some, particularly those who were concerned that public opinion should in general not be too harsh, even took up the defence of the beautiful widow. Others, less complacent, did not dare close their doors to her, for fear of being the first to do so. One local playwright, hearing her referred to as belonging to the '*demi-monde*', quipped that she represented 'neither the world, nor the half-world, but a quarter to the world'. But since in larger cities everything becomes accepted, so the situation of Mrs Elzen became accepted. Her friends would say: 'Of course, one cannot expect too much from Helenka, but she does have her good points.' And without anyone noticing it, she was allowed greater freedom than anyone else. From time to time someone would mention the fact that for some years before his death she had no longer lived with her husband: someone would observe that she was bringing up Romulus and Remus as a pair of clowns, or indeed that she hardly cared for them at all, but such murmurs of censure would only have been heeded if Mrs Elzen had been less beautiful, less wealthy, and less hospitable. On the other hand, men showed little restraint in their conversations about 'the wife prodigy'. Even those who were enamoured of her slandered her out of jealousy; the only man who kept silent on these occasions was the one who was favoured at the time, or wished to appear to be more favoured than the others. Indeed, human malice went so far that it was said Mrs Elzen had one man for the winter season in town, and another for the summer. And Swirski knew of all this. He knew even more than most, since a certain Mrs Broniszowa, whom he had known in Warsaw, a close friend of the beautiful widow, had told him of a particularly unhappy accident in Mrs Elzen's life which had culminated in a serious illness. 'What that poor Helenka went through then God only knows! Perhaps in His divine mercy He ordered it so that it should come prematurely, to save her from even greater moral suffering!' Swirski had in fact suspected that this 'premature accident' might well be an invention, but he could in no sense have harboured any illusions as to Mrs Elzen's past, or at least he could under no circumstances believe that she was a woman to whom one could safely entrust one's peace of mind.

Yet all this knowledge had in fact only drawn him to her, by awakening his curiosity. Hearing of her arrival in Monte Carlo, he had felt a desire, perhaps not entirely innocent, to make her acquaintance more closely. As an artist, too, he was interested to assess the charm exerted on men by this woman who was everywhere badly spoken of.

To begin with, he had been disenchanted. She was certainly beautiful, and sensually attractive, but he noticed that she lacked goodness and real feeling. A person interested her only insofar as he might be useful to her. Aside from this consideration, he was a creature of complete indifference to her. Swirski also noticed in her a total absence of respect for spiritual life, for literature, and for art. She culled from them what she needed, giving nothing in return. As an artist and a thinking man, he understood perfectly well that such an attitude betrayed a vain, crude and barbaric nature, however elegant the appearances. He had known other such women. He knew

that they impressed people with the strength which comes
from decisiveness and boundless, ruthless egoism. He had
heard people say when talking of such women: 'She's a cold
but clever woman', but he had always felt only disdain and
contempt for them. They were, to his mind, creatures devoid
of any higher spiritual culture, and even of reason, for such
intelligence which only snatches everything for itself, without
thinking of others, is the intelligence of animals. Both in Mrs
Elzen and in Romulus and Remus he saw people in whom culture begins and ends on the skin, covering a plebeian and
crude vacuum. He was also struck by her cosmopolitanism.
She was like a coin so worn that it was difficult to ascertain to
which country it belonged. This filled Swirski with distaste,
not only because he was a man of entirely contrary disposition,
but also because he was familiar with real society, and knew
that the higher circles in England, France or Italy did not forsake the land in which they had grown, and looked with
wholesome contempt upon these Riviera weeds without true
roots.

Wiadrowski was quite right when he declared that Romulus
and Remus were being brought up as travelling salesmen or
porters in great hotels. It was well known that although Mrs
Elzen's father had managed to obtain a title, her grandfather
had been an estate manager, and Swirski, with his developed
sense of humour, could not help being amused at the thought
that the great-grandchildren of the farm manager could not
speak Polish properly and pronounced the letter 'r' like true
Parisians. They also offended his artistic sense. The boys were
handsome, very handsome even, but Swirski's subtle artistic
sense told him that in these two identical bird-like skulls and
bird-like faces, beauty was not something refined over several
generations, but a sort of accident, almost a physiological freak
stemming from their being twins. And it was in vain that he
said to himself that their mother too was beautiful; he was
always left with the feeling that neither the mother nor her
sons deserved it, and that both in this respect and in the matter of their wealth, they were parvenus. It was only prolonged
close contact with them that weakened these impressions in
him.

From the very beginning, Mrs Elzen singled him out and

did her best to attract him. He was worth far more than the
rest of her acquaintance: he bore a fine name, he possessed a
notable fortune and a great reputation. It was true he was not
young, but then she too was thirty-five years old, and his her-
culean figure more than made up for his lack of youth. The
prospect of marrying him was, for a woman of whom people
spoke so lightly, equivalent to regaining her honour and position. She may have suspected that he had different tastes and
a different nature from hers, but he possessed goodness and,
like every artist, a certain degree of naivety in the depths of his
heart. So Mrs Elzen believed that she would be able to bend
him to her purpose. And it was not only calculation that moti-
vated her; as she attracted him, he began to attract her. She
began to say to herself that she loved him, and eventually came
to believe it.

What happened to him was something that sometimes happens even to the most intelligent people. His reason gave up
the moment his senses were aroused. Worse still, his reason
became their slave, and instead of fighting against them, it fur-
nished them with arguments. In this way, the wise and clever
Swirski began to justify everything, presenting it to himself in
a favourable light, soothing and explaining. 'It is true,' he
would say to himself, 'that neither her nature nor her past con-
duct offer any evidence of this, but who can prove to me that
she is not indeed tired of this life, and that she does not aspire
with her whole soul to something different? There is undoubtedly much coquetry in her behaviour, but who can swear that
she has not deployed this coquetry because she has fallen in
love with me sincerely? To pretend that a person, whatever his
faults and vices, has no good in him is infantile! Ah! What a
mixture is the human soul! It is only necessary to provide the
right conditions for that goodness to flourish for the evil to
die. Mrs Elzen has passed her first youth. How stupid it would
be to imagine that there is no voice inside her calling for a
quiet and virtuous life, for peace, for contentment! Indeed, for
these very reasons such a woman more than any other might
value an honest man who can give her all this.' This last observation seemed to him to be particularly apt and profound. Earlier, his common sense had told him that Mrs Elzen was out
to catch him. Now he replied to it: 'You are quite right; one

can say of even the most ideal woman who wishes to join herself to a man she loves that she is out to catch him!' Another
thing that reassured him as to the future was the hope of children. He thought that then she would have something to love,
and that she would have to break with her empty worldly life,
for which she would have no time – and by the time the children would have grown up, her youth would have passed completely, and then the home would attract her more than
society. Finally, he would say to himself: 'It'll work out somehow! Life has to be lived, and before I reach old age I shall
have lived a few years with a woman who is beautiful and
engaging, by whose side every day will seem to me a great
day.'

It was in fact these 'few years' that constituted the greatest
attraction for him. There was of course something a little
humiliating for Mrs Elzen in the fact that he did not foresee
any great complications largely because her youth, and therefore their opportunity, were shortly to pass. But he did not
admit to himself that this was the thought that lay at the bottom of his optimism, and he continued to deceive himself, as
people always do when reason plays the pimp to the senses.

But now, after the events of the previous evening, he awoke
in a state of great anxiety and discouragement. He could not
avoid two recurring reflections. One was the knowledge that if
someone had told him a month before that he would declare
himself to Mrs Elzen, he would have called him a fool. The
other was that the particular charm of his relations with her,
which lay in uncertainty, in the mutual guessing of looks and
thoughts, of unfinished sentences, of incomplete declarations
and in mutual attraction, was far greater than that which
derived from the new situation. It had been far more agreeable
to Swirski to prepare the engagement than to be engaged – and
when the thought struck him that the pleasure might be simi-
larly diminished still further by marriage, then the devil could
take the whole thing. There were moments when the reflection
that he was committed, that he had no way out, and that he
was obliged to take Mrs Elzen along with Romulus and Remus
on board for life whether he liked it or not was downright
insufferable. Being a loyal person, he did not wish to curse
Mrs Elzen, so he cursed Romulus and Remus, he cursed their

Parisian accents, their tight, bird-like skulls and their bird-like faces.

'I had my cares, but at least I was free and I was able to put all my soul into painting,' he said to himself. 'Now, the devil knows what will happen!' And here the artistic problems that he was going through spoiled what remained of his good humour, although they at least distracted his thoughts on to a different subject. Mrs Elzen and the whole business of marriage were eclipsed by thoughts of his painting 'Sleep and Death', on which he had been working for several months, and to which he attached enormous weight, since it was to constitute a protest against the generally accepted view of death.

In conversations with other painters, he would inveigh against Christianity for introducing the skeleton into life and art as the symbol of death. To Swirski this seemed a terrible injustice done to Death. The Greeks saw Thanatos as a winged genius, and this was quite right. What could be uglier and more terrifying than a skeleton? If anything, it was the Christians, who see in death the gateway to a new life, who should not have depicted it in this manner. According to Swirski this notion had been born of the gloomy German soul, the same that had given birth to Gothic, which was grandiose and splendid, but so gloomy as to suggest that the church was not a passage to the brilliance of heaven, but to hope-forsaken subterranean chasms. He always expressed surprise that the Renaissance had not reformed the symbol of death. Indeed, if death were not eternal silence, if it could complain, it would exclaim: 'Why do people imagine me in the form of a skeleton! The skeleton is precisely what I reject and leave behind!' In Swirski's painting, the genius of sleep calmly and gently presented the genius of death with the body of a young girl, and the genius of death gently extinguished the flame of a lamp burning by her head as he bent over her. As he painted, Swirski repeated to himself: 'I want people who look at this to say to themselves: Oh, how wonderfully serene!' And he wanted to communicate this serenity to the spectator through the lines, the figures, the expressions and the colour. He believed that if he managed to create this atmosphere, and if the painting succeeded in explaining itself, then it would become an important and novel work.

He also had another thought in mind. In line with current views, he believed that painting ought to avoid the literary statement, but he saw a great difference between this and thoughtless reproduction of the external world in the manner of a photographic plate: shape, colour, shade, and nothing more, as though it were an artist's duty to suppress the thinking being in himself! Whenever he viewed the paintings of the English artists, for instance, he was always struck above all by the high degree of thought in their work. One could see from their canvasses that they had spiritual culture and psychological grasp, that they were thinking people, and highly educated. In the work of the Poles, he saw something quite different. With the exception of a few, the general picture was one of talented but thoughtless people, immature and lacking in cultivation. They lived on the mouldy crumbs of doctrines falling from the French table, not realising for a moment that it was possible to entertain independent thought, even less to create autonomous Polish art. It was clear to Swirski that the doctrine of objectivity in art was made for them. To proclaim oneself an artist but to remain a spiritual lackey was a very comfortable existence. Why should they wish to read, know, think – it was such a bore!

But Swirski was of the opinion that even if a landscape only reveals a state of mind, then that mind must be adjusted not only to the lower orders; it must be subtle, sensitive, developed and cultivated. He argued with his colleagues about this, in fiery discussions. 'I do not demand of you that you should paint as well as the French, English or Spanish – I demand that you should paint better, and above all in your own way! And anyone who does not want to try should become a tinker!' he would say, and he insisted that whether a picture represented a haystack, or hens pecking in a farmyard, or a field of potatoes, or horses at pasture, or the still corner of a pond, the most important element in it would always be the soul. That was why he poured as much of his own soul as he could into his portraits, and aside from this he would 'declare himself' in other paintings, the latest of which was to be *Hypnos and Thanatos*.

The two geniuses were almost finished, but the head of the girl was proving difficult. Swirski realised that she had to be not only beautiful, but also very distinctive, and all the models who came to him were beautiful, to be sure, but not very individual. Madame Lageat, from whom Swirski rented the studio, and who was an old acquaintance, had promised to look for others, but it was not easy. A new model was supposed to have come that very morning, but had failed to show up, although it was long past eleven o'clock.

All this, taken together with the declaration of the day before, caused Swirski to have doubts not only about his future peace of mind, but also about his artistic future, and particularly about his painting. Hypnos suddenly seemed rather heavy, Thanatos rather stupid. At last he decided that since he could not get down to work, he might as well go down to the shore, where the sight of the sea and sun might brighten up his thoughts and his feelings.

Just as he was about to go out, the bell tinkled in the hall, and two tartans, two fringes, and the two bird-like heads of Romulus and Remus appeared in the room, followed by Kresowicz, who looked paler and gloomier than ever.

'*Bonjouh Monsieur! Bonjouh Monsieur! Maman* sends you these roses and invites you to luncheon,' shouted the boys, brandishing clusters of tea and moss roses. They handed these to Swirski, and began to run about the studio, looking at everything. They were particularly taken with some sketches representing naked bodies, and as they looked at them, they elbowed each other.

'*Tiens!*'

'*Regahde!*'

Swirski, who was irritated by this, looked at his watch and said: 'If we wish to be on time for luncheon, we had better go right away.' He took his hat and they went out. There were no cabs to be found in the vicinity of the study, so they walked. The painter walked along behind with Kresowicz.

'How are your pupils?' he asked.

Kresowicz turned his hostile, sneering face on him. 'My pupils? Fine. They're bursting with health and they're happy in their Scottish suits. They may be a joy to someone – but not to me!'

'Why?'

'Because I am leaving tomorrow.'

'How so?' exclaimed Swirski with surprise. 'I knew nothing of this! Nobody has mentioned it. What a pity!'

'No pity for them!' answered Kresowicz.

'Only because they are probably too young to see it.'

'They will never be in a position to understand . . . Not now or ever in their lives. Never!'

'I hope you are mistaken,' replied Swirski drily. 'In any case I am sad to hear of your departure.'

But the student went on, as though he were talking to himself. 'Yes, it's a pity! But what a waste of time! What am I to them or they to me? It is perhaps better that they should be as they will be. If you want to sow corn, you must plough up the grass, and the thinner that is the easier the task should be. Much could be said on that subject, but it's not worth it, certainly not worth it for me. The microbes will get me anyway.'

'You have never been threatened by consumption. Before she took you on, Mrs Elzen enquired after your health from a doctor, which should not surprise you, for she was anxious for her children. And the doctor assured her that there was no danger.'

'Certainly, there is no danger. Anyway, I have found a sure method to deal with the microbes.'

'What method is that?'

'You will read about it in the papers. Discoveries of that kind are not hidden under a bushel.'

Swirski looked enquiringly at Kresowicz as though he were trying to make out whether the man was feverish. But by then they had come to the railway station, which was teeming with people. The holidaymakers of Nice were, as usual in the mornings, setting off for Monte Carlo. As Swirski was buying his ticket, Wiadrowski, who had espied him, came up.

'Good morning! Off to Monte?'

'Yes. Have you got your ticket already?'

'I have a monthly one. It'll be crowded on the train today.'

'We can travel in the corridor.'

'It's a real exodus, what? And everyone is carrying his widow's mite. Good morning, Mr Kresowicz! What do you think of life here? I'd like to hear your comment from the point of view of your political party.'

Kresowicz blinked, as though he did not understand what

was being asked of him, and then replied: 'I'm joining the party of the silent.'

'I know, I know . . . A remarkable party: it either holds its tongue or it explodes . . .' He began to laugh.

The bell rang, and they had to hurry. Cries of *'En voiture! En voiture!'* sounded along the platform. A moment later, Swirski, Kresowicz, Wiadrowski and the two boys were standing in the corridor of a carriage.

'It's no joke with my sciatica – look at this crowd! Quite impossible to get a seat. A real migration of the nations!'

Not only the compartments, but also the corridors were thronged with people of every nationality. There were Poles, Russians, Englishmen, Germans, Frenchmen – all setting off for the conquest of the bank, which daily repelled the attack, breaking these ranks like a rocky outcrop breaks the waves of the sea. The places by the windows were taken by women, from whom emanated the scent of iris and heliotrope. The sun illuminated the false flowers on their hats, the velvets, lace, the real or paste jewels in their ears, the jet gleaming like armour on their protruding breasts, the darkened eyebrows, the powdered or rouged faces, excited by the prospect of amusement and the game. The most experienced eye could not have distinguished between the sluts playing at being ladies and the ladies playing at being sluts. The men, with bunches of violets in the buttonholes of their frock-coats, cast over this crowd of women with an inquisitive and brazen eye, looking over the dresses, faces, shoulders and hips with the same cold interest with which one views objects set out for sale. This crush had something of the chaos of the market-place, and was animated by a sort of haste. From time to time the train would plunge into the darkness of tunnels, then the windows were once again illuminated with the sun, the sky, the sea, palm groves, olive-trees, villas, white clusters of almonds, and a moment later night would descend again. Station after station flashed past. New crowds of people squeezed into the carriages, dressed up, elegant, as if setting off for a great, joyful feast.

'What a true picture of life . . . like pigs to the trough!' exclaimed Wiadrowski.

'What is this true picture?'

'This train. I could philosophise on the subject until lunch, but since I prefer to philosophise after lunch, then perhaps you would care to join me for it?'

'You must excuse me,' answered Swirski, 'I have been invited by Mrs Elzen.'

'In that case – I retreat!' He began to smile. The idea that Swirski might marry Mrs Elzen had not crossed his mind. He was, in fact, quite sure that the painter's interest was the same as that of the others, but being an admirer of all artists, and of Swirski in particular, he felt a certain satisfaction that Swirski had beaten his rivals. 'I represent wealth,' he thought to himself, 'Porzecki a title, the young Kładzki youth, and de Sinten the world of fashionable idiots. All these possess considerable value, particularly in this place, yet 'the wife-prodigy' has chosen him. It has to be said that the woman has taste.' And looking at the artist, he began to mumble: '*Io triumphe, tu moraris aureos currus . . .*'

'What did you say?' asked Swirski, through the thundering of the train.

'Nothing. Just a hiccup after Horace. I say that since you have refused me, I shall offer a consolation lunch to myself, de Sinten, Porzecki and the Kładzkis.'

'And for what do you need to console yourselves?' asked Swirski, moving closer and looking into his eyes almost menacingly.

'For the loss of your company,' answered Wiadrowski coolly. 'And what did you suppose I meant, dear sir?'

Swirski bit his lip and did not answer. He felt his own conscience burning him, for he knew that if he were marrying any ordinary girl back home then he would never assume that idle slanders could be meant for her.

They had arrived. Mrs Elzen, refreshed, young and beautiful, was waiting for them at the station. She had obviously just arrived too, as she was still breathing hurriedly, and her face was flushed with what could easily have passed for emotion. When she held out both hands to Swirski, Wiadrowski said to himself: 'Yes! He has beaten us all by seven lengths. She looks really in love.'

He gazed at her almost with tenderness. In a white flannel dress with a sailor collar, with her radiant eyes, she seemed to him, in spite of the light traces of powder on her face, younger and more charming than ever. For a moment he even felt sad that he was not the lucky man she had come to meet – and he reflected that the method with which he had tried to gain her favours, which consisted of being consistently malicious, was stupid. But he comforted himself with the thought of how he would mock de Sinten and the other 'also rans'.

After greeting her, Swirski thanked her for the roses. She listened with a touch of embarrassment, occasionally casting a look at Wiadrowski, as though she were unhappy that he should be a witness of this scene.

He too felt it would be best if he took his leave. But they still had to go up together in the lift to the place where the casino and the gardens were situated. By then, however, Mrs Elzen had recovered all her ease.

'To lunch! To lunch!,' she shouted gaily, 'I'm as hungry as a whale!'

Wiadrowski muttered to himself that he would not mind playing at Jonah in this particular case, but he did not say it out loud, reflecting that if Swirski were to take him by the neck and throw him out of the lift, as he would have every right to do, the journey down would be a long one. In the gardens he took his leave of them and walked away, but, turning round, he saw from a distance Mrs Elzen leaning gently on Swirski's shoulder, whispering something in his ear.

'They're talking about the dessert after lunch!' he thought.

But he was mistaken. Turning her charming face to the painter, she had in fact asked him: 'Does Wiadrowski know already?'

'No,' answered Swirski, 'I only met him at the station.'

As he said this, he felt uneasiness return at the thought that Mrs Elzen was referring to the engagement as to an accomplished fact, and that everyone would have to be told about it. At the same time her close presence, her beauty and her calm began to take effect, and he relaxed and took heart.

Lunch took place in the company of Romulus and Remus, and Kresowicz, who did not say a word from beginning to end. But after coffee Mrs Elzen allowed the boys to go to Roquebrune with the young man, and then asked Swirski: 'Would you prefer to go for a walk or a drive?'

He would in fact have preferred to go to her room and 'go

halfway to paradise' but he thought that if she did not wish this, it was clear proof of how seriously she took their relationship, and in his heart he said to himself that he ought to be grateful to her for it.

'If you are not tired, then I would prefer to walk,' he answered.

'Good. I am not in the least tired. But where shall we go? Would you like to go and watch the pigeon-shooting?'

'Gladly. Only we shall not be alone there. De Sinten and young Kładkzi will be practising after lunch.'

'Yes, but they will not disturb us. When it comes to pigeons, they grow deaf and blind to everything around them . . . Anyway, let them see me with my great man!' Tilting her head, she smiled at him: 'Unless the great man himself does not wish it? . . .'

'Of course! Let them see us!' answered Swirski, raising her hand to his lips.

'Then let us go right down – I quite enjoy watching.'

'Very well.'

A moment later they were on the steps leading down to the shooting gallery.

'How bright it is here, how good, and how happy I feel!' exclaimed Mrs Elzen. Then she asked, in a whisper even though there was nobody close by: 'And you?'

'My brightness is beside me!' he answered, pressing her arm to his breast.

They began to descend. The day was indeed uncommonly bright, the air was full of gold and azure, and the sea in the distance was a dark blue.

'Let us stop here a moment,' said Mrs Elzen. 'One can see the cages perfectly from here.'

Just below them a green grassy semicircle jutted out into the sea. Cages with pigeons were laid out in an arc on the grass. Every now and then, one of them would suddenly flip open, and a frightened bird would take flight, after which one would hear a shot, and the pigeon would fall to the ground, or into the sea, where boats were bobbing with fishermen awaiting their booty. Sometimes, however, the shot would miss, the pigeon would fly out to sea, and then, turning about, return to seek shelter in the eaves of the casino.

'From here one cannot see the guns, and we cannot tell who is shooting,' said Mrs Elzen gaily. 'So let us use it to foretell the future. If the next pigeon falls, we shall stay in Monte Carlo, and if it gets away, we shall go to Italy.'

'Agreed,' said Swirski. 'Look, there it goes!'

A cage fell open at that moment, but the pigeon seemed stunned, and did not move. It was at last goaded into flight by a wooden ball thrown at it. A shot rang out, but the bird did not fall at once. It rose high into the air, and then glided out towards the sea, losing height as it went, as though it were wounded, and then disappeared altogether from sight in the glare of the sun.

'Maybe it went down, maybe it didn't! The future is always uncertain!' said Swirski with a laugh. But Mrs Elzen pouted like an angry child.

'It's that insufferable de Sinten,' she said. 'I'll wager anything it is him! Let us go down.' They descended towards the shooting gallery, down the steps lined with cactuses, morning glory and honeysuckle, which was trained over the walls. Mrs Elzen would pause at every shot, and then, standing on the great steps in her white dress against a background of greenery, she looked like a statue.

'No other cloth falls into such magnificent folds as flannel,' remarked Swirski.

'Ah, these artists!' returned the young woman. There was a note of irony in her voice, for she felt a little piqued that at this moment Swirski should be thinking not of her but of the folds into which various types of cloth fell.

'Let us go!'

A few minutes later they were under the roof of the shooting gallery. Of their acquaintance, only de Sinten was there. He was shooting for money against some Hungarian count. Both of them were dressed in ruddy English suits, with similar caps, pulled down at the peak, and check stockings, both looking very distinguished, both of them with the faces of idiots. But, just as Mrs Elzen had predicted, de Sinten was so absorbed in the shooting that he did not notice them, and it was only some time later that he came up to greet them.

'How is it going?' she asked.

'I'm winning! I am almost sure to collect the whole pool.'

Here he turned to Swirski.

'Do you not shoot?'

'Certainly I do, but not today.'

'Today,' he said, looking meaningfully at Mrs Elzen, 'I am *heureux au jeu!*' After this he was called away to take his shot.

'He wanted to say that he was unlucky in love,' said Swirski.

'*Imbécile*! Could it be otherwise?' But in spite of these angry words, one could see from the face of the beautiful woman that she was not displeased that Swirski had been given fresh evidence of her charms. It was not to be the last such evidence that day.

'I wanted to ask you something,' said Swirski after a moment's silence. 'But during lunch I couldn't, in the presence of the children and Kresowicz. Kresowicz told me on the way here that he is leaving, or at least that this is his last day as the boys' tutor. Is this true, and why?'

'It is true,' replied Mrs Elzen. 'First of all, I am not sure of his health. A few days ago I forced him to go to a doctor. It is true that the doctor repeated his opinion that there was no risk of tuberculosis – otherwise I should not keep him for a single hour, but all the same, he looks worse every day . . . he is eccentric, irritable, sometimes insufferable . . . that is the first reason. And secondly, you yourself know his political convictions. These will not affect Romulus and Remus, I know. The way they have been brought up, such principles could never gain a hold on them. But I do not wish them to know of such things in their childhood; they should not be exposed to such fanaticism and such hatred of the social sphere to which they themselves belong . . . You expressed the wish that they should speak with someone in their own language, and that was enough for me . . . It was like an order for me . . . That is the way I am . . . And I understand myself that it is right that they should get to know their own language a little . . . Nowadays the world takes note of this, and I confess that people are right. But even in this respect, Kresowicz was a little too passionate . . .'

'A pity! He has curious lines in the corner of the eye which betray fanaticism. An interesting face . . . and actually quite an interesting man.'

'Again, it's the artist in you speaking,' said Mrs Elzen, smiling. But after a moment she grew serious, and her face even displayed a certain embarrassment.

'I have another reason, also,' she said. 'it is difficult for me to speak of it, but I shall nevertheless mention it, for whom am I to confide in if not my . . . great man . . . so dear and kind, who can understand anything . . . Well, I noticed that Kresowicz has lost his head and fallen head over heels in love with me, and in these conditions he cannot remain close to –'

'What? Him too?' exclaimed Swirski.

'Yes,' she replied, with downcast eyes. She did her best to pretend that this confession was causing her unhappiness, but, just as earlier, after de Sinten's words, a smile of gratified self-love and female vanity hovered on her lips. Swirski noticed it, and an unpleasant, angry feeling gripped his heart.

'So I have succumbed to an epidemic,' he said. She looked at him for a moment.

'Are those the words of a jealous man or an ungrateful one?' she asked softly.

'You are quite right . . .' the painter answered evasively. 'If that is the case, then Kresowicz must go . . .'

'I shall settle up with him today, and that will be the end of it.'

They fell silent. All that could be heard were the shots of de Sinten and the Hungarian. But Swirski could not forgive her that smile, which he had caught on the wing. He told himself that Mrs Elzen had behaved towards Kresowicz quite correctly, and that there was nothing for him to cavil at, but he nevertheless felt irritation building up in his heart. Once, right at the beginning of his acquaintance with Mrs Elzen, he had seen her riding a bicycle: she was riding along in front, and several yards behind her rode de Sinten, young Kładzki, Porzecki, Wilkisbey and Waxford. At the time this group had made a horrible impression on him, as though he had witnessed some animal rite of males pursuing a female. Now this picture loomed up once again before him, and his sensitive artistic nature suffered at the memory. 'That's how it really is,' he said to himself, 'everyone is running after her, and if I were to fall over some obstacle, then the next one in line would catch up with her!' . . . But his thoughts were interrupted by

Mrs Elzen, who was beginning to feel cold in the shade, and wanted to go out into the sun.

'Let us go to your apartment so you can get something to cover yourself with,' answered Swirski. They started up towards the upper terrace, but halfway up the stairs, she stopped suddenly.

'You are annoyed with me,' she said. 'What have I done wrong . . . did I not act as I should have?'

Swirski, who had calmed down a little on the way, and who was touched by her anxiety, replied: 'Please forgive an old eccentric. It is I who should be begging your forgiveness.'

Mrs Elzen wanted to know what had brought on his gloom, but she could get nothing out of him. Half in jest and half in sadness, she began to inveigh against artists. What strange and difficult people: offended at the slightest thing, hurt by a trifle, they clammed up and took refuge in their lonely studios. Today she had already felt the artist in him three times . . . It was bad . . . As a punishment, this unworthy painter must stay all afternoon, for dinner too.

But Swirski declared that he must go home. He explained his artistic problems, his trouble in finding a model for *Sleep and Death*, and the importance he attached to this picture.

'I can see from this,' said the widow, smiling, 'that I shall always have one terrible rival in the shape of Art.'

'Art is no rival,' answered Swirski. 'Art is a deity which you will worship by my side.'

The beautiful widow's regular brow furrowed lightly for an instant, but they had already come to the hotel. That afternoon Swirski went very far on the road to paradise. When he left, it was with a shudder of delight in his bones, and also with the knowledge that only marriage would open its doors for him completely.

And, having cooled down a little in the carriage, he thanked Mrs Elzen for her determination to impart this knowledge.

IV

Before beginning her toilette for dinner, she summoned Kresowicz for the settling up, and she did so with a certain curiosity as to how the leave-taking would pass off. In the course of her life she saw so many average people, people who seemed to have been turned out by the same tailor to a similar pattern, that this young eccentric had intrigued her for some time. Now that he was about to leave with a broken heart, he intrigued her all the more. She felt sure that his passion would betray itself in some way, and she even had a hidden hope that it would, promising to herself not entirely frankly that she would stem it with a look or a word if it were about to exceed certain bounds.

But when Kresowicz presented himself, he was cold, and his face wore a threatening rather than a loving expression. Looking at him, Mrs Elzen thought that the artist in Swirski had been right to single out this head, for it had something quite remarkable about it. The features seemed to be made of steel, proclaiming that the will dominated the intelligence, and this gave them an expression that was dull as well as implacable. Swirski had long ago guessed that this was one of those people who once they grasp a certain idea will never allow any breath of scepticism to shake their faith in it, and whose capacity to act will never be undermined by doubt precisely because their strong, resilient character is harnessed to a certain narrowness of mind. Fanaticism flourishes in this sort of soil. For all her worldly wisdom, Mrs Elzen was too shallow to recognise this by herself. Kresowicz would only have caught her attention if he had been a handsome boy, but since he was not, she had originally treated him like an object – until Swirski had unknowingly prompted her to take a second look.

She received him politely, and paid him the money due. Then, in the same cold and indifferent tone in which she usually addressed him, but with greater courtesy, she expressed regret that her projected departure from Monte Carlo, which was imminent, meant that they would not meet again.

Kresowicz put the money into his pocket and replied: 'I myself declared to you yesterday that I could no longer teach Romulus and Remus.'

'That has made it easier for me to dispense with your services,' she replied, raising her head. She wanted, at least to begin with, to keep the conversation decorous, and to force this on Kresowicz, but one only needed to look at him to see that he was determined to say everything he had to say.

'You have paid me off in good money,' he said, 'so please do not add any counterfeit words for the road.'

'What do you mean?'

'I mean,' he went on, 'that neither are you parting company with me because of your departure, nor I because I wished to leave your service. The real reason is quite different, and you know what it is as well as I do.'

'If I do know it, then perhaps I do not wish to hear of it or speak of it,' she replied with hauteur.

He moved a step closer, putting his hands behind his back and thrusting his head forward, like a threatening bird.

'But you must!' he said with emphasis. 'First because in a moment I shall leave you, and second, for other reasons, of which you will hear tomorrow.'

Mrs Elzen rose, frowning, and assumed the somewhat theatrical manner of an offended queen.

'What does this mean?'

He came closer still, so that his face was now only a few inches from hers, and he began to speak, with concentrated energy.

'It means that I should have loathed you and your whole world, and yet I fell in love with you. It means that because of you I have rendered myself contemptible in my own eyes, for which I shall punish myself. But it is precisely because of that that I have nothing to lose, and that you must pay me for it, otherwise there will be trouble!'

Mrs Elzen did not take fright, for she was not at all afraid of men. Nor was she afraid of Kresowicz's tuberculosis, since the local doctor had laid her mind at rest entirely on that score. But while the anger and fear she displayed were only apparent, her astonishment was real enough. She suddenly felt admiration rising inside her. *'Mais c'est un vrai oiseau de proie,* who is ready to tear me apart! . . .' Her nature was quite used to corruption and thrived on excitement, so any adventure, particularly when it flattered her feminine vanity, had an inexpressible charm for her. Besides, her moral sense was not alarmed by trifles. Had Kresowicz begged her for a moment of happiness, for the right to kiss the hem of her dress, with humility, with tears in his eyes, on bended knee, she would have had him thrown out at once. But this threatening and almost demented man, this representative of a sect, about whose terrifying activity fabulous things were said in her world, seemed to her to be so demonic, so different from other people she knew, that she was quite simply filled with delight. Her senses were avid for novelty. She reflected, also, that if she were to resist, the whole affair might take on quite unforeseen dimensions and turn into a scandal, for this madman was quite clearly ready for anything. Kresowicz went on, bathing her face with his warm breath.

'I love you, and I have nothing to lose! I lost my health, I ruined my future, and I have humiliated myself! . . . I have nothing to lose! – Do you understand that? I don't care if your screams bring in ten or a hundred people . . . But for you, it would matter a great deal! Afterwards, I shall go away, and the secret will perish – I swear!'

Mrs Elzen was by now only concerned with keeping up the appearances that feminine hypocrisy always tries to maintain, and with fooling herself. Turning eyes full of false terror on his face, which really did look like the face of a madman, she asked:

'Do you want to kill me?'

'I want payment – not in money!' he answered, his voice choking.

He went even paler, reached out and took hold of her, while she began to defend herself. But she did this weakly, like a fainting woman whom terror has robbed of her senses and her strength.

V

When the train reached Villefranche, Swirski alighted and went down to the harbour, as he had suddenly felt the impulse to return to Nice by boat. Just by the entrance to the harbour he came across a fisherman he had used before. The man was delighted to see the generous customer and with typical Ligurian bravado undertook to take him anywhere, 'even to Corsica, and even if the Sirocco were churning up the sea to its very bottom'.

In fact, it was only a question of a short trip, made all the easier by the fact that there was not a breath of wind. Swirski sat down by the rudder, and the boat began to glide forward over the smooth sea. Having passed a number of luxurious private yachts, they came up to the ironclads, whose quiet black masses rose up hard and distinct in the afternoon sun. The deck of the *Formidable* was already festooned with garlands of multicoloured lights for the next day's ball, to which Swirski would be receiving an invitation. Seen from below, the sailors at the gunwale looked like pygmies in contrast to the bulk of the ship. The steel sides of the hulls, the funnels, the masts and the yardarms were reflected in the water as in a mirror. From time to time a naval boat would pass between the ships like a black insect moving rows of feet with regular strokes. Beyond the ships began the open sea, whose surface, as usual at the entrance to a harbour and in spite of the lack of wind, rose and fell slowly, lifting and lowering the boat in which Swirski sat with a movement that was at the same time gentle and powerful. They drew close to the tall rocks by the right side of the harbour wall along which ran the white dusty road. Below the road stretched a parade ground where some soldiers were practising on their trumpets. At last, rounding the point, against which surged the waves coming in from the deep, they sailed out to sea.

Outside the harbour there is always a little breeze, so the fisherman hoisted a sail, while Swirski, manning the rudder, turned not towards Nice, but southwards, on to the open sea. They sailed straight ahead, borne gently by the swell. The sun was beginning to dip low, and the rocky outcrops and the sea turned red. Everything around them was calm, quiet, and so vast that Swirski could not help reflecting on how small and contemptible life was in the presence of the boundlessness that surrounded him. He suddenly felt as though he had sailed very far away from all his own and other people's preoccupations. Mrs Elzen, Romulus, Remus, all his acquaintance and that whole seaside anthill, full of fever, anxiety, futile ambitions

and contemptible passions, grew insignificant. As a man used
to analysing what was going on inside him, he was alarmed at
this sensation: it occurred to him that if he were really in love
with Mrs Elzen, then the image of her would never be occlud-
ed or blurred, it would never shrink or disappear. He remembered how, long before, when a woman he loved had married
another, he had set off abroad. It was the first time he saw
Italy, Rome, Sicily, the sea, the coast of Africa – yet none of
these impressions had been able to erase the memory of the
beloved woman from his mind. In the galleries of Florence and
Rome, on the sea and in the desert, she was always with him
and he experienced everything through her. Everywhere, he
would exclaim 'Look!' as though she were by his side. The difference between that time and the present filled him with sadness.

But the calm of the evening and the sea were like a healing
balm. They had sailed out so far that the shore was hardly dis-
tinguishable. Then the sun went down. A star came out, then
another. The dolphins that had been breaking the surface
around the boat with their sharp backs in the light of the sunset now retreated into the depths, and no sound came from
anywhere. The surface of the water was smooth, and the sail
was almost limp. After a while, the moon rose from behind the
hills, suffusing the sea with a greenish brilliance and illuminat-
ing everything up to the horizon. The southern night had
begun, mild and still. Swirski wrapped himself in a cloak lent
by the fisherman, and gave free rein to his thoughts.

'Everything that surrounds me now is not only beautiful, it
is also the truth. Human life, if it is to make any sense, must
be grafted to the trunk of nature, grow out of it like a branch
grows out of a tree, and exist by virtue of the same laws. Only
then will it be true, and at the same time moral, for morality
is in essence no more than the accordance of life with the universal law of nature. Here I am surrounded by simplicity and
peace, but I understand them and feel them only as an artist:
I do not have them within me as a man, for my own life and
that of the people amongst whom I live has parted with nature,
has ceased to be governed by its laws, is no longer their consequence, and has become nothing more than a lie. Everything
that is in us is artificial. Even the sense of the truth of nature

has perished within us. Our relationships are founded on falsehood, our minds are distorted, our souls and our impulses are
sick. We deceive each other and ourselves, and in the end
nobody is certain whether he really wants what he is striving
for, or whether he knows how to strive for what he wants.'

In the midst of this night, the boundlessness of the sea, the
stars, the whole of nature, its peace, its simplicity and its vast-
ness, he was suddenly gripped by the sense of the enormous
falsehood of human relations. His love for Mrs Elzen appeared
to him as a great lie, and so did her feelings towards him,
towards her children, towards other men and towards the
world. The whole of life on that bright shore was a lie, the
whole present was a lie, and so was his own future. 'I am
caught in a net,' he thought, 'and I do not know how to break
out of it!' It was true. For if the whole of life was a lie, what
was he to do about it? Should he return to nature? Start some
kind of half-primitive, half-bucolic life? Break with mankind
and become a kind of radical? Swirski felt too old and too
sceptical for this. For that one needed some of the dogmatism
of a Kresowicz and to see in evil a spur to battle and reform,
and not experience it merely as a sensation that the morrow
would efface! Then another thought struck him. If one has not
the strength to change the world, then one can at least escape
from it, if only for a time, and draw breath. Tomorrow he
could be in Marseille, a couple of days hence out on the ocean,
hundreds of miles from the shore, from the sick life, from its
lies and deception. Everything would be solved, or rather, cut
through as with a knife.

All at once he was seized by such eagerness to translate this
thought into action that he gave the order to make for Nice.
'The first instinct of the animal caught in a trap,' he thought
to himself, 'is to break free. It is his right, it is natural, and
therefore it is moral. My trap is not just Mrs Elzen, it is made
up of everything that surrounds me. By marrying Mr Elzen I
should be marrying a lifetime of falsehood. This would not
stem only from her, it would result from the nature of things
– and from such prospects it is always permissible to escape.'
Here he began to imagine other prospects, which he would see
in his flight: great deserts of water and sand, unknown lands
and peoples: the honesty and harmony of their primitive life,

and above all variety and contrast to his present life. 'I should have done this a long time ago!' he said to himself.

He was then struck by a notion that could have occurred only to an artist – that if one jilts one's betrothed and goes off, to Paris for instance, that is the sort of dastardly act one reads of in cheap novels, but if one bolts beyond the Equator, to the land where spices grow, then the act of leaving her is diminished by the sheer scale of distance, the whole thing looks quite different, becomes more original and therefore in better taste altogether. 'And I shall go devilish far!' he thought.

Meanwhile Nice appeared in the distance in the guise of a string of lights. In the middle of this string the building known as the Jetée Promenade shone forth like a huge lantern. As the boat, urged on now by a strong breeze, neared the harbour, each one of these lights seemed to turn into a fiery pillar, shimmering on the waves by the shore. The sight of all this light sobered Swirski.

'The city – and life!' he thought. And all his earlier plans began to dissolve like visions born of the wild and the night. That which only a moment before had seemed justified, feasible and essential now seemed to him a whim devoid of reality, and slightly dishonest as well. 'Whatever it may be like, one nevertheless has to take life into account. Anyone who has lived by its laws as many years as I have must feel a certain responsibility towards them. It is too easy to say to oneself: I took advantage of them while it was convenient, and the moment they do not suit me I return to nature.' He then fell to thinking more specifically, not about general theories, but about Mrs Elzen herself.

'By what right would I abandon her? If her life has been artificial and false, if her past is a little murky, I knew about it and I could very well have refrained from proposing. Now I should only have the right to break off with her if I discovered in her some vice that she had been hiding, or if she were to commit some wrong against me. But she has committed no wrong against me. She has been honest and sincere with me. And there must be something in her that attracts me, for otherwise I would not have proposed. At times I do feel that I am in love with her, and if occasionally I am visited by doubts, why should she be the one to suffer on that account? In any case, my flight would be a great injustice to her, and possibly a severe blow.'

He forced himself to face the fact that dreaming of escape and carrying out the plan were two very different things for a decent man. He could permit himself only to dream. To flee from danger was quite contrary to his personal nature, as well as that of his caste, which was thoroughly civilised, and he would rather have stood before Mrs Elzen and demanded that she release him from his word. Besides, the very thought of hurting a woman moved his heart, and Mrs Elzen suddenly seemed closer and dearer to him.

They had sailed into the harbour, and a moment later the boat tied up. Swirski paid the fisherman and hailed a carriage to go home. Driving along the streets amid the noise, light, clatter and movement, he was again seized with longing for that silence, that boundless expanse of water, that peace, and that great Divine truth which he had only just left. When he was quite near the studio, he was arrested by a new thought: 'A strange thing – that I, who have always feared women and been so wary of them, should have eventually chosen a woman who arouses more reservations than any other.'

There was something fatalistic here, and Swirski would certainly have found in this combination of facts enough material to reflect on for the whole evening, had it not been for the fact that as he entered the servant handed him two letters. One contained an invitation to the next day's ball on the *Formidable*, and the other was from Madame Lageat, his landlady.

She informed him of her own departure to Marseille for two days, and at the same time announced that she had found him a model who ought to satisfy his most exacting taste, and who would call on the morrow.

VI

The promised wonder turned up the following morning at nine o'clock. Swirski was dressed and waiting impatiently, half-expecting disappointment. But the first glance satisfied him that his fears had been unfounded. The model was tall, slender and very graceful. She had a small head, a fine face, beautiful brows, long lashes and a very fresh complexion. What delighted Swirski above all was that she had 'her own face', and something girlish in her expression. 'Her movements are noble,' he thought, 'and if she is built as she seems, then I think it is a case of 'Eureka!' I shall engage her for a long time, and take her about with me!'

He was also struck by her shyness and the look of fear on her face. He knew that models sometimes feign timidity, but he suspected that this one was not pretending.

'What is your name, my child?' he asked.

'Maria Cervi.'

'Are you from Nice?'

'Yes sir.'

'Have you posed before?'

'No sir.'

'Trained models know what is expected of them, but there is always trouble with novices. Have you never posed at all?'

'No sir.'

'What made you want to be a model?'

The model hesitated with her answer, and coloured a little.

'Madame Lageat told me that I would be able to earn a little . . .'

'Yes, but you seem to be afraid. What are you afraid of? I won't eat you! How much do you want per sitting?'

'Madame Lageat said that you pay five francs . . .'

'Madame Lageat was mistaken: I pay ten francs.'

Joy lit up the girl's face, and her cheeks coloured even more.

'When am I to begin?' she asked, her voice trembling a little.

'Today, at once!' said Swirski, pointing to the half-finished picture. 'There is a screen: go and undress! To the waist only! You will pose for the head, the breasts, and part of the stomach!'

She turned on him a face full of astonishment, and her arms dropped slowly to her sides.

'How is that, sir?' she asked fearfully, looking at him with frightened eyes.

'My child,' he answered a little impatiently, 'I understand

that the first time can be a little difficult. But either you are a model or you are not. I need a head, breasts and part of the stomach; I need them, understand? And you should know that there is nothing wrong in this. Think it over, but hurry, because if you decide you do not want to, then I shall have to find someone else.'

But he felt uneasy as he spoke, for deep down he wanted her to stay, and he certainly did not want to have to look for another model. There was a silence. The girl had grown very pale, but after a moment she went behind the screen. Swirski began to move the easel up to the window, making a lot of noise as he positioned it. 'She'll get used to it, and in a week's time she'll laugh at her scruples,' he said to himself. Then he moved the sofa on which the model was to lie, took up his brushes, and began to grow impatient.

'Well? Are you ready?'

There was silence.

'Come on, make up your mind! What is this nonsense!'

A trembling voice came from behind the screen.

'Please, sir!' it implored, 'I thought that . . . There is poverty at home, but this way . . . I . . . cannot! . . . If only you would be so kind . . . just the head . . . even for three francs . . . even just for two . . . If you would be so kind! . . .' and the words turned into sobbing.

Swirski turned towards the screen and dropped his brushes. His mouth fell open in astonishment: the model had spoken in his native language.

'Are you Polish?' he exclaimed, unconsciously assuming the more polite form of address.

'Yes, sir! . . . That is . . . my father was Italian, but my grandfather is Polish . . .' Again there was silence. Then Swirski recovered his composure.

'Please get dressed . . . You will sit for the head only.' But she had evidently not even begun to undress, for she came out from behind the screen immediately, her face full of embarrassment, confusion and fear, and with traces of tears on her cheeks.

'Thank you . . . You are so . . . I'm sorry, but . . .'

'Please calm yourself,' interrupted Swirski. 'Here's a chair! Please calm yourself. You can sit for the head . . . What the

devil, I had no wish to offend you. You see this picture. I
needed a model for this figure . . . But since it means so much
to you, then that is different, particularly as you are a Pole.'

Tears once more began to flow down her cheeks, but gratitude looked out at him through her blue eyes. He found a bottle of wine, poured out a glass, and, handing it to her, said:

'Have a drink. I have some biscuits too somewhere, but the
deuce knows where. Please calm yourself.' Saying, this, he
gazed at her with sympathy in his honest eyes, and after a
moment added: 'Poor child!'

He began moving the easel back to its former position, saying: 'There will be no posing today. You are too agitated.
Tomorrow we shall set to work from early morning, but now
we shall have a little talk. Who would have guessed that Maria
Cervi was a Pole! So your grandfather is a Pole? Yes? Is he
alive?'

'He is alive, but for the past two years he has been unable
to walk.'

'What is his name?'

'Orysiewicz,' she said, pronouncing it with a slight accent.

'I know the name. Did he leave Poland a long time ago?'

'Grandfather has not been in Poland for sixty years. He was
in the Italian army, and then worked in a bank in Nice.'

'How old is he?'

'Grandfather is nearly ninety.'

'And your father was called Cervi?'

'Yes. He came from Nice, but he also served in the Italian
army.'

'How long ago did he die?'

'Five years ago.'

'And your mother is still alive?'

'Yes. We live together in old Nice.'

'Good. And now, one more question: does your mother
know that you wanted to become a model?'

To this, the girl answered in a hesitant voice.

'No. Mama does not know. Madame Lageat told me that I
could earn five francs a day in this way, and since there is such
poverty at home . . . it's terrible . . . so . . . I had no choice . . .'

Swirski took in the whole figure of the girl at a glance, and
realised that she was telling the truth. Everything testified to

poverty, beginning with her hat and her dress, which was so worn, or rather so consumed by age, that one could see every thread in it, down to her faded and heavily darned gloves.

'Now you must go home, and you must tell your mother that there is a painter called Swirski who wishes you to model for the head in his picture. Tell her also that this painter will call, on the recommendation of Madame Lageat, to ask whether you and your mother would come for sittings at his studio, for which he will offer ten francs a day.'

Miss Cervi began to thank him, stammering and confusing her words, in a voice full of tears and joy at the same time. Seeing the confusion she was in, he interrupted:

'All right! All right! I shall call in an hour's time. You seem an honest girl. You can trust me. Sometimes I can be a bit of a bear, but I can be understanding too. We shall sort everything out and forget about all this unpleasantness. Ah! and one other thing! I won't give you any money now, so that you do not have to go into explanations, but when I come I shall bring as much as is necessary on account. I have also had my ups and downs, so I know the value of speedy assistance. You have nothing to be grateful for, it is nothing! Goodbye, my child – in an hour.'

Having enquired further about the address, he conducted the girl downstairs. An hour later he got into a carriage and asked to be driven to old Nice. Everything that had happened seemed to him so singular that he could think of nothing else. He also felt that glow which any honest man feels when he has behaved as honour dictates, and when he is in a position to be of real assistance.

'If she is not a decent and good woman,' he reflected about Miss Cervi, 'then I am the stupidest mule in the whole of Liguria.' And he did not for a moment believe that. He was convinced that he had come across a remarkable and fine female soul, and at the same time he was glad that it should have been enclosed in such a young and comely body.

The carriage stopped at last before an old and crumbling house near the harbour. The concierge indicated the apartment of Mrs Cervi with a certain disdain.

'It really is poverty!' thought the painter as he climbed the steep steps. A moment later, he knocked on the door.

'Come in, please!' a voice sounded from within.

Swirski went in. He was received by a woman of about forty, dressed in black. She was sallow, sad, thin, and clearly broken by life, but there was nothing vulgar about her. Beside her stood Miss Maria.

'I know everything, and I thank you from the bottom of my heart and my soul!' said Mrs Cervi. 'May the Lord reward you, and may He shower blessings upon you.' With these words, she took his hand and bent over it, as though she intended to kiss it. But he took it back quickly, and then, wishing to dispel the formality as soon as possible and break the ice of the first meeting, turned to Miss Maria, and wagging his finger at her with the familiarity of an old friend, said:

'Aha! I see this little person has spilled the beans!'

Miss Maria smiled at him, a little sadly, and a little embarrassed. She seemed to him lovely, more beautiful than in the studio. He noticed that she had put around her neck some sort of old lilac ribbon, which she had not had on before, and this touched him, for it was a sign that she did not see him as just an old man.

'Yes, Marynia has told me everything,' said Mrs Cervi. 'God watches over her and over us, and He has sent you to us.'

'Miss Maria herself told me of your difficulties,' answered Swirski, 'but you must believe me, madam, that even in such conditions, to have such a daughter as her is real happiness.'

'Yes,' answered Mrs Cervi calmly.

'Actually, it is I who owe you ladies a debt of gratitude. I had been searching high and low, all in vain, when suddenly this magnificent head drops down from heaven. Now I am quite confident about my painting. I only have to insure myself, so that my model does not escape from me!'

Saying this, he took out three hundred francs, which he forced Mrs Cervi to accept, assuring her that he was getting a tremendous bargain, for thanks to Miss Maria he would get a fabulous sum for his painting. He also declared that he would like to meet the grandfather, as he had a weakness for old soldiers.

Hearing this, Miss Maria went next door. After a while the rumble of a wheelchair was heard, and the grandfather, who had obviously been decked out in anticipation, trundled into the room, dressed in his uniform and wearing all his decorations.

Swirski beheld the face of an old man, shrunken, wrinkled, with hair and whiskers as white as milk, and wide-open blue eyes which looked a little like the eyes of a child.

'Grandfather,' said Miss Maria, bending down so the old man could see her lips, and speaking not loudly but slowly and distinctly, 'this is Mr Swirski, a fellow-countryman and an artist.'

The old man turned his blue eyes on him and began to look with intensity, blinking, as though he were trying to collect his thoughts.

'A fellow-countryman?' he repeated. 'Yes! . . . A fellow-countryman! . . .' Then he smiled, looked at his daughter, his granddaughter, then at Swirski once again, apparently searching for words, and then asked, in an old, trembling voice: 'And what will the spring bring with it? . . . Eh?'

He had apparently been struck with some thought, one that had outlived all others, but which he could no longer express . . . After a moment he leant his shaking head against the back of his chair and looked out of the window, smiling at the thought, and repeating: 'Yes! Yes! It will come! . . .'

'Grandfather's always like this,' said Miss Maria.

Swirski gazed at him with emotion, while Mrs Cervi began to tell him about her father and her husband. Both had taken part in the wars against Austria for Italy's independence. For a time they had lived in Florence, and it was only after the capture of Rome that they had come to Nice, which was Cervi's native town. It was here that Orysiewicz had given his daughter in marriage to his younger companion-in-arms, and with the help of his relatives they had both found work in a bank. Everything had gone quite well, until, a few years previously, Cervi had been killed in a railway accident, while Orysiewicz had been obliged to retire for reasons of age. It was then that poverty visited them, as the three of them had nothing to live off beyond the six hundred lire that the Italian government paid the old soldier. It was just enough to keep them from dying, but not enough to live on. The women earned a little extra by sewing or giving lessons, but the summer, when life in Nice came to a standstill and there was no opportunity for extra work, always consumed their meagre reserves. Two years earlier the old soldier had completely lost the power of his legs. As he was frequently ill, he required medical care, and since then things had got worse and worse.

Listening to this account, Swirski made two mental observations: first that Mrs Cervi spoke Polish less well than her daughter. Evidently the old man had not been able to devote as much attention to teaching his daughter during his soldiering years as he had to teaching his granddaughter. The second observation seemed more significant to Swirski. He reflected that this granddaughter, being such a beautiful girl, could have, particularly in Nice, on this coast visited yearly by idle millions, put herself in a position to throw money about by the handful, keep carriages and servants, and have a velvet-lined boudoir. Instead, she had a worn-out dress and a faded lilac ribbon as her only finery. So there must have been some force that kept her from evil. 'For this,' he reflected, 'she must have two things: an innate purity of nature and an honest upbringing. There can be no doubt that I have stumbled on both here.'

He felt at ease with these people. He had also noticed that in both of the women poverty had not worn out the traces of good breeding and that inborn elegance which comes from within. Both the mother and the daughter had received him as the messenger of providence, but at the same time it was clear from their words and their behaviour that they were more delighted at having met an honest man than at receiving the help he brought. The three hundred francs would probably save the family many worries and humiliations, but he felt that both mother and daughter were more grateful to him for the fact that he had behaved like a man with a heart, a true and kind heart, that he had understood the girl's pain, her modesty and her sacrifice. What delighted him most of all was that in the bashfulness and grateful looks of Miss Cervi there was a hint of the embarrassment of a young girl faced with a man to whom she owes a debt of the deepest gratitude, who is also not entirely, to use his own expression, 'past it'. He was forty-five, and in spite of the fact that he felt young at heart, he occasionally had his doubts, so the lilac ribbon and this last observation caused him real pleasure. He was now speaking to them with all the respect and attention due to ladies of the highest rank, and the knowledge that he was charming them all the more caused him added satisfaction. He pressed the hands of both when taking his leave, and when Miss Cervi returned the pressure with downcast eyes, but with all the strength of her warm young hand, he went out a little dazed, with his head so full of the beautiful model that the coachman had to ask him twice where he wished to go.

On the way, he began to think that it would not be quite right to put the head of 'Miss Maria' on a half-naked body, and he began to convince himself that the picture itself would benefit if he covered the breasts of the sleeping girl with some light drapery. 'The moment I get back I shall get hold of any old model, cover her with a veil, and alter it all at once, so that when they come tomorrow everything will be ready,' he said to himself.

Then it occurred to him that he would never be able to hire a model such as Miss Cervi on a permanent basis, to take her with him, and this thought saddened him. But the carriage had stopped at his front door, so he paid and got out.

'A telegram for you, sir!' exclaimed the doorman.

The painter awoke as from a dream.

'Aha! Very good! Give it here!' Taking the telegram from the doorman he opened it with impatience. But he had scarcely glanced at it before his face registered surprise and alarm. The telegram ran:

'Kresowicz shot himself an hour ago. Come.

Helena.'

VII

Mrs Elzen came out to meet Swirski in a state of some confusion, with irritation clearly visible on her face. Her eyes were dry, but very red, as though she had a fever, and they betrayed burning impatience.

'Have you had a letter or anything?' she asked hurriedly.

'No, just your telegram. What a tragedy!'

'I thought he might have written to you.'

'No. When did it happen?'

'This morning. They heard a shot from his room. The servants rushed in and found him dead.'

'Here, in the hotel?'

'No. Fortunately he moved to the Condamine yesterday . . .'

'And what was the reason?'

'How should I know?' she answered pettishly.

'As far as I know he didn't gamble.'

'No. They found plenty of money on him.'

'Yesterday you dismissed him.'

'Yes, but that was at his own request.'

'He didn't take it to heart?'

'How should I know,' she repeated feverishly. 'He might have gone away somewhere first if he was going to do it! But he was a madman – that explains everything! Why couldn't he go away somewhere?'

Swirski observed her carefully for a moment.

'Please calm yourself,' he said.

But, failing to grasp his meaning, she went on: 'It is all so embarrassing, and just think what trouble it might cause me! Who knows, I might even have to give some explanations, make a deposition, or something . . . What a dreadful business! . . . And then there will be people talking. Wiadrowski will be the first! . . . I think you had better tell everyone that the unfortunate man had lost money, you could even say some of it was my money, which would explain his action. If it became necessary to speak in court, then it would be best not to say this, because it might be revealed as untrue, but in society, I think this would be the best course . . . If only he had gone off somewhere – at least to Menton or Nice! And God only knows if he didn't write something before his death to take revenge on me . . . God forbid that some posthumous letter should find its way into the papers! . . . Anything is possible with people like that. I had wanted to leave this place anyway, and now I shall be obliged to . . .'

Swirski was looking with more and more attention at her angry face with its set mouth, and finally said: 'What an extraordinary . . .'

'Quite extraordinary!' cut in Mrs Elzen. 'But won't it set

tongues wagging even more if we leave this place tomorrow?'

'I doubt it,' said Swirski.

He began to ask about the hotel in which Kresowicz had shot himself, and then announced that he would go there to get further information from the staff on the spot and to take care of the body. But she tried to hold him back, with unusual insistence, until he finally snapped at her:

'Madam, he is not a dog, but a man, and he deserves to be buried decently.'

'Someone will bury him anyway.'

But Swirski took his leave and went out. On the steps of the hotel he passed his hand across his forehead, then put on his hat and repeated to himself:

'Quite extraordinary! . . .'

He knew from experience how far selfishness can be carried in human beings. He also knew that in egoism as in self-sacrifice, women far surpass the potential of men. He had already come across people in whom a polite veneer covered a crude animal selfishness, and in whom every moral considera-tion ended at the precise point where personal interest began – but still Mrs Elzen had astonished him. 'The poor wretch was the tutor of her children, lived under the same roof, and was even in love with her . . . And she? Not even a word of pity, not a glimmer of sympathy, not a shred of interest! Noth-ing! She's furious with him for causing her trouble, for not having got out of the way, for having spoiled her season, for exposing her to the possibility of having to appear in court and becoming the object of gossip. It never even occurred to her to wonder what was going on inside the man, why he killed him-self, and whether it was not on account of her. In her irritation she has even forgotten that she is betraying herself in front of me. If not her heart, then her brain at least should háve told her to behave differently in front of me. Oh, what spiritual barbarity! Appearances, appearances, and under that French corset and French accent there's no soul – just the primitive black nature of a worthy daughter of Cham! Civilisation stuck to the skin like powder! . . . And the woman even wants me to tell everyone that he gambled away her money . . . Ugh! May the devil take her!'

Similar thoughts and imprecations were still whirling round

his head when he reached the Condamine. Without difficulty he found the little hotel in which the tragedy had taken place. In Kresowicz's room he met a doctor and a court functionary, who were delighted by his arrival, since they assumed Swirski would be able to enlighten them about the dead man.

'The suicide,' said the functionary, 'left a note saying that he wishes to be buried in a common grave, and asking for all the money found on him to be sent to an address in Zurich. He burnt all his other papers, as you can see from the grate.'

Swirski looked at Kresowicz, who lay on the bed with wide open, terrified eyes, his lips pursed as though he were about to whistle.

'The dead man believed himself to be incurably ill,' he said. 'he told me so himself, and that is probably why he took his own life. He certainly never went gambling.' He then told them everything he knew about Kresowicz. Before leaving he left enough money for a private grave.

On the way he remembered what Kresowicz had told him about microbes, as well as the young man's declaration to Wiadrowski that he belonged to the 'party of the silent', and he concluded that the student had probably been intending to kill himself for some time, and that the main reason for his action was the conviction that he was condemned to death anyway. But he also recognised that there might have been other circumstantial reasons, among them his unhappy love for Mrs Elzen and the necessity of parting with her. These thoughts filled him with sadness. The corpse of Kresowicz, with its lips set to whistle and the look of terror in anticipation of death in its eyes was vivid in his memory. He reflected that nobody can face that terrible night of death without fear, and that in the face of its inevitability the whole of life is one great absurdity. He returned to Mrs Elzen in a state of spiritual depression.

She gave a sigh of relief on hearing that Kresowicz had left no papers. She declared that she too would send a suitable amount of money for his funeral, and it was only now that she began to speak of him with any pity. But it was in vain that she attempted to keep Swirski with her for a couple of hours. The artist replied that he felt out of sorts and must go back home.

'But we shall see each other this evening?' said Mrs Elzen as she gave him her hand. 'I had even thought of coming to Nice and going on from there with you.'

'Going where?' asked Swirski with surprise.

'Have you forgotten? To the *Formidable*, of course . . .'

'So you are going to go to this ball?'

'If only you knew how much it costs me, particularly after such an unfortunate event, you would spare a tear for me . . . I feel sorry for the poor man too . . . But one must! . . . One must, if only to prevent people from jumping to any conclusions . . .'

'Really? Goodbye!' said Swirski.

A while later, as he sat in the train, he said to himself: 'If I go to the *Formidable* or anywhere else with you, then I'm a dead crab!'

VIII

It was with a much lighter heart that he received Mrs Cervi and Miss Maria on the following morning. At the sight of the beautiful, fresh face of the girl he was even overcome by joy.

Everything in the studio was already prepared. The easel was in the right place, the sofa for the model was positioned and covered. Madame Lageat had received the strictest instructions to let nobody in, even if 'Queen Victoria herself' should turn up.

Swirski was drawing and undrawing the blinds on the ceiling light, but as he pulled on the strings he gazed intently at his charming model. The ladies had taken off their hats, and Miss Maria asked: 'What should I do now?'

'First, you must let down your hair,' said Swirski.

He came up to her, while she lifted both hands to her head. It was plain that the act seemed strange and embarrassing to her, but also quite pleasant. Swirski looked at her confused face, her lowered eyelids, at the whole figure arching backwards, at the exquisite shape of her hips – and he said to himself that in this great rubbish-heap of Nice he had indeed discovered a real pearl. A moment later the hair cascaded onto her shoulders. Miss Cervi shook her head to disentangle it, and it covered her completely.

'*Corpo Dio!*' exclaimed Swirski.

The next thing was the more difficult task of positioning the model. Swirski could tell that the girl's heart was beating faster, that her breast was rising and falling more quickly, that her cheeks were burning, that she was fighting and restraining an instinctive resistance, and that she was surrendering with an anxiety that was akin to subconscious delight.

'No, this is no ordinary model,' he said to himself. 'This is something quite different. And I am not looking at her as just a painter.' He too felt embarrassed, and his hands trembled a little while positioning her head on the pillow. But wishing to dispel his own embarrassment, he began chiding her jokingly, pretending to be bad-tempered.

'You must keep still! Like this! One must make some sacrifices for art's sake! Now, that's better! How perfect that profile looks against the red background. If only you could see it! But you cannot. Smiling is not allowed! You must sleep! In a moment I shall be painting.'

He began to paint, and as was his habit, he chatted the while, asking Mrs Cervi about old times. He learnt, amongst other things, that 'Marynia' had in the previous year found very rewarding work as a reader to Countess Dziadzikiewicz, who was the daughter of the great Łódź industrialist Atrament. But the job came to an end the moment the countess discovered that Marynia's father and grandfather had fought in the Italian army. This was a great disappointment, as both mother and daughter longed for her to find such a position with a lady who spent all winter in Nice.

The painter had awoken in Swirski. He frowned, concentrated, measured the figure of the reclining girl with his brush, and painted with intensity. From time to time, however, he would put down the palette and brush, approach the model and, lightly touching her brow, correct her position. While doing so, he would lean over perhaps a little more than was absolutely necessary in the interests of art alone, and when he could feel the warmth of the young body, when he looked at the long lashes and the slightly open mouth, a quiver would go through his whole being, his fingers would tremble nervously and in his heart he would reprove himself: 'Steady, old man!

What the deuce! Steady!'

He was in fact besotted by her. He was excited beyond measure by her embarrassment, her blushes and her shy looks, which were not entirely devoid of girlish coquettishness. All this indicated that she did not see him as an old man. Her grandfather must have told her wonderful things about his countrymen, and had probably set her dreaming on the subject – and here at last one of them had crossed her path, not any old one either, but a kind, famous one, who had, to cap it all, appeared at the moment of greatest need bearing succour with a kind heart. How else was she to look at him but with sympathy, interest and gratitude?

All this meant that the morning slipped by before Swirski had had time to notice. It was Miss Marynia who brought up the fact that it was noon, by declaring that they must be getting back because grandfather was alone, and it was time to think of his lunch. Swirski begged them to return in the afternoon. If they did not wish to leave the old man on his own, then perhaps they could ask a friend to sit with him for a couple of hours . . . Perhaps the concierge, or her husband, or someone of her family? It was a question of the picture! Two sittings a day would be an excellent thing for both parties. If the finding of company for the grandfather entailed any costs, he, Swirski, would consider it a favour if he were allowed to bear them, as he could think of nothing but his picture.

Two sittings were indeed too profitable in the light of the poverty at home for Mrs Cervi not to assent. It was agreed that the ladies would return at two. Swirski was so delighted that he decided to accompany them home. In his own doorway he was met by the housekeeper, who handed him a bunch of moss roses, saying that they had been left by a couple of beautiful small boys with a strangely dressed servant who had wanted at all costs to go up to his studio, but, in accordance with his instructions, she had refused to let them in.

Swirski told her she had done well, and, taking the roses, he handed them to Miss Cervi. A moment later they were on the Promenade des Anglais. Nice seemed more beautiful and lively than ever to Swirski. The variety and bustle on the Promenade, which he had always found irritating, now amused him. On the way he saw Wiadrowski and de Sinten, who stopped to greet him. Swirski merely bowed and went on, but as he passed he noticed how de Sinten put in his monocle to have a better look at Miss Marynia, and he distinctly heard his astonished *'Saprrrristi!'* The two men even followed them for a while, but opposite the Jetée Promenade Swirski hailed a cab and drove the ladies home.

On the way he felt the urge to invite the whole family to lunch, but he realised that it might be difficult with the old man, and that in view of their very recent acquaintance Mrs Cervi might be a little taken aback by such a sudden invitation. But he promised himself that once the question of company for the grandfather had been sorted out, he would in the interests of gaining time arrange to have lunch served in the studio. Having taken his leave of the mother and daughter at their front door, he went into the first hotel he could find and ordered lunch. He swallowed several dishes in a hurry, without noticing what he was eating. Mrs Elzen, Romulus and Remus, and bunches of moss roses flashed through his thoughts, but in a way that seemed unreal. Only a few days before, the beautiful widow and his relationship with her had been subjects of the greatest weight, over which he had tortured himself. He still remembered that internal crisis which he had gone through at sea on the way back from Villefranche. But now he said to himself: 'All that no longer exists for me, and I shall not think about it any more.' And he felt no twinge of alarm or anxiety. In fact, he felt as though a great load had fallen from his shoulders. Instead, all his thoughts now kept rushing back to Miss Cervi. His head was full of her, his eyes were full of her. He saw her in his imagination with her hair undone and her eyelids closed, and when he thought that in an hour's time he would once again be touching her brow, leaning over her, feeling the warmth emanating from her, he felt quite intoxicated and once again said to himself: 'Come on, old man, steady.'

When he got home, he found a telegram from Mrs Elzen, which read: 'I am awaiting you for dinner at six.' He crumpled it and put it in his pocket, and when Mrs Cervi arrived with her daughter, he forgot about it so completely that when after he had finished work he heard five o'clock strike, he began to wonder where to go and have dinner, and even felt a little annoyed at having nothing to do that evening.

IX

As she brought lunch into the studio for the three of them the next day, Madame Lageat announced that only an hour before the same two beautiful young boys had turned up, this time not with a strangely dressed servant, but with a young and beautiful lady.

'The young lady wanted absolutely to see you, but I told her that you had gone to Antibes . . .'

'To Toulon! To Toulon!' exclaimed the painter gaily.

But the day after that Madame Lageat had nobody to give this message to, for the only thing that turned up was a letter. Swirski did not bother to read it. On that very day, while he was trying to improve the 'position' of Miss Marynia, he placed his hands behind her shoulders and lifted her in such a way that their breasts almost touched, and her breath suffused his face. She changed colour from emotion, while he said to himself that if only one could make such a moment last, it would be worth giving one's life for.

That evening he had another discussion with himself. 'Your passions are playing up again,' he told himself, 'but this time it is different, for the soul is rushing forth after them, and it rushes forth because she is a child who has managed, in this dung-heap of Nice, to remain as pure as a teardrop. It is not even a question of her own merit; it is her nature – but where else would one find a nature like that? This time I am not deluding myself, and I am not talking myself into anything: it is reality that speaks in me.' He felt as though he were living in a sweet dream. Unfortunately, dreams are followed by awakening, and this came for Swirski two days later in the shape of another telegram which slipped through the letter-box and fell to the floor in the presence of the two ladies.

Miss Cervi, who was just about to let her hair down for the sitting, was the first to notice it. She picked it up and handed it to Swirski.

He opened it without enthusiasm, but after a single glance, the expression on his face changed.

'You ladies must excuse me,' he said, 'I have received news that obliges me to leave at once.'

'Nothing bad, I hope?' asked Miss Cervi anxiously.

'No! No! But I may not be able to get back for the afternoon sitting. However, I shall deal with it today, and tomorrow we shall be back to normal.' He bade them goodbye somewhat feverishly, but almost too warmly, and a few moments later was sitting in a carriage making for Monte Carlo.

As he passed the Jetée Promenade he took out the telegram and read it again. It ran as follows:

'I expect you this afternoon. If you do not come by the four o'clock train, I shall know what to think and how to act.
Morphine'

Swirski had panicked when he saw that signature, partly on account of the recent memory of the Kresowicz tragedy. 'Who can tell,' he thought, 'what a woman might be driven to by wounded love, or at least by wounded self-love. I should not have behaved as I have. It would have been easy to answer the first letter and break everything off. It is not a good thing to trifle with anyone, regardless of whether they are good or bad people. I shall now break off definitely, but I must go to her, and I had better not wait for the four o'clock train.'

He told the coachman not to spare the horses. He tried to reassure himself with the thought that Mrs Elzen would never take her own life. It seemed entirely out of character. But then he was beset by doubts. That monstrous egoism of hers, transformed into offended pride, might drive her to some act of madness.

He remembered that she was also endowed with determination, decision, and not a little courage. The thought of her children ought to restrain her, but would it? Did she ever really care for those children? His hair stood on end at the thought of what might happen. His conscience stirred and began to torment him. The image of Miss Cervi hovered before his eyes, evoking a bitter and boundless grief. He kept telling himself that he was on his way to break off, and that he would do so decisively, but in the depths of his soul he felt scared. What if that evil, vain, determined woman were to say to him: 'You or Morphine!' Next to the feelings of fear and uncertainty he felt disgust welling up: only the heroine of a bad novel could behave in such a way. But what if she did? The world, and particularly the world of Nice, was full of heroines of bad novels.

Enveloped in these thoughts and in clouds of whitish dust he at last reached Monte Carlo. He told the coachman to stop before the Hôtel de Paris. But before he had got down from the carriage, he noticed Romulus and Remus armed with racquets hitting a ball about on the lawn, under the supervision of their Cossack, who was the strangely dressed servant described by Madame Lageat.

They too noticed him, and ran up.

'Good mohning, sir!'

'Good mohning!'

'Good morning. Is your mother upstairs?'

'No, Mamma has gone out on a bicycle with Monsieur de Sinten'.

There was a short silence.

'Ah! So Mamma has gone out on a bicycle with Monsieur de Sinten!' repeated Swirski. 'Splendid!' A moment later he added: 'Of course! She was not expecting me until four o'clock!' And he began to laugh. 'The drama ends in farce . . . But of course, this is the Riviera! What an ass I am!'

'Will you be waiting for Mamma!' asked Romulus.

'No. Listen, boys. Tell Mamma that I came to say goodbye to her, and that I am sorry not to have found her at home, as I am leaving today.'

Having given this message, he told the coachman to drive him straight back to Nice. That evening, however, he received yet another telegram, which contained only the single word: 'Scoundrel!' This put him in an excellent mood, for the telegram was not signed 'Morphine'.

X

Two weeks later the picture *Sleep and Death* was finished. Swirski started work on another, which he wanted to call *Euterpe*, but progress was slow. He complained that the light was too bright, and spent whole sittings gazing into the pretty face of Miss Marynia instead of painting, claiming that he was trying to find the most appropriate expression for Euterpe. He would stare at her so relentlessly that Miss Cervi blushed, and he himself felt increasing disquiet in his breast. One morning, he suddenly began to speak in a strange voice they had not heard before.

'I have observed that you ladies have a great love for Italy . . .'

'We do, and so does grandfather,' answered Miss Cervi.

'So do I. In fact, I spend half of my life in Rome or Florence. The light there at this time of year is not so bright, and one could paint whole days long. Oh, yes! Who doesn't love Italy! And do you know what I sometimes think!'

Miss Marynia lowered her head and opened her mouth a little, gazing at him with attention, as she always did when he spoke.

'I think that every man has two motherlands: his own, which is the most dear, and Italy. You only have to consider that all culture, all art, all knowledge, everything has come from there . . . Take the Renaissance for instance . . . Really! We are all of us if not children, then at least grandchildren of Italy . . .'

'Yes!' exclaimed Miss Cervi.

'I don't know if I mentioned that I have a studio in Rome, on via Margutta, and now that the light has grown so bright here, I find myself longing for it . . . What if we were all to set off for Rome, would it not be wonderful? . . . And then we could go to Warsaw.'

'That is impossible!' answered Miss Marynia with a sad smile.

But he suddenly came up to her and, taking her hands and looking into her eyes with great tenderness, said: 'There is a way, dear lady, there is a way! Can you not guess what it is?' She grew pale with happiness. He pressed both her hands to his breast and added:

'Give me your hand, be mine . . .'

Notes

CHARCOAL SKETCHES

In this story *Barania Głowa, Osłowice, Wrzeciądz* and other proper names such as *Burak, Rzepa* and *Zołzikiewicz* which are clearly intended for comic effect, have been given translated forms, but all other names left in their original form.

Page 17: *Village office, Elder, Clerk.* The Emancipation decree of 1864 set up village councils whose members were elected by the peasants. The Elder *(Wójt)* presided over the council. The only Tsarist functionary was the *pisarz* or secretary/clerk.

Page 18: *Governor.* Tsarist civil governor of a district.

Page 18: *Head.* Head of the bureaucracy of a district.

Page 18: *Inspector . . . distilleries.* After the emancipation, which hit many of them financially, landowners branched out more and more into the cheap and lucrative business of distilling vodka. Duty was payable on this which gave rise to much bribery of fiscal *inspectors.*

Pages 19/20: *Army lists, military lists, draft lists.* Poles were regularly conscripted into the Russian army.

Page 22: *roubles.* After 1840 the Polish areas within the Russian Empire used Russian currency.

Page 22: *distant period.* This and all subsequent references to *stormy times* and so on allude to the recently quelled Insurrection of 1863–4.

Page 23: *'All hail to you.'* Revolutionary song composed by Gustav Ehrenberg, 1818–95.

Page 23: *Rinaldo Rinaldini.* Famous Sicilian bandit.

Page 24: *unfriendly implement of plaited hide.* The knout, the Russian whip used for flogging.

Page 24: *St Ignatius Loyola.* Religious revelation came to the founder of the Jesuits (1491–1556) as he lay recovering from a war wound.

Page 24: *The Pacification* was a meticulous operation to ferret out anyone who had fought, hidden arms, tended wounded, transported supplies, or in any other way helped the insurgents in 1863–4, and was accompanied by bribery and denunciation.

Page 25: *Isabella of Spain:* Queen Isabella II of Spain (1833–68).

Carlos Marfori, governor of Madrid, was her lover.

Page 30: *Jews.* In central and eastern areas of the country, Jews were the universal middlemen, and they appear in this story in the figures of Srul the tailor, Szmul the innkeeper, Drysla the merchant, Herszek and Icek Zweinos the factors.

Page 30: *woods . . . easement.* Among the bones of contention after emancipation were the so-called *serwituty,* the peasant's rights of wood-gathering over parts of the manor woods, which often precluded their felling or sale.

Page 31: *The enfranchisement.* The emancipation of the peasants (1864) gave them the land which they were currently renting from the manor.

Page 33: Francisco *Serrano* (1810–85) was one of Isabella' s generals.

Page 33: *Carlists.* Supporters of Don Carlos, Isabella's rival for the Spanish throne.

Page 35: *Rural Guard.* The Tsarist police in rural areas.

Page 35: *Military Commission.* The body that went through the draft lists rejecting the unfit, the married etc.

Page 37: *Garibaldo.* Many of Garibaldi's officers fought in the Polish Insurrection of 1863–4, and it was even thought he might join it himself.

Page 37: *The French.* A reference to 1812, when the Grande Armée passed through Poland on its way to Moscow.

Page 42: *village court.* The village councils adjudicated minor disputes and settled the business of the locality.

Page 42: *non-intervention . . . John Bright.* Sienkiewicz takes a swipe at the policy of the British statesman John Bright (1811–89), and particularly his agitation against British involvement in the Crimean War.

Page 44: *Mr Floss . . . Red.* Floss is clearly not a noble name, and the local gentry assume that he is a Red, the name given to the more radical populist faction in the 1863–4 Insurrection.

Page 45: *Galicia* was that part of Poland under Austrian rule, which, after 1871, obtained wide-ranging autonomy and self-rule.

Page 45: *Vistula Region.* The official name given by Russia to its Polish territories after the Insurrection of 1863–4.

Page 49: *Nevadendeh and Bezendeh.* An inseparable pair of doves from a fable by Ignacy Krasicki (1735–1801).

Page 49: *Surveyor* was a dirty word amongst peasants, who always assumed that land-surveyors were cheats. Peasants also seized on any bombastic words that they did not understand and used them as insults – hence the absurd use and effect of *Suffragan*.

Page 54: *Imogen*. A reference to the daughter of Cymbeline in Shakespeare's play, whose virtue is wrongly impugned, and finally vindicated.

Page 58: Julian *Ochorowicz* (1850–1917) was a Positivist philosopher and writer.

Page 59: *Touching his knees:* The old Polish form of respectful greeting took the form of bending down and symbolically embracing the knees of the older or socially superior person.

Page 61: Adam *Asnyk* (1838–97), the only lyrical poet of the Positivist period.

Page 61: Kornel *Ujejski* (1823-97). Patriotic lyrical poet concerned with the plight of the peasantry.

Page 62: Leonard Sowiński (1831–87). A less popular but more socially radical poet.

Page 64: Józef Ignacy *Kraszewski* (1812–87). The Polish Dumas, a prolific writer of mainly historical novels.

Page 73: *Nielzya!* Russian for 'forbidden'.

Page 77: *The Gomon*. An imaginary procession of folk-lore, including dancing animals, plants and even stones.

Page 80: Salustiano *Olozaga* (1803–73). Spanish statesman and ambassador to the court of Napoleon III. The Empress *Eugenie* was Napoleon's Spanish-born wife.

BARTEK THE CONQUEROR

In giving his hero the name of Bartek, Sienkiewicz alludes to an earlier peasant hero. In 1794, at the Battle of Racławice against the Russians, the Polish peasant units armed with scythes won the day. A certain Bartosz Głowacki, a peasant from the region of Kraków, was first to reach the Russian battery and captured the guns.

The names of places and people have been left in their original form here, as the story does not rely on them for comic effect. But all the place-names set the scene: *Pognembin* is derived from the word for 'oppression'; *Krzywda* from 'injustice'; *Wywłaszczynce* from 'expropriation'; *Niedola* from 'adversity'; *Mizerów* from 'misery'. Of the other names only that of Squire *Jarzyński* (derived from *jarzyna*, a vegetable) has a comic connotation.

Page 87: *The Duchy of Poznań* (Posen in German) was the official name of that part of the Polish Commonwealth annexed by Prussia in the second and third partitions of Poland (1792 and 1795). It had semi-autonomous status until 1871, when it was incorporated into the German Reich.

Page 88: *The odd German colonist.* It was Prussian and then German policy to integrate the annexed Polish territories into the German mainstream by encouraging German colonists from all over the country to settle there.

Page 88: *The 'Wacht am Rhein'.* 'The Watch on the Rhine' was a German patriotic song.

Page 89: *Landwehr.* The territorial reserve of the German army.

Page 94: General Friedrich *Steinmetz* (1796–1877). In the Austro-Prussian war of 1866 he commanded the 5th Army Corps composed mainly of Poles.

Page 94: The *Kingdom* was that part of the Polish Commonwealth incorporated into the Russian Empire by the second and third partitions of Poland, and later renamed the Vistula Region.

Page 96: *Podolian cattle.* Podolia was a province of the old Polish Commonwealth.

Page 97: *Unser Fritz.* 'Our Fritz', later Frederick III. He commanded the 3rd Army Corps in 1870.

Page 101: *Zouaves.* A type of French colonial infantry.

Page 101: In the Battle of *Gravelotte* on 18 August 1870, the Poznanian regiments played an important part.

Page 105: *'While still we live'.* Second line of the *Song of the Legions,* later the Polish national anthem.

Page 113: *Franc-Tireurs.* Special units of volunteer riflemen. Many Poles, particularly veterans of the 1831 and 1863 uprisings, fought in them.

Page 118: *Hay, Straw:* In the Prussian army it was customary to tie a straw to one leg and a wisp of hay to the other for the benefit of those recruits who could not tell their right from their left.

Page 121: Teofil von *Podbielski* (1814–79). Prussian quartermaster-general during the 1870–71 war.

Page 128: *Posener Zeitung.* The German daily Poznań newspaper.

Page 128: *Reichstag.* The German parliament, in which delegates for the province of Poznań sat after the incorporation into the Reich.

Page 129: *Zentrum.* The German Catholic Party, which became an ally of the Polish delegates in the Reichstag after Bismarck launched the *Kulturkampf,* his campaign against the Catholic Church.

Page 135: *Landrat.* Regional Governor in the Prussian administration.

ON THE BRIGHT SHORE

Page 154: Joseph *Chamberlain* (1836–1914). British colonial secretary between 1895 and 1900.

Page 155: Lord *Salisbury* (1830–1903). British Prime Minister, 1886–1902.

Page 156: *Pyrrho* of Elis (c.360–270 BC). Greek sceptic philosopher.

Page 195: *Cham* or Ham. The cursed son of Noah.

Page 198: *Countess Dziadzikiewicz,* the daughter of a Jewish industrialist from the great boom town of Łódź, where vast fortunes were being made in Sienkiewicz's day, is clearly an arch-conservative, hence her reaction to hearing of Orysiewicz and Cervi serving in the Italian wars for independence.

Fiction published by Angel Books

ALFRED DÖBLIN

A People Betrayed *and* Karl and Rosa

(The trilogy November 1918: A German Revolution *complete in 2 volumes)*

Translated by John E. Woods

0 88064 008 1 *and* 0 88064 011 1 *(paperback)*

Published in the USA by Fromm International Publishing Corporation, New York

FYODOR DOSTOYEVSKY

The Village of Stepanchikovo

Translated by Ignat Avsey

0 946162 06 9 *(cased)* 0 946162 07 7 *(paperback)*

VSEVOLOD GARSHIN

From the Reminiscences of Private Ivanov *and other stories*

Translated by Peter Henry and others

0 946162 08 5 *(cased)* 0 946162 09 3 *(paperback)*

GERHART HAUPTMANN

Lineman Thiel *and other tales*

Translated by Stanley Radcliffe

0 946162 27 1 *(cased)* 0 946162 28 X *(paperback)*

HEINRICH VON KLEIST/LUDWIG TIECK/E. T. A. HOFFMANN

Six German Romantic Tales

Translated by Ronald Taylor

0 946162 17 4 *(paperback)*

ALEXANDER PUSHKIN

The Tales of Belkin

with The History of the Village of Goryukhino

Translated by Gillon Aitken and David Budgen

0 946162 04 2 *(cased)* 0 946162 05 0 *(paperback)*

ADALBERT STIFTER

Brigitta

with Abdias; Limestone; *and* The Forest Path

Translated by Helen Watanabe-O'Kelly

0 946162 36 0 *(cased)* 0 946162 37 9 *(paperback)*